"Bah humbug," she said.

Noelle had worked with people from varying cultures around the world; she could surely handle a bad-tempered Navy SEAL. Besides, the way his face looked whenever he was talking to Mishka... Noelle's heart turned over. He was one of the most striking men she'd ever met, but the warm tenderness he revealed to his niece was even more compelling than his looks.

She told herself to forget it. She'd just gotten divorced and her life was upside down; the next few weeks were supposed to be about getting her head and emotions sorted out. Anyway, while she might be attracted to Dakota, she wasn't ready for romance, even presuming he found her attractive in return...

Dear Reader,

My series Big Sky Navy Heroes pivots around a harsh grandfather who drove his grandsons away from Montana. Saul Hawkins deeply regrets the past and hopes to bring these three Navy heroes home again by offering a challenge—prove yourself as a rancher and receive a third of the family's Soaring Hawk Ranch.

With a relative of my own in the Special Forces, I wanted to tell a story about someone who is badly hurt in the line of duty. Dakota resents his injury because it means he can't keep helping people. I've paired him with Noelle, a doctor with an international relief organization. While exhausted from her work, Noelle loves Christmas and tries to help this bah humbug ex-SEAL find his yuletide spirit. Being such a fan of Christmas myself, how could I resist?

Classic Movie Alert: If you've never seen the 1955 movie *We're No Angels*, now is the time. With stars like Bogart, Ustinov and Joan Bennett, it's a delightful holiday tale about three escaped convicts. Hearts of gold? You decide. But when all is said and done, who can beat Bogie and Ustinov together?

Please visit my website at sites.google.com/view/juliannamorris--author/home, where I share information on my books and other news. I'm also on Twitter, @julianna_author, and can be contacted on my Facebook page at julianna.morris.author. If you prefer writing a letter, please use c/o Harlequin Enterprises ULC, 22 Adelaide Street West, 41st Floor, Toronto, Ontario, Canada M5H 4E3.

Best wishes,

Julianna Morris

HEARTWARMING

The SEAL's Christmas Dilemma

—

Julianna Morris

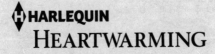

HARLEQUIN
HEARTWARMING

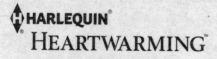

HARLEQUIN®
HEARTWARMING™

ISBN-13: 978-1-335-58472-4

Recycling programs
for this product may
not exist in your area.

The SEAL's Christmas Dilemma

Copyright © 2022 by Julianna Morris

For questions and comments about the quality of this book,
please contact us at CustomerService@Harlequin.com.

Harlequin Enterprises ULC
22 Adelaide St. West, 41st Floor
Toronto, Ontario M5H 4E3, Canada
www.Harlequin.com

Printed in U.S.A.

Julianna Morris barely remembers a time when she didn't want to be a writer, having scribbled out her first novel in sixth grade (a maudlin tale she says will never ever see the light of day). She also loves to read, and her library includes everything from history and biographies to most fiction genres. Julianna has been a park ranger, program analyst and systems analyst in information technology. She loves animals, travel, gardening, baking, hiking, taking photographs, making patchwork quilts and doing a few dozen other things. Her biggest complaint is not having enough hours in the day.

Books by Julianna Morris

Harlequin Heartwarming

Big Sky Navy Heroes

The Cowboy SEAL's Challenge

Hearts of Big Sky

The Man from Montana
Christmas on the Ranch
Twins for the Rodeo Star

Visit the Author Profile page
at Harlequin.com for more titles.

To everyone out there making the world
a better place.

PROLOGUE

"COMMANDER, CAN YOU hear me?"

The insistent voice filtered into Dakota's fuzzy brain and he opened his eyes to see a woman in uniform standing over him. An officer.

Standing?

He tried to banish the pain muddling his head, but didn't quite succeed. A glance around told him he was in a ship's medical bay.

Memory of a bomb blast returned. Aside from that, the last thing he could recall was telling a dumb joke, then grinning at his SEAL team and giving the signal to move.

"What about my men?" he croaked through a dry throat. "And the mission?"

"Don't worry about that now."

"Is my team all right?"

The Navy doctor sighed. "Your mission is classified and above my pay grade, so to speak. All I can say is that you arrived by helicopter two days ago. I've operated twice. You're lucky to be alive."

Dakota slowly realized there were bandages on his face and leg. Actually, he was bandaged all the way down the right side of his body. He painfully wiggled his fingers and toes. They seemed to work. Something in the doctor's face suggested there was more to his injuries than she was revealing, but he doubted she would provide any details at the moment.

"The ship has been on radio silence," the doctor said, "but we'll be able to notify your emergency contacts later today, and they can speak with the rest of your family. The names I have are Jordan and Wyatt Maxwell. Is that right?"

Dakota didn't want to explain that his brothers were the majority of the family he had left. His grandfather didn't count, his mom had passed away when he was just a kid and his father had been missing for so long, he was presumed dead.

"Yes, but I'll talk to them myself," he said. "When I'm able."

His brothers were going to be concerned and Jordan's new wife would worry, something she didn't need during her pregnancy.

The thought of his eldest brother's unexpected marital contentment was curiously soothing and Dakota let his eyelids drift downward.

At least one of the Maxwell brothers was happy.

CHAPTER ONE

NOELLE HUMMED A Christmas carol as she drove a rental car toward her family's ranch, the Blue Banner.

She'd flown into Bozeman the night before and gone straight to a hotel, unable to face the two-hour-plus drive right away. She was worn out from everything that had gone on over the last year, but was determined to enjoy the extended holiday season with her family. That, and take stock of her life.

Being a doctor doing international disaster relief was the only thing she'd ever wanted; now she needed to step back and think. And what better place to do that than her childhood home?

Not that home would be the same. Her three brothers still lived there, but not her sister and niece. Paige had married former Navy SEAL Jordan Maxwell, who'd grown up near the Blue Banner. They'd just had a baby boy and Jordan was a devoted daddy to

Mishka, Paige's adopted daughter. Still, they wouldn't be far, they lived across the way at the Soaring Hawk Ranch.

The house came into view, partially framed by sycamore trees still dotted with a few yellow leaves that hadn't fallen for the winter. Sheaves of dry cornstalks were tied to the posts on the porch steps and piles of pumpkins sat on either side of the door. No doubt all had been grown in the Blue Banner's large kitchen garden.

Her mother must have been watching for her arrival, because she came hurrying down the steps as soon as Noelle parked next to the other ranch vehicles.

"Darling."

"Hi, Mom."

Her warm, enveloping hug soothed Noelle. She hadn't been in Montana since Paige's wedding, fifteen months earlier. So much had happened between then and now, it seemed a lifetime ago.

"You've lost weight," Margaret Bannerman said, frowning as she stepped back and looked at her. "Is everything all right? Steffen didn't do anything horrid, did he?"

"*No.* He's a good person—we simply weren't right for each other. A doctor and an engineer, flying off to different parts of the globe all the time? Our home base may have been Atlanta, but we were rarely there at the same time. How did we think a marriage was going to work with that between us? Anyhow, I'm fine, just tired."

It was true, though not the entire story. The time might come when Noelle spoke more about her divorce, but for now, she thought it was best for the family to think that she and Steffen had merely discovered they weren't compatible.

Sorrow filled her for what might have been, but it was for the baby she'd lost, rather than her marriage. Talking about it might help, except she wanted to relax during the holidays without everyone watching, concerned she was going to break apart at any moment. She also didn't want to do anything to diminish her parents' pleasure in their second grandchild, which was why she'd stayed silent after her own unexpected pregnancy ended in emergency surgery this last spring.

Her mother hugged her again. "I wish you'd let us meet you at the airport, or at least that you had stayed with your aunt Trish instead of at a hotel. She'll be unhappy you didn't call her."

"I'll apologize. My flight was delayed several times and I just wanted to crawl into bed." Noelle loved her extended family, but she'd also needed some peace and quiet. "You know Aunt Trish, she's a night owl and would have wanted to talk for hours."

"I understand. Come inside and have a cup of hot cider. One of your brothers can fetch your suitcases when they get back to the house. With that storm coming, they're putting winter feed down with your father and the cowhands."

"In one of Dad's emails he said the forage left in the pastures was especially good this year," Noelle said with a frown. "Surely the snow won't get deep enough that the cattle can't reach it. Not this early."

"We've had several storms, right on top of each other. We talked about it at the last ranching association meeting and most of us decided to put feed out if another one hit too soon. I'm relieved you arrived before the weather turned."

Noelle might have left for college at thirteen, but she still understood that on a ranch certain things had to be done, and taking care of the cattle was a priority. Each season presented demands to a rancher and winter was no exception.

"I can get my own luggage," Noelle said, taking her medical bag and suitcases from the trunk. Over the years she'd learned to travel light. Nobody needed a doctor who dressed like a fashion plate during a flood or earthquake.

Going inside the house was a return to childhood. Margaret Bannerman decorated for the holidays with a zest and everything glowed with autumn colors for the upcoming Thanksgiving gathering. Yellow, amber and rusty-red chrysanthemums vied for space by the fireplace and every other available surface. Fruits, vegetables and nuts spilled from wicker containers, along with winter squash and more pumpkins.

"That's new," Noelle murmured, gesturing to a basket by the fireplace, full of pine cones, with miniature white lights peeking out between them.

Margaret smiled fondly. "Mishka made it in school. She refused to make pine cone turkeys and her classmates joined her in the revolution. The teacher had to improvise."

Mishka. Any remaining chill in Noelle was chased away at the thought of her darling niece.

It seemed impossible she was old enough to attend school. Wasn't it just yesterday that she was a baby, needing her diapers changed?

"I always thought it was ironic to have children make 'happy turkey' art, and then turn around and expect them to eat turkey on the holiday."

"You're a nonconformist, too."

Noelle grinned. They went into the kitchen and she accepted a mug of hot cider. The makings for one of her mother's feasts were evident on the counters—potatoes, apples for her deluxe caramel apple pie, along with containers of pecans, flour and butter. Two bowls covered with dish towels probably contained rising bread dough. No doubt there were big containers of marinating steaks in the refrigerator.

"I realize Mishka must be at school, but is Paige bringing the baby over?" Noelle asked as they chatted.

"The whole family is coming tonight, including Jordan's grandfather, Saul Hawkins and his wife. You heard Saul also got married, right?"

Nicole nodded, knowing her mother would explain everything if given a chance.

"I should say Saul and Anna Beth will be

here if they aren't too tired," Margaret continued. "They went to Billings for a checkup with the orthopedist and are driving back this morning. Saul finally had his hip replacement operation this summer."

"Long overdue from what Paige says. I understand it was delayed several times."

"Oh, yes. She wanted to be here when you arrived, but Daniel had colic most of last night, so she hated to disturb him when he finally got to sleep. She sounded pretty tired herself."

Instant concern caught Noelle. While colic wasn't unusual with babies, Daniel was her nephew—a nephew she had yet to meet. She felt bad about not getting home sooner. "I brought my medical bag. I'll go over and see if there's anything I can do."

"I'm sure Paige would appreciate that. She's anxious to see you. I'd go along, but I might be needed here." Margaret worked actively on the ranch, often assisting with winter feeding or pulling calves in the spring, and all the other tasks required. Not to mention the coffee and chow she kept ready for anyone who'd spent long hours in the cold and needed to refuel. The ranch hands had a cook for their dining hall, but on a day like this, he'd be out helping to feed the herds.

Teamwork was vital for a family ranch to run successfully. There were times that Noelle felt guilty for leaving, but her parents had encouraged her to follow her heart, and her heart had wanted medical school. Anyway, the Blue Banner had her father and brothers and would still need a bunkhouse filled with ranch hands, so they were doing fine without her.

Noelle drank the rest of her spiced cider and donned her jacket again. It was lovely to bundle up and feel the crisp air on her cheeks. She'd mostly worked in warm climates over the years. Even on her last emergency medical posting in the Himalayas, the weather had been temperate.

Outside, the wide, intense blue of the Montana sky belied the approach of a storm. Still, there were dark clouds on the horizon and she hadn't been gone for so long that she didn't remember the sensation of shifting weather.

She'd only driven up the Soaring Hawk Ranch road once, when she'd rushed home for her sister's summer wedding. The ranch belonged to Saul Hawkins and it was odd to think Paige and her husband lived here now with Saul and his wife. Saul might have been a neighbor, but his cantankerous reputation was legendary in Shelton County.

The condition of the ranch had vastly improved since the wedding and Noelle smiled at the cornstalks and pumpkins in front of the house, similar to the ones at the Blue Banner. As she was about to knock, the door opened to reveal a grim-looking man wearing a heavy coat. He wasn't her brother-in-law or old Saul Hawkins, though there was a distinct resemblance to the Hawkins side of the family. She'd once thought the description of eyes as dark as night was fanciful, but now she changed her mind. It fit.

"Yes?" the man said sharply.

"I'm Noelle Bannerman, Paige's sister. And you're, um, Dakota Maxwell," she said, belatedly recognizing him. Neither of Jordan's brothers had been able to come to his wedding and childhood was a long time ago.

Dakota had been a lanky rebel when they were kids, swift with a joke and equally swift at stepping in when the school bullies got rowdy. His first strategy had been defusing tense situations with laughter, rather than his fists. All these years later he looked as if he'd gone through hell and back a few times.

He didn't say anything and Nicole held up her medical bag. "I'm a doctor now, making a house call."

"I don't need a doctor."

His terse, angry response made Noelle purse her lips. "Good, because I'm not here for you. Mom told me that my nephew has colic, so I came over to see if there's anything I can do to help."

DAKOTA WAS INSTANTLY CHAGRINNED.

Sometimes he didn't like himself very much, and it seemed clear from Noelle's face that she didn't care for him, either. He remembered her as a quiet squirt who'd skipped grade after grade in school. It couldn't have been easy for Noelle to be much younger and smarter than her classmates. He even recalled she'd taken online college courses at the same time she was in high school.

She'd changed. In fact, he wouldn't have known her if she hadn't introduced herself. She was taller, for one thing. And her hair was a waterfall of dark, rippling gold instead of being a pixie cut, while her brown eyes were now confident, rather than diffident.

"Of course," he said. "But Daniel may be asleep."

"I'd still like to come in and say hello."

Noelle tucked the collar of her jacket more snugly around her throat. As if in response, a chill breeze blew across the porch and swirled through the partially open door. If Dakota had been capable of turning red from embarrassment, he would have. He stepped aside to let her in, awkwardly pivoting on his right leg. Determined not to react, he ground his teeth and didn't let the twinge of pain show on his face. The specialists had told him his knee and other muscles and bones would strengthen, but they'd never be quite the same as before the mission.

"I didn't know you were in Montana," Noelle said as she set her bag on a table. It was worn, with a first responder insignia and a medical symbol. "Are you visiting for the holidays?"

"No."

Amusement filled her eyes at his curt response and he sighed. He wasn't accustomed to volunteering information, but he wasn't a SEAL any longer, protecting military secrets. Not only that, Noelle was his brother's sister-in-law. They ought to be on civil terms.

Jordan had mentioned that getting along with neighbors and the people in Shelton was important to being a successful rancher, a message his wife had impressed on him from the start of their courtship. Dakota intended to get along with everyone, but he wasn't a novice; he'd worked on the Soaring Hawk as a cowhand, waiting for his younger brother Wyatt to graduate high school so they could enlist together. And that wasn't counting all the years when he was a kid, doing chores with Saul as an unrelenting taskmaster. His grandfather hadn't believed in hiring a foreman or ranch manager. Instead he'd filled the role himself, preferring to be called either ramrod or boss.

"I got in last night," Dakota said reluctantly. "I'm moving back to Montana. Permanently."

"I see."

"*Noelle*, I can't believe you're finally here," cried Paige, his sister-in-law, as she rushed down the main staircase.

As the sisters hugged, Dakota searched for the fastest polite exit. Paige had insisted he sleep in the house last night, though he'd fully intended to use the foreman's quarters from the start, regardless of their condition. Jordan hadn't helped, grinning like a lovesick fool as his wife insisted the quarters weren't ready and they couldn't possibly let him sleep in a chilled bed when they had so much room.

Seriously?

Jordan had refused to stay in the main house with Saul when *he* first returned to Montana; why had he thought his brother would feel any different?

Marriage had changed Jordan. But even before that, he'd forgiven their grandfather for the harsh way he'd raised them. Dakota had trouble doing the same, though it wasn't their lousy childhood that bothered him. Saul had taken them away from their father after their mother died, refusing to even let them see Evan Maxwell. His dad had eventually left the area and all of their efforts to locate him had failed.

A familiar tight sensation gripped Dakota at the thought. Evan Maxwell had no reason to hide, and the only work he knew was ranching. He shouldn't have been difficult to find, which could mean he was dead and they'd never know what had happened to him. That was Jordan's assumption, but Dakota refused to give up hope. Maybe his father was ashamed to get in contact. Alcoholism wasn't an easy thing to face. He'd messed up his family and abandoned his ranch, all for the sake of forgetting his sorrows.

"Dakota, let's all go to the kitchen for something hot to drink," Paige said before he could make a discreet getaway. As soon as he and Paige had gotten reacquainted, he'd recognized she was a perfect match for his brother.

He shook his head. "I appreciate the offer, but I'll leave you and your sister to visit. I need to turn up the heat in my quarters and get back to work."

"But you've been working in the barn and paddock since four a.m."

"And Jordan will be out with the cowhands for most of the day, distributing winter feed. That's where I should be, too," he returned more sharply than he'd intended.

He didn't want to be treated as an invalid. His brother had refused to let him go with the group, saying somebody had to stay at the main ranch and keep an eye on things. But that was just an excuse, which meant even Jordan must question whether he was physically able to do the work.

"Come on," Paige coaxed, "there's no rush about moving into the foreman's quarters. In fact, we wish you'd live in the house."

Dakota couldn't take the risk. He was still having dreams about the explosion that had ended his Navy career, and the thought of frightening his young niece or nephew if he woke up yelling was unacceptable. Equally unacceptable was Saul finding out about the nightmares. They'd eventually go away—Dakota figured it was just the way his brain was processing the violent end of his mission—but his grandfather had a habit of zeroing in on anything he perceived as a weak spot.

He forced a smile. Funny, there was a time he remembered smiling a great deal. "I appreciate the offer, but this way I'd have my own space. More or less."

His sister-in-law seemed disappointed and Noelle wore a quizzical expression that would have made him suspicious in his days as a Navy SEAL. He'd spent enough time on special reconnaissance that he had a sixth sense when someone was taking an undue interest in him or his actions.

She's a doctor, he reminded himself.

It was natural for her to take an interest in his injuries and treatment.

"All right. But you're always welcome. This is your home, too."

Dakota managed another smile, hoping she wouldn't hug him, the way she had the previous night. He didn't know how to react to such enthusiastic affection from adults. It was different with Mishka, Paige's adopted daughter. Mishka was a sweet kid who seemed to love everybody without reservation.

"Thanks," he said, "but I just came in to get my keys."

He left quickly and closed the door behind him. The air was becoming colder by the moment and clouds were skidding across the sky. With any luck he could get his new quarters sorted and more work done before the storm arrived. And before his grandfather returned from Billings.

Aside from a brief visit to meet his new sister-in-law, Dakota hadn't seen Saul since enlisting and would have been fine with never seeing him again. Yet now he was living on the Soaring Hawk and would be trying to prove to the old man that his injuries wouldn't get in the way of doing what needed to be done.

It wasn't a step Dakota had expected to make so soon in his life.

NOELLE MADE A face at her sister when they were alone. "Dakota Maxwell takes after Saul Hawkins in more ways than one."

"Saul has improved," Paige said lightly. "And don't forget, now he's also my grandpa-in-law."

"He was pleasant at your wedding, but I haven't forgotten how much he scared Mom when she was a kid. We used to be pretty nervous of him, too."

Paige scrunched her nose, a gesture typical of the Bannerman women. "True, but he grows on you. And Anna Beth has lightened him up. Beneath her no-nonsense exterior, she has a heart of gold. I'm thrilled she and Saul fell in love with each other. She's just what he needs."

"I'll take your word for that. Do you need me to take a look at Daniel?"

"Thanks, but he's doing okay for now. Let's have some coffee."

Noelle followed her sister to the kitchen, a bright, cheerful room, redolent with the scent of coffee. "Are you drinking a lot of coffee these days?" she asked casually.

"Mostly the last week or two. It's the only way I can stay awake and get anything done. Daniel hasn't slept well since he was born, and now he's started to get colic," Paige explained as she filled two large mugs from the pot. "We didn't brew any in the house for a long time because Saul isn't supposed to have caffeine. We'd have to run out to the crew's dining hall where a pot is always going. But he's promised not to drink any, so we're making it inside again."

"I see." Noelle walked over and took both mugs from her sister's hands. "You need to avoid coffee, too, at least until you know if it's a problem for Daniel. When a nursing mother drinks caffeine, it can cause colic in her baby, along with some other foods. I'm surprised your doctor didn't tell you that."

Paige looked dismayed. "The colic is pretty new, so I haven't had a chance to discuss it with Dr. Wycoff. You mean I've been doing this to Daniel? Mishka had colic when she was little and I wasn't nursing *her*."

Paige had adopted Mishka as an infant from India five years earlier, so she had experience with babies.

"Try not to worry," Noelle soothed. "If the colic is related to food or beverages, it should clear up fast. I'll get you a list of the most likely suspects. Start by eliminating anything you began eating or drinking recently. But caffeine seems the likely culprit to me."

She eyed Paige, who had already lost her pregnancy weight. Paige had always munched on whatever she wanted and stayed slender, which had frustrated Noelle when they were kids. It had been hard to watch her little sister eat chocolate and other sweets without gaining an ounce.

"Uh, I hate reminding you that chocolate also has a small amount of caffeine," she added. "If Daniel has been restless at night since he was born, I'm guessing he might be bothered by any chocolate you were eating."

"All right." Despite agreeing, her sister yawned and looked longingly at the coffee.

"Take a nap," Noelle suggested. "I'll watch Daniel if he wakes up."

"Maybe later. I haven't seen you in forever. And we barely talked when you were in the Himalayas because you could only get reception on a satellite phone. You were too busy, anyhow."

Noelle's midriff tightened with the reminder. She'd managed a two-minute call each week to the family on her team's satellite phone, but that was all. It was just as well. They would have asked about the earthquake recovery efforts and she would have had trouble keeping her composure.

"All right," she agreed. "Then sit down and

tell me what's going on with your brother-in-law. Dakota doesn't seem happy to be here."

Paige sighed as they settled at the kitchen table. "It's that challenge Saul sent Jordan and his brothers a while back. Basically, if they spend a year on the Soaring Hawk and prove themselves as ranchers, they'll get a third of the acreage through a trust, along with cattle and some other stuff. Jordan did it, and now that Dakota has left the Navy, he's accepted."

"It's a great opportunity," Noelle agreed, "though I don't understand why Saul doesn't just leave the ranch to them. He doesn't have any other family to inherit. Right?"

Paige kept her gaze downcast. "No. But the relationships are complicated and Dakota is as unhappy about the situation as Jordan was when he first arrived. Maybe more, which is strange because Jordan says Saul wasn't as demanding with the two younger boys after he was gone. Anyway, I hoped returning would be easier for Dakota."

"Moving home after so long would be complicated for most people."

"I wanted to fix a big homecoming meal and Dakota refused," Paige went on unhappily. "He seems angry and Jordan is worried about him. But please don't repeat that."

"Of course not." Noelle traced a circle on the table with her finger, trying to choose the right words. Dakota Maxwell wasn't any of her concern, but her sister was involved, so it mattered. "I noticed the recent scars on Dakota's face. Does that have something to do with him being here?"

The original lacerations had obviously been treated by an expert. There was also a slight hesitation and stiffness in Dakota's stride, suggesting his injuries were extensive.

Paige nodded. "He had to take a medical discharge because of his leg. I know you're on vacation, but Jordan says Dakota is supposed to get physical therapy. Is there any chance you could, I don't know, encourage him to do it? Maybe even work with him while you're here. We don't have a physio in Shelton and I doubt he'll go to Bozeman or Helena."

Noelle suspected Dakota wouldn't be open to encouragement. She was also sure he'd be a monster of a patient for any doctor or physical therapist. He might be even worse as a friend. Still, while the last year had exhausted her in every way, she felt a hint of exhilaration at the prospect of going toe-to-toe with him.

"I'm not an orthopedist or trained in therapy," Noelle said slowly, "but I could show him a few exercises if he's interested. As your sister. He's already made it very clear he doesn't want a doctor."

"Whatever you can do would be wonderful."

Paige's earnest concern for her husband's family made Noelle wistful. Steffen's parents had welcomed her, yet a barrier had risen when they discovered she wasn't going to stop flying around the world for her work. It turned out that Steffen had assumed they would both resign and get jobs in the states, while she'd believed they would keep doing disaster relief.

Her marriage had been a case of totally mixed signals, along with mistaking a mutual respect for love. There hadn't been any real attraction between them. She still cared about her ex as a friend, but they should have *stayed* friends.

An image of Dakota crept into Noelle's mind.

He was a warrior. Obstinate and currently projecting the personality of an injured grizzly bear, though his old, devil-may-care attitude might resurface once he'd had more time to recover. He was wounded, not defeated. There was even something a little dangerous about him, which shouldn't intrigue her.

But did.

CHAPTER TWO

"I'M STAYING HERE, not eating with your in-laws," Dakota told his brother a few hours later as he cleaned stalls in the horse barn. "You married into the Bannerman clan, which makes them your family, not mine. I have no intention of being a stranger at their dinner table."

Jordan gave him an exasperated look. "You're my brother, that makes you family to them. Saul and Anna Beth are going, too. Besides, you grew up in Shelton, so you're hardly a stranger."

Dakota was glad his brother had found a place he felt at home, but returning was a different story for him. He hadn't chosen to leave the Navy; they'd discharged him because of his leg, which stuck in his craw for multiple reasons. But the worst part was that two members of his SEAL team had died in the explosion—good men he'd served with for years.

"Bro?" Jordan prompted. "You aren't self-conscious about how you look, right? You were never as handsome as me, but no one can have everything."

Beneath his brother's teasing comment, Dakota knew Jordan was really asking if he was uncomfortable about the maze of red scars on the right side of his face. He didn't think much about them, aside from having to be cautious while shaving. One of the doctors had suggested growing a beard if he didn't want plastic surgery, but Dakota preferred being clean-shaven. The marks weren't pretty, but he had more important things to think about. Anyhow, getting banged up wasn't unusual for a SEAL, whether in training or on assignment. He'd accepted scars as a matter of course. Most of them faded with time.

"I always thought Wyatt was the handsome Maxwell brother," Dakota said easily. "But someone needs to be at the Soaring Hawk to keep an eye on things while the storm moves in. That's what you said when you insisted I stay behind while everyone else was putting down hay and protein cake for the herd."

Truthfully, he just wasn't interested in socializing. It was one thing to have a beer with his SEAL team, another to be surrounded by family chitchat that had nothing to do with him.

Jordan shook his head. "One of the things I've learned is that being in charge doesn't mean you have to do it all yourself. The hands can keep watch. I give a fair amount of responsibility to Melody James, in particular. Regardless, with the weather changing we won't be gone for long. We don't want to cancel—it means a lot to my mother-in-law to have everyone there tonight for Noelle."

"I'm new and don't know the ranch hands yet. I'm staying here."

Dakota's mind was made up and he wasn't backing down. More than anything, the thought of eating with his grandfather was impossible—he wasn't a hypocrite, so sitting with Saul at a convivial dinner table would make him choke. He could never forget the old man had prevented them from seeing their father after getting custody.

"Do whatever you want," Jordan growled, visibly annoyed as he left the barn.

Dakota knew his brother didn't understand. On the surface his relationship with Saul hadn't been as difficult as the one between Jordan and their grandfather. But underneath, Dakota would have done anything to get away. He'd even played practical jokes around the area as a form of rebellion. Looking back, he was appalled at his behavior—if anyone had found out he was responsible, it would have caused serious problems for him and Wyatt. Saul was the type to always come down hard on both of them, no matter who was responsible.

A few minutes later he heard a vehicle drive away. Relieved, he put out a hand and rested his weight on the gate of a horse stall. The pain in his leg and knee had grown through the day; he would have to do something about it once the work was done.

His grandfather had come out to check up on him after getting back from Billings. Sixteen years had passed, yet Dakota had still gone defensive when Saul asked about his injuries. To someone else the old man might have sounded concerned, but Dakota knew better.

Saul was looking for a weakness.

Any weakness.

He'd believed his grandsons would turn out like their father and been determined to work the "bad genes" out of them. He was probably convinced he still needed to do the same thing.

"You should elevate your leg to take down the swelling," Noelle Bannerman said from the barn door, startling him. "Also use an ice pack. The cold air probably isn't enough."

Dakota quickly straightened. "I don't know what you're talking about."

She walked toward him with the same easy grace he'd noticed in his sister-in-law. "I can tell your knee is swollen, even covered by your jeans."

Doctors.

He scowled. "That's none of your concern— I'm not your patient."

The smile faded from her face. "I'm glad you aren't. My patients are in desperate circumstances because of natural disasters or epidemics or war. Or sometimes simply because of backbreaking poverty. You're healthy, have a home and are able to work. But that doesn't mean you're an iron man."

"I never said I was."

"From what I've seen of Navy SEALs, you believe you're out to save the world."

"I could say the same for doctors who dash around the globe to hot spots in order to practice medicine," he retorted.

"I'd rather prevent people from getting sick or injured in the first place. But I'm a doctor, no more or less, and there are limits to what any of us can do." For an instant, a palpable wave of sadness seemed to come from her, then she lifted and dropped her shoulders and it was gone.

Dakota sighed. Noelle may have witnessed as many horrors in her work as he'd seen himself. Was that what she'd expected when she was in high school, determined to get into medical school?

"You've always wanted to be a doctor, haven't you?" he asked.

Though both from ranching families, they'd moved in different circles at school. As a matter of fact, she'd skipped so many grades, the age difference between Noelle and her classmates must have made her "circle" a circle of one by the time she graduated.

"I can barely remember when I wasn't planning to go to medical school." She gestured to his leg. "Jordan and the rest of the family have left for the Blue Banner. Is there any harm in letting me check your knee before I leave myself? As a concerned bystander, not a physician. You needn't worry that I'll tell anyone. I'm licensed in this state, but I wouldn't want the Shelton medical clinic to think I'm competing with them."

The request was so reasonable, it seemed churlish to refuse. The Navy docs had made a point of saying he needed to consult a physician when he reached Montana. He might do that eventually, but the VA didn't have a facility in Shelton and taking the better part of a day to drive to a larger community and back was out of the question for a while.

"All right, just not in my quarters. I don't want the ranch hands to think I'm already entertaining guests in case they come out for a breath of air or something."

"How about the tack room? We can close the door to protect your reputation. Or keep it open, if you think that's better." Noelle sounded amused, but he was serious about projecting the correct image to the Soaring Hawk employees. Starting right meant fewer problems along the way.

Without another word he headed for the tack room, still making an effort not to limp. Once the door was shut, he sat on a chair and pulled off his boot. But when he began tugging his jeans up his right leg, he was stymied by the hem of the aging fabric. It wouldn't go all the way over the swollen joint.

"I'm not dropping my pants for you," he warned.

"I don't recall asking." Noelle sank onto a footstool and pulled off the gloves she wore. Her slim hands eased under the denim and their softness seemed to instantly soothe the hot, tight swelling. She traced the scars left by both the original injury and the corrective operations since then.

"So, what do you think?"

Noelle looked up. "I can't tell you more than you already know, less because I can't determine much beyond the swelling. Recovery takes time. I'm guessing you've pushed yourself too hard today." Her fingers continued moving in small circular motions, sometimes firmer, sometimes lighter, and he could swear the pain eased with each stroke.

"I'm working, that's all. I've pushed even harder during training or on a mission."

"I'm sure of that, though probably not while recovering from surgery. Without reviewing your medical records, I wouldn't know if you're in danger of reinjuring yourself."

"Not to worry—the Navy docs cleared me for work on the ranch."

WITHIN REASON, Noelle qualified silently.

She doubted a doctor had given Dakota carte blanche to pursue any activity he wanted, however he wanted—though not being an orthopedist, she couldn't say for certain. However, since the scars on his face couldn't be more than a few months old, he must still be healing. And Navy doctors wouldn't have much experience with the demands put on a cowboy.

"As I recall, this is one of the lighter periods on a ranch," she said, dropping her hands. "So you should be able to enjoy the holidays, do your rehab and settle in as the Soaring Hawk's foreman."

As if in response, a gust of wind hit the side of the barn. The sturdy structure shuddered.

Dakota snickered and she made a face.

"All right," she agreed, "it's a lighter period if the weather cooperates. I know the incoming storm is causing a ton of work, but at least it isn't on top of calving season."

Calving season, which could begin as early as February, was a brutal period. A good percentage of cows, especially first-time mothers, needed assistance with birthing their babies. Then there were the various diseases that new calves could contract.

"It doesn't matter—I don't celebrate the holidays. Just call me the local Christmas grouch." Dakota gestured to his chest. "The guy with a heart that's a few sizes too small."

Noelle stared.

Perhaps that was his idea of a joke, but she didn't think it was funny. Christmas in Shelton was wonderful. They had a lighted tractor parade, craft bazaars, weekly gatherings in the park for groups to perform—an event known as the Park Carolers—a community tree-lighting ceremony, a holiday Bake-Off along with a house-decorating contest, tours and other celebrations. It pushed off the chill of winter and the unrelenting effort to keep the herds healthy. Since graduating from medical school she'd had little chance to spend the entire holiday season in Montana and she was determined to take part in *all* the festivities this year.

"I'm surprised you didn't go with 'bah, humbug,'" she said finally.

"I'll leave that to my grandfather. He used to call Christmas a bother and refused to celebrate."

"Don't look now, but you're taking after

him," Noelle returned in a dry tone that made Dakota scowl.

She heard a truck driving into the ranch center and the sound seemed to make him restless. He shoved the hem of his jeans down over his boot and stood. "You'd better get going or you'll be late for dinner with your family."

In other words, *leave me alone*.

Okay, fine. She would do as she'd promised her sister and try to help Dakota with some exercises, but a temporary strategic retreat was in order. Of course, that didn't mean she couldn't give him a parting shot across his proverbial bow.

"It's too bad you aren't coming," she said casually. "My mother is a fabulous cook. She's making steak and her cheesy scalloped potatoes, with caramel apple pie for dessert. The pie has a buttery pecan crumb topping that's positively decadent. Mom always makes it the first night I get home."

Noelle resisted smiling at Dakota's expression. She wasn't playing fair to describe the menu, but food was a great icebreaker. In her work she'd often discovered that eating together took down barriers that might otherwise have remained insurmountable.

She thought Dakota had almost been convinced to join the Bannerman gathering, then he shook his head. "Enjoy your homecoming dinner."

Regret niggled at Noelle. They'd both come home after a long absence, his much longer than her own. In Dakota's case he was back for good, but he had refused a celebratory meal in his honor. A variety of explanations flitted through her mind; she just didn't know enough about him to do more than speculate.

"Thanks. I'm sure Mom will send food back with Paige and Jordan."

He shrugged, revealing nothing in his expression, and Noelle clenched her jaw in frustration. It shouldn't matter, but his attitude might upset Paige, who had one of the softest hearts in the world.

Noelle collected her gloves and stood up. "I should be back tomorrow or the next day, depending on the storm. Maybe I can check your leg again."

"That isn't necessary."

His tone didn't brook argument, so she'd have to find another way to help out. Noelle wasn't accustomed to people ducking her medical care, but he'd made it clear she wasn't his doctor. Not that she thought friendship was an option with him, either.

Outside the temperature had dropped another few degrees and she shivered. The timing of her arrival in Shelton could have been better and she wished her mother had postponed the homecoming gathering for a few days. With any luck they'd finish quickly, letting Paige and her family return to the Soaring Hawk before the weather became too hazardous for driving.

Noelle scrunched her nose.

She might also be overreacting. It had been years since she'd experienced a serious Montana blizzard. The Blue Banner and Soaring Hawk ranches weren't far from each other and she was the only one in the family driving a small compact. Maybe she should have rented something larger, but it had seemed a waste.

"Excuse me?" said a voice and she turned to see someone getting out of a battered pickup truck. From what she could tell through his winter wraps, he was young, perhaps in his early twenties. "My name is Alex Sorenson. Are you Mrs. Maxwell?"

"I'm Noelle Bannerman, Mrs. Maxwell's sister. I'm acquainted with your parents. They own the Sunny Crest Ranch, north of Shelton, right?"

"Yes, ma'am. Is the new ramrod around?"

"That would be me," Dakota said as he stepped from the barn and closed the door.

Alex shuffled his feet. "I heard there's a newspaper want ad coming out, looking for ranch hands. Came to apply."

Dakota's black eyebrows rose and Noelle was surprised as well. It was late in the afternoon and a storm was brewing. He could have phoned.

"I'll get going," she told the men. "Have a good evening."

Behind the thick western clouds, the sun was dropping toward the mountains. She loved this time of day. When she was little she'd believed the worlds of her imagination intersected at twilight. Her imagination hadn't been welcome in medical school, but once she was doing disaster relief work in the field, the ability to come up with creative solutions had proven useful.

She got in the car and turned the heat to full blast. If the weather stayed like this, she'd have to buy extra winter gear in Shelton or borrow some from her mom and sister.

As she backed out, she saw the two men in

her rearview mirror. She watched for a moment, hoping Dakota would change his mind about going with her, but Alex Sorenson's arrival had made it even more unlikely.

Ramrod.

A few of the older ranchers continued using the old term for foreman—men like Saul Hawkins, who had been a stern boss to the people who worked for him. But modern times or not, ranching life in Montana still required tough, resilient people.

DAKOTA REGARDED THE kid in front of him. This might be his first day on the job as foreman, but he already knew getting and keeping cowhands was an ongoing challenge. With a long, hard winter predicted, his brother had expected to advertise for another couple of employees.

"Come into the office," Dakota said, motioning to the foreman's quarters on the other side of the paddock, on to which his brother and sister-in-law had built a ranch business office and storage area. The heat had been on long enough it should be reasonably warm, though in this kind of weather, it would take a while for the walls to lose their chill.

Once inside, Alex seemed to hesitate, then

took off his hat and the knitted scarf that covered the lower part of his face. His chin jutted as burn scars on his jaw and neck were revealed.

Dakota gestured to a chair. "If your family owns a ranch, why are you looking for work elsewhere?"

"I was in an accident a few years ago and Mom and Dad still think I can't handle doing anything too physical. They mean well—they're just overprotective. But I can do the work—you don't need to worry about that. I won All-Around Best Cowboy once in the junior rodeo and I grew up helping run the Sunny Crest. I can pull a calf, operate and repair haying equipment, muck stalls. Anything you need."

"Have you talked to your parents about this?"

"They know I planned to go job hunting. A buddy called me. He said the Soaring Hawk would be hiring and that…" His voice trailed off and he looked miserable.

Dakota didn't need to ask what the friend had said. He'd stopped in town before coming out to the ranch and seen a few curious glances at his own scarred face. The cold air made the scars stand out more, turning them a deep purplish red. He had also met with the ranch hands this morning in the bunkhouse dining hall, before they'd left to put down feed for the cattle. Even with the weather turning, there would have been time for a phone call or two.

"Someone told you that I have scars on my face," he said bluntly. "And you figured I'd understand how you feel."

"Well, uh…" Alex's voice trailed off again and he flushed. "There's a lot of stuff going on. Mr. Maxwell, I just want to prove myself somewhere. Is that so awful? My folks try to make everything easy on me and I *hate* it. The hands at the ranch know I'm not pulling my weight, but that's because Mom and Dad won't let me. If you call, Dad will probably say he's worried I can't handle the job. Except it isn't true. I'm strong—I can do whatever you need."

Dakota understood Alex's frustration and sat back with a frown. Should he get a doctor's release for the kid, or accept his word that it wouldn't be detrimental to do physically demanding tasks? This was one of the sticky parts of being the boss. On the other hand, Alex was of age and could make his own decisions. He'd lack references if he had always worked on his family's spread, but it would be obvious soon enough if he wasn't able to do the work.

"You must want the job pretty badly to come down before the ad was even published," Dakota said.

"I wanted to be the first to apply."

"All right. You'll need to fill out paperwork and I'll have to do the necessary checks before it's official."

Another broadside of wind hit the building. But it was nothing to what it would soon be like. Dakota remembered blizzards from his childhood. The temperature would plummet and it would seem as if a raging curtain of white was sweeping over the land.

"In the meantime," he continued, "there's an empty bed in the men's half of the bunkhouse if you'd care to stay and not drive back in this wind."

A broad smile crossed the young man's face. "Yes, sir. That would be fine. I carry an emergency pack of clothes and supplies in winter, so I'm set. Can I do the paperwork now?"

Clearly he didn't want to take any chance Dakota would change his mind. That was fine. An eager recruit was always preferable to someone who didn't care.

Not a recruit, Dakota reminded himself. *A new employee.* After spending most of his adult life in the Navy, he thought in military terms. That would have to change.

The swift assessment he'd given the office earlier had showed a well-organized filing system, including a prominent "new hires" folder lying on the desk. Courtesy of his sister-in-law, no doubt. Jordan's wife helped with the cattle and horses whenever she had time, but she primarily did accounting and was the business manager for both the Soaring Hawk and her parents' ranch. He opened the file and handed Alex a pen and a set of the employment forms inside, then settled down to wait.

Without intending to, his hand found his injured knee, though not because it hurt. Instead he was remembering the sensation of Noelle's fingers, soothing the pain.

Nonsense, his brain told him.

It was just the normal reaction to an attractive woman, his senses focusing on her, rather than the throb in his leg. He didn't believe in a healing touch.

For that matter, he didn't believe in much of anything.

"I'm finished," Alex said fifteen minutes later.

He held out the pages he'd completed and Dakota locked them in a desk drawer, knowing he would have to discuss the Soaring Hawk's hiring procedures with Jordan. In essence, he now worked for his brother and grandfather. He had to do things their way, and doing a good job meant he'd end up with one-third of the ranch in a trust.

Before the mission had exploded in his face, he wouldn't have doubted being able to show he could be a rancher. After all, he'd succeeded in becoming a Navy SEAL, perhaps the most rigorous training course in the world. Except now it was harder not to question himself.

His hand tightened briefly on his keys before he shoved them in his pocket.

No one had come out and said it, but despite the official findings, he wondered if senior command thought he was responsible for the deaths on the mission. He wouldn't blame them.

Not when he also blamed himself.

CHAPTER THREE

THE SUN WAS shining through the bedroom window when Noelle woke after her third night back in Shelton; the storm had lasted two days but finally blown over while she slept. She inhaled the rich scent of apples and spice rising from the first floor of the house. For a moment she was ten years old again.

She yawned and looked at the clock, then shot upright, the blankets tumbling from her shoulders.

How could it be after nine o'clock?

She didn't sleep in, and on a ranch, nobody else slept in, either.

"Drat," she muttered.

"Mrrrrooow," grumbled the cat who was curled up on the pillow next to her.

"Sorry, Asa."

When Noelle stroked Asa's neck, he rolled to his back, waving his white paws in the air. The family had adopted him a few years after she'd left for college, a scrawny kitten they'd found on the public road that ran by the ranch.

He was showing his advanced age, but he was still gorgeous, with long black fur, a large white spot on his tummy and a smaller one on his chin to match his feet. Hopefully he would be around for years to come, a lovable goofball, demanding his place on laps and purring his head off. Once he'd discovered the comforts of an indoor life, he had shown no interest in venturing out again, even to the barns. He liked to lounge on pillows, not nests of hay or straw.

"I'd better get dressed," she whispered to the little purr machine.

As if in protest, Asa wrapped his paws around her wrist and gave her a kitty kiss. His raspy tongue tickled her palm and prompted a smile.

"I should have been up hours ago," Noelle murmured, not feeling particularly motivated, though she'd slept for twelve hours straight. "Mom is going to think I'm lazy."

Finally she freed her hand from the feline's grasp and swung her feet to the floor. She still felt the bone-deep weariness which had brought her home in the first place. A part of her knew it was emotional—both grief from losing the baby, followed by her most recent assignment that had strained the entire medical crew to the limit. It was terrible to lose one patient, but the earthquake in the Himalayas had taken an unbelievable toll. So many wonderful people gone, along with their homes and livelihoods.

How many times could someone's heart break and still be able to heal?

She tried to think about something else as she dressed and headed down to the main floor.

"Mom?" she called.

"In here."

Here was the kitchen, where her mother was busily canning applesauce, apple butter and other assorted apple products. The Bannermans had experimented over the years and found apple varieties that did well in Montana's relatively short growing period. A large orchard lay behind the house, along with the kitchen garden.

"You should have woken me up to help," Noelle said.

"Nonsense. You need to rest. That's why you're home longer than usual, right?" Margaret asked shrewdly.

"Nothing gets by you, Mom."

"I can see it in your face, darling. You haven't seemed terribly upset about the divorce, but I can't help wondering if that's the reason."

Noelle shook her head. "Not really, though I feel guilty for not listening to my instincts. Steffen is a great guy, but we were fooling ourselves about being in love. It seemed as if we should be perfect for each other with our interest in international relief projects, then it turned out we weren't."

"I'm so sorry, dear. Sit down and I'll get your breakfast ready."

"Just coffee is fine."

"It isn't fine—you need something in your stomach." Margaret was a firm believer in the restorative power of food. She swiftly prepared scrambled eggs and ham, along with a stack of fluffy pancakes.

With a wry sigh, Noelle sat at the table. The family had refused to let her help during the storm and now her mother wouldn't let her assist in the kitchen. She felt positively useless.

"Paige called," Margaret said. "Daniel didn't have any colic last night and they were able to get some sleep for the first time in two weeks. She's so grateful for the advice about caffeine.

It didn't occur to me since you kids never had trouble with colic. I practically lived on coffee when you all were babies."

Noelle was glad to hear she'd accomplished much more than just sitting around and visiting since arriving in Montana.

"Did she say anything about her brother-in-law?"

Margaret blinked. "Is there any reason she should have?"

"Just wondered. I ran into Dakota at the Soaring Hawk the other day. He's even more intense than when he was a kid, minus his old smile. I remember he used to kid around a lot."

Noelle pictured Dakota's dark, serious eyes. The Maxwell brothers were part of her childhood, but she'd had little contact with them. She didn't even recall them being on the school bus until after they'd gone to live with their grandfather. But the three of them *must* have been there. Their father's old ranch, the Circle M, was on the same bus route. And they would have attended the same community events before their mother died, either with the ranch association or somewhere else.

"Did you know Dakota's mom?" she asked.

Margaret looked up from the apples she

was paring. "Not well. Victoria had a good sense of humor and played jokes on people. Gentle jokes—she never did anything unkind. Dakota's rambunctious boyhood pranks were much more like his father's when he was a teenager. We knew Dakota was the one painting the water tower and such, but didn't want to say anything to make things more difficult for him with Saul. Anyhow, Dakota used water-soluble paint, so it didn't cost much to fix. Sheriff Cranston did the cleanup himself."

Noelle cut a wedge of pancake, trying to find the right words. "If things were bad for Dakota and his brothers, why didn't anyone do something about it?"

Her mother's expression saddened. "We didn't think it was bad, but it must have been difficult to go from having two loving, outgoing parents to living with a stern, loner grandfather."

"I see." Noelle swirled the pancake wedge through maple syrup. "Would it have been better if they'd stayed with their dad?"

Margaret sighed. "I'm afraid not. Evan Maxwell's drinking problem after his wife died wasn't a secret. He'd pass out at the bar in Shelton and Sheriff Cranston had to bring him home. There were brawls and other problems, including drunk driving, though the boys were never with Evan as far as anyone knows."

Noelle shuddered at the thought. "What does Jordan say about it?"

"Very little. His childhood is off-limits. But we know Evan stopped taking care of the Circle M, to the point he couldn't even sell it. Then one day he just left. Paige thinks he might have wanted to get away and pull himself together, so he kept paying the property tax on the ranch for a while, then that stopped, too. Basically, after they went into the Navy, his sons got ownership of the Circle M by paying the back taxes."

"Jordan must talk about his childhood with Paige."

"I'm sure he does—they're very close. He's a fine man and such a wonderful daddy to our little Mishka. We're thrilled to have him in the family." Margaret would have welcomed any spouse chosen by one of her children, but her sincere affection for Jordan Maxwell was unmistakable.

Fresh melancholy hit Noelle and she shook herself. "Are you certain I can't help with the canning?"

"Positive. I have a rhythm going. The roads should be plowed by now. Why don't you visit Paige or some of your friends?"

Noelle didn't remind her mother that she'd been so fixated on leapfrogging through school and taking online college courses, she hadn't made many friends. There was a price to be paid for that kind of dedication. She didn't mind, but lately had wondered if there were other options to consider.

Like a family?

She shoved the thought away. Dwelling on something that couldn't be changed was no help. She'd been fortunate to be back in the States when she started having a problem; with an ectopic pregnancy, she could have bled to death if she'd been too far from a hospital and proper diagnostic equipment.

She got up. "I'll grab my coat and go over to see Paige."

Margaret frowned at her plate. "I meant you should go for a visit after you finished breakfast. You haven't eaten nearly enough."

"I've had plenty, Mom."

Noelle kissed her mother and went out to the foyer for her coat and bag.

It was good to know her nephew was doing better. The doctor would have advised Paige about the colic on her next well-baby visit, but at least she'd helped her sister and brother-in-law get some rest in the meantime.

ALEX DIDN'T HAVE to think while mucking the horse stalls; the task was so familiar, he could do it in his sleep. Right now they needed cleaning twice a day because the ranch's horses had spent the entire storm in the barn.

The day before yesterday, in the middle of the storm, Dakota had officially hired him, assigning him the task of making sure the horses in the barn were fed and had plenty of fresh water, along with cleaning the stalls.

The Soaring Hawk's horses were awesome: some of the best Alex had ever seen. With so many stabled in the frigid weather, cleaning up after them was more than a full-time job, so the other hands were rotating to help him out.

Alex hoped that eventually he'd be assigned other duties as well, but was grateful Dakota had given him a chance. That was all he'd wanted from his parents; they just couldn't see beyond his injuries. Besides, taking care of animals was an important job and he was proud to be given the responsibility of ensuring they were all right.

Alex ran the loaded wheelbarrow behind the barn to empty it on one of the compost heaps, then headed back inside. He spread more fresh straw, moved the horse to its clean stall and grabbed the shovel again.

The temperature was still below zero. Only when it warmed up would the horses be allowed to spend time in the paddock. He'd need to learn the various quirks and personalities of the different animals, but he could tell they were restless now that the storm had passed, eager to be in the open air with space to move.

Some were out working—Dakota and the hands were checking the herds to see how they'd fared during the blizzard. Having a few of the horses gone made it easier to muck out the stalls.

"Hey, girl," he murmured to Dolley Madison. She was Mrs. Maxwell's horse, along with Cinnamon. Both mares were gentle and closely bonded to Mrs. Maxwell, who'd come to visit during the storm with her husband. The Maxwells were great, though Alex was still sorting out who did what on the Soaring Hawk.

After another few stalls, the wheelbarrow was full and he was rolling it out of the barn when an old green truck came down the ranch road.

He groaned.

It was Blair Darby. She parked, got out and slammed the door with a bang.

Alex tried to pretend she wasn't there, once again directing the wheelbarrow around the end of the barn.

"I see you, Alex," she called, following.

"What of it? I'm working."

"You shouldn't be working here—you should be on the Sunny Crest. It's your family's spread. They need you."

He dropped the wheelbarrow handles and turned around. "Dad doesn't need me—he hired two extra hands when I was in the hospital. One who's still there, by the way. Anthony is okay, but I should be doing his job."

Blair glared at him, so beautiful he ached to look at her. But he had to ignore the way she made him feel, the way he'd been ignoring it since waking up in a Seattle hospital and finding out his life had fallen apart. He couldn't marry Blair and live with her feeling sorry for him.

"That was over two years ago and he was back and forth to Washington, seeing you at the hospital. He needed the help. Anyhow, the

Sunny Crest has more cattle now," Blair retorted. "So your dad needs more employees."

"Not if he'd let me work properly."

"You *do* work there. Or did, until you took a job at the Soaring Hawk." She lowered her voice. "Honestly, this place belongs to Sourpuss Hawkins. Don't you remember the stories about him?"

Alex dumped the mixed straw and horse manure. "Don't call him that. I talked to Mr. Hawkins this morning and he seems okay. Besides, Dakota Maxwell is the ramrod. Uh, I mean, the foreman. I work for him."

"Whatever. But your mom and dad—"

"Dakota will let me do my part, my parents don't. Just go away. I wouldn't want anyone thinking I'm slacking off and already having visitors."

"Please don't do this," Blair begged. "Maybe I shouldn't have pushed about us getting back together. Don't take it out on your mom and dad."

Alex was furious. "I'm not taking anything out on them. I simply made a decision not to be treated as half a person any longer. No more plastic surgery or counseling or pretending nothing happened. I am what I am."

BLAIR WOULD HAVE cried if she wasn't still so angry she could spit. She'd loved Alex since they were eleven and been friends with him for years before that—did he honestly think she was so shallow that a few scars would change her mind? Okay. So life wasn't going the way they'd planned—life rarely went as planned.

He lifted the handles of the wheelbarrow. "I don't want to talk any more. Go find someone else. Did you ever stop to think that I'm a different person now, or that I no longer want the same things I used to want?"

Blair sucked in a breath…marrying *her* was one of the things he'd wanted. They'd planned a future together all through high school, yet clear as anything, he was suggesting he didn't love her any longer. But was he trying to be noble, or did he really mean it?

She was still trying to come up with something to say when he disappeared with the wheelbarrow into the barn.

Blair looked around the snowy ranch center. Never in her wildest imagination had she ever expected to be on the Soaring Hawk or anywhere close to Sourpuss Hawkins. The stories about him were epic, not that she believed most of them.

"Hi. Are you here to apply for the ranch hand opening?" Blair wheeled to see a tall man approaching her. "We still have one position available."

A job. That was an interesting idea. If she worked for the Soaring Hawk she'd get to see Alex some of the time. He couldn't avoid her if she was living at the same place *he* was living.

"I'd love to apply," she said. "My name is Blair Darby and I've worked with horses and cattle since I was a kid. I have a degree in computer science, but I started out studying ranch management. I also helped at my aunt and uncle's ranch every summer during college and on the weekends when I could get home. They raised me from when I was eight."

"Excellent. You'll need to talk to my brother, Dakota Maxwell. He's just taken over as foreman and is doing the hiring. I'm Jordan Maxwell, part owner of the Soaring Hawk."

"It's nice to meet you, Mr. Maxwell."

"A pleasure, Blair. Dakota is out with the other cowhands. I'll check to see when he's coming back."

Blair glanced at the horse barn, half expecting Alex to come out yelling a protest, but maybe he couldn't hear enough from inside the building to realize what was going on.

"I don't want to be a bother, Mr. Maxwell."

Jordan took out his phone. "It's no bother. Let me step away while I talk to him."

She was glad he hadn't asked why she wasn't working in information technology or on her family's spread. She'd been doing freelance web designs, but her latest contracts were almost completed and she was ahead of schedule. As for her aunt and uncle, they'd known she and Alex planned to get married, so they'd never anticipated her working on the Canary Diamond. Naturally she helped out, but her cousins were there and could more than handle the ranch with Uncle Will and their cowhands.

Aunt Sarah and Uncle Will were wonderful. As a wedding gift to her and Alex, they'd promised to buy a starter herd of twenty-five certified organic heifers and two certified organic bulls, their one proviso being that Blair get her college degree before the wedding.

It was ironic, since converting the Sunny Crest to an organic operation had originally been Alex's dream. He'd even started the process of certifying the family ranch when they were college freshmen. She didn't know if the organic certification was done or had gotten dropped. Perhaps that was another thing he no longer wanted or cared about. Why else would he go work for a different ranch?

She sighed, wishing she hadn't said anything about his father's decision to keep an extra cowhand on the payroll. As much as she loved Alex's parents, she didn't want him to think she was taking their side.

"Good news, Blair," Jordan Maxwell said, returning. "Dakota will be back at the main ranch before long. You're welcome to wait up at the house or in the foreman's office."

"The foreman's office," she said hastily. Sourpuss Hawkins couldn't be as bad as the stories told about him, but she didn't want to find out the hard way.

Mr. Maxwell escorted her to the office and she sat down, looking around curiously. Though the room blended with the rest of the building, she'd heard they had been doing construction on the Soaring Hawk. The office was probably new. It *smelled* new.

She took off her jacket, loving that a large black-and-white tuxedo cat was stretched out on the desk, unconcerned about their arrival. Blair gave the cat his due attention after Mr.

Maxwell left, then pulled out her phone and dialed her aunt.

"Is Alex listening to reason?" Aunt Sarah asked immediately.

"No. In fact, he pretty much said we're over. But I'm going to apply for a job on the Soaring Hawk so I can be near him."

There was a brief silence on the phone. "Are you sure that's a good idea, Blair?"

"What choice do I have? At least he can't dodge me this way. Maybe if he sees me every day, he'll remember how much we're in love."

"He's already hurt you once."

Blair pulled in a deep, miserable breath. Actually, Alex had hurt her numerous times over the last two and a half years. First by telling his parents he didn't want to see her at the hospital, and later again at the rehab center. He also hadn't taken any of her calls. Then he'd sent a message that he'd decided not to finish college. And how about rarely letting her visit once he got home from Seattle? Or never *ever* letting her kiss him?

Each rejection had been like a knife in her chest. But he'd never actually broken up with her. Her hope now was to change his mind.

"I know, Aunt Sarah," Blair admitted through a tight throat. "But I need to do this."

"Well, maybe it's an opportunity to figure out if you still love him, or discover whether you've grown too far apart to make a life together. That *does* happen," her aunt said gently. "You need to be prepared for the possibility."

Blair had trouble imagining a future that didn't include Alex, but her aunt and uncle worried that she was too much like her mom, who'd been wildly unrealistic about romance. Renee Darby was the poster child for finding love in all the wrong places. Ultimately, she'd left her daughter in Montana to pursue a relationship that landed her in prison.

As for Blair's father? Nobody even knew his name.

"I realize that," Blair said reluctantly.

"Promise you'll think about it," Aunt Sarah pleaded. "I care about Alex, but you're my niece. Your happiness is my first concern."

Don't be like my sister.

Blair knew that was what her aunt was thinking. But she wasn't going to self-destruct over Alex; she just needed to know with absolute certainty that he didn't love her any longer. And maybe she needed to sort out her own heart after spending so much time waiting for him to stop pushing her away. The only consolation was knowing he'd pushed almost everyone else away, sticking close to his family ranch except when he went to Seattle for treatment. The shock was that he'd applied for a job where he would be forced to encounter people he didn't know well.

"I'll be fine," Blair assured her aunt.

"But what about the holidays? Thanksgiving is next week. You can't spend it in a bunkhouse."

"If I get the job, they'll probably give us time to visit our families. That's what you and Uncle Will and most of the ranchers do around here. I'll have to wait and see. I can't ask right off—it would sound as if I'm already being difficult."

However much Blair loved family gatherings, she didn't want to spend the rest of her life wondering if there was more she could have done to get through to Alex.

"I suppose."

An idea suddenly occurred to Blair. "Why don't you invite the Sorensons over on Thanksgiving? You know, like before Alex's accident."

"We'd love to have them here. But won't it upset you?"

"Why should the rest of us stop being friends because he wants to be a recluse? Maybe he should realize that he's isolating his parents, too. They've had zero social life since he came home from the hospital."

Aunt Sarah laughed softly. "Isolating? Is that what the counselor told you?"

"In a way."

At her aunt and uncle's urging, Blair had visited a college counselor when Alex refused to see her. Talking with someone who didn't have a stake in the situation had helped. But even if the psychologist had been willing to offer advice, which she hadn't, Blair would have made her own decisions. As a little girl living with an unreliable mother, she'd learned to be independent a whole lot younger than most kids.

She heard the sound of a horse outside. "Ooh, have to go. I think the foreman is back. Love you, Aunt Sarah."

"Love you, too. I'll talk to Donna and Jeff about coming on Thanksgiving. It would be lovely to have them. Just like old times."

"Okay, bye." Blair put the phone back in

her pocket and waited. After another couple of minutes the door opened and a man came inside, pulling off his hat. He was about the same height as Jordan Maxwell, but his hair was black and he wasn't smiling.

Blair stood up. She was gutsy, but she'd heard the new foreman was a former Navy SEAL and it made her nervous. "Um, hi. I'm Blair Darby," she said. "Should I shake your hand or salute you?"

He frowned. "I'm not in the Navy any longer."

"Sorry," she said hastily. "I want to apply for a job as a ranch hand."

Mr. Maxwell nodded, his mouth still straight. "My brother mentioned you have a degree in computer science. Why would you want to work on the Soaring Hawk?"

Wow.

He came right to the point. She should have known the question would be asked by someone.

"I love ranch life and there aren't many information technology jobs around Shelton," she explained.

It was true, though with the advances in computers and the internet, someone could live on one side of the world and work remotely for a company on the other side. She had standing job offers from several large companies and might accept one if things didn't work out with Alex. She might accept, regardless. Having a second income would be useful on a ranch where anything and everything could happen.

Blair cleared her throat, her discomfort growing under Dakota Maxwell's silent scrutiny. "I haven't given up on computer science completely. For example, I maintain the Shelton Ranching Association website as a volunteer, but I can do that here. Not on work hours, of course," she added quickly.

The expression on his face turned more thoughtful. "We don't have a website for the Soaring Hawk. That's something you might be able to handle for us. My brother has started a breeding program with the ranch's registered horses. Some weanlings have been sold already and we'll have more available next year. A website would be useful."

"I'd be happy to create and maintain a website, but I can do all types of work needed on a ranch. My uncle, William O'Brien, owns the Canary Diamond. He can verify my skills."

DAKOTA FELT A faint sense of déjà vu. Not three days earlier, Alex Sorenson had sat there talking about his experience on the family ranch. But Alex had suggested his parents would probably say he wasn't physically strong enough, while Blair didn't seem concerned about getting a reference from her uncle.

"Why aren't you working on the Canary Diamond?" he asked, the feeling of déjà vu growing even stronger.

"They don't need me." Unhappiness flickered in Blair's blue eyes. "You see, I expected to get married right after college, but it didn't happen."

Dakota knew all too well how someone's life could get derailed at a moment's notice. Blair looked fit and the two female ranch hands his brother had previously hired were excellent—so far, they'd impressed him the most with their sheer grit and work ethic. Well, along with Alex Sorenson, who'd thrown himself into mucking the horse barn the last two days as if he was cleaning Buckingham Palace.

Dakota gave Blair the forms to complete and poured them both a cup of coffee, thinking he ought to have done that at the start.

He'd gotten thrown off by her artless comment about whether to shake hands or salute him and knew his gruff response had embarrassed her, something he hadn't intended. It just had been another reminder of having to leave the Navy, which wasn't anyone else's fault.

Get over it, his brain ordered.

His job now was running the Soaring Hawk. The idea of having to prove anything to Saul Hawkins was galling, but returning had seemed the best option with his Navy career coming to a screeching end. At least the agreement with Saul included a third party who would ultimately decide if Dakota had met the terms of the contract. Like Jordan, Dakota had chosen Liam Flannigan of Kindred Ranch to be that third party. If Wyatt ever returned to accept their grandfather's challenge, he'd probably do the same.

Dakota's biggest concern was how much Saul might influence the final decision.

CHAPTER FOUR

AFTER BLAIR DARBY LEFT, Dakota started going over the stock records. Based on reports received from the ranch hands and his own visual survey, all the cattle seemed to be accounted for and healthy, coming through the storm without a problem.

When he was satisfied, he put the records away and went out to check conditions in the horse barn. Alex Sorenson was doing well, but he was new and Dakota wanted to strike a balance between trusting the kid and being sure the animals weren't neglected. He walked the long length of the building and found Alex finishing the last few stalls.

"Hey, Alex. Nice job."

"Thanks. Gosh, the Soaring Hawk has awesome horses."

"I agree. My brother has high hopes for next year's foals. You can move them out to the paddock now. It's warm enough."

"Yes, sir."

Dakota stroked the nose of a mare who'd reached her head over the door of her stall, asking for attention. Stormy was a blue roan, uniform in coat color, with a thick black mane and tail. He would have loved having her as his personal mount, but she wasn't large enough for his height and muscle mass. Besides, Jordan had recently purchased a stallion that needed working. Tucker had excellent bloodlines and Dakota planned to alternate riding him with some of the geldings.

"I saw you talking to Blair Darby," Alex said as he moved the wheelbarrow to another stall. "I hope she didn't, like, *bother* you with, uh, anything."

"You know Blair?"

"We went to high school together. And we were at Montana State University in Bozeman. For a while."

Interesting.

"Blair might come to work for the Soaring Hawk," he said in a casual tone, curious what Alex's reaction might be.

The kid spun around. "But she *can't*. Blair isn't a ranch hand, she's into computers and stuff."

Dakota hiked an eyebrow, ever so slightly. "Hiring is a foreman's decision."

Alex went red. "I didn't mean… I apologize, sir. Better get busy." He put his head down and began collecting dirty straw and manure as if his life depended on getting every last scrap.

Dakota turned and walked from the barn. Earlier he'd noticed Noelle's small compact parked near the main house. It was still there. He supposed she would be at the Soaring Hawk a good deal while she was in Montana, visiting her sister, niece and nephew.

The way she'd changed still amazed him. She had been much too young to think about romantically, but he remembered getting annoyed when other kids teased her for being shorter and smaller than them. There was no doubt that Noelle had turned into a striking woman who could look out for herself. In other circumstances he might regret not having time to socialize more. But then, she hadn't shown any awareness of him, so it wasn't an issue.

"Dakota, come in for lunch," his sister-in-law called from the porch of the main house.

"Thanks, but I'm getting ready to ride out again."

Paige wasn't wearing her coat and she rubbed her arms. "Please come, Dakota. Saul wants to talk."

He groaned. As a rule, a foreman wouldn't spend much time with the family—he'd go in, give a report on conditions affecting the ranch and get out. At least that's how Dakota expected to do things, but his sister-in-law had other ideas. He could see why Jordan had succumbed to Paige; she had a charm and determination that must have been irresistible.

"All right. But first I have to wash up. You need to get back inside," he told her, concerned about her getting chilled. She might be sweet, but she was also stubborn enough to argue with him until she turned into an ice cube.

She smiled and returned to the house, while he went into the foreman's quarters for a quick change of clothes before crossing the wide area between the buildings once more.

Winter was a dreary time of year in Montana, with short days, wind, frequent gray weather and brown grass when it wasn't covered by snow. He didn't remember feeling that way before his mother's death, but he'd been young when she died. Now it just seemed bleak here.

Dakota wiped snow from his shoes and started to knock, thinking it would demonstrate he saw himself as a ranch employee, but the door opened before his knuckles could make contact.

"Hey, Dakota."

It was Noelle and she looked anything but bleak.

Her dark gold hair contrasted warmly with her red pants and long-sleeved sweater, the fine red knit hugging her curves. She stepped to one side and he came in, catching a faint whiff of peach and spice. He inhaled appreciatively.

"That's Coco Chanel, right?" he asked.

Her mouth opened in surprise. "Yes. I wouldn't take you as a guy who knows women's fragrances."

"It's the only one I recognize. One of my men had a bottle dumped in his boots after his wife suggested they needed deodorizing."

"Um, Chanel is a pricey deodorant."

"One of his children did it. Anyhow, it was all we could smell for weeks. Frank ended up having to buy new boots before the next mission—you can't waft upscale perfume on a covert assignment. We also chipped in and got another bottle for his wife. It seemed only fair. His boots really *did* stink and his kid was trying to be helpful."

Noelle's smile wavered as she closed the door. "I don't wear perfume when I'm working. It wouldn't be right since so many people are sensitive to fragrances. But I indulge in a hint during the holidays. I can wash it off if there's a problem."

Dakota hesitated, not wanting her to get the wrong idea. He hadn't been hitting on her or anything; the fragrance had simply caught his notice. He'd joked about it to his men on several occasions, saying Frank's boots smelled better than they did. And the scent was a whole lot more pleasant than what came out of the business end of a cow or horse.

"An entire bottle was overpowering, but yours is nice. Very light."

"Thanks. We should go in—lunch is already on the table."

He followed her to the dining room, which had mostly been used for storing ranch records and calf medicines when he was growing up. Like the rest of the house, the walls were freshly painted. The table was covered with a white cloth and had a centerpiece of candles, fall leaves and gourds. There was nothing to remind him of the past except his brother and grandfather.

"It's about time, Dakota—have you been avoiding me?" Anna Beth asked. "Other than waving at me across the yard, this is the first I've seen of you. You haven't even come into the dining hall when I was there."

"I haven't been here for long and I've been busy because of the storm," he said. "Besides, you were in Billings when I arrived."

Anna Beth was a no-nonsense retired marine who'd been friends with his eldest brother for over twenty years. Jordan had asked her to move to Shelton as their grandfather's housekeeper; the shock was that she'd ended up marrying Saul. Each to their own, Dakota supposed, though it made Anna Beth his step-grandmother, which seemed odd. It was also odd to call her Anna Beth instead of Sarge, a moniker she'd gone by since being promoted to sergeant in the marines.

"I'm back now," she said.

"Sure. But I should point out that you didn't come to see me, either. It goes both ways."

While Dakota was mostly acquainted with Anna Beth through his eldest brother, he knew the feisty former master sergeant was as tough as nails. She liked when someone didn't take guff from her or anyone else.

Saul frowned. "Dakota—"

He was interrupted by his wife's hearty chuckle. "That's right," Anna Beth agreed, "but I've lived in Montana long enough now to understand the livestock comes first."

"Not quite first." Saul gave his wife a fond look and squeezed her hand, a gesture that made Dakota's eyes widen. His grandfather had never hugged them as children or patted their backs. Or even shaken hands. The only times he'd shown a modest amount of approval were when Dakota had won All-Around Best Cowboy in Shelton's annual rodeo.

"Have a seat," his brother urged.

The only open spot was next to Noelle, which meant Saul was directly across the table. Dakota hadn't spent the years since leaving Montana simmering with resentment toward his grandfather, but being back on the ranch was raising unpleasant memories.

For most of lunch he stayed out of the conversation except to answer questions about how the herds had managed during the two-day blizzard.

"Excellent," Saul said when he learned

the cattle were accounted for and healthy. "Let's hope this won't be as bad a winter as they're predicting. We've already gotten our fair share of storms and it isn't even December yet."

Dakota shot a look at his brother. "I can't take any credit. Jordan took charge of putting out winter feed."

Saul just shrugged. He shifted in his chair, seeming uncomfortable.

"Are you all right?" Anna Beth asked.

"A little stiff."

"You haven't been doing all the exercises you're supposed to do, have you?"

"I'm not a physical therapist, but I'd be happy to help," Noelle volunteered.

"That would be wonderful," Anna Beth said.

Saul didn't appear happy, but in the face of his wife's enthusiasm, he didn't seem inclined to argue. "Yeah, I suppose that would be all right." Then he brightened and a calculating expression filled his face. "I've always thought it would be nice to have a doctor in the family."

"Oh, yeah, that was subtle," Jordan remarked and his wife grinned.

Dakota was aware of his grandfather giving him and Noelle a speculative look. He clenched his jaw. Saul might decide to try his hand at matchmaking—he'd done it with Jordan and Paige—but he could forget it. Dakota had a year to prove himself as a rancher and he wasn't going to risk the agreement on a romance *or* let his grandfather try to control his life in any way. That wasn't part of the deal they'd made. And that didn't even take into account Noelle's chosen career and lack of interest.

The situation had been different for Jordan. Paige had become a surrogate granddaughter to Saul before Jordan ever returned to Montana. Their relationship would have received his unqualified approval. Besides, Jordan had fallen head over heels for his wife, while Dakota wasn't sure he was capable of that kind of passionate love.

WHILE NOELLE USUALLY laughed when people talked about the benefits of a doctor in the family, she sensed tension radiating from Dakota and there didn't seem to be a way to lighten the moment without making things worse. The joke was nothing new. Before she'd married, her friends had tried to fix her up with their brothers, cousins or other relatives, saying the same thing.

"Noelle, your sister tells me you're single," Saul said.

Ouch.

"That's right. Divorced and not looking," she replied promptly.

"What kind of fool would let you go?"

She shrugged. Saul Hawkins was old enough he probably felt he could ask the kind of questions most people avoided. "It was a mutual decision. And since you're already taken, Mr. Hawkins, I guess I'm out of luck for the future."

The small bit of humor produced smiles around the table, while Saul Hawkins—the ogre she'd heard stories about her whole life—guffawed and slapped the table. "You're quick. I like that. Call me Saul."

Next to Noelle some of Dakota's uptight energy seemed to dissipate.

It was just as well. She hadn't offered to assist with *his* therapy—at least not yet—and she didn't want him thinking too much about her being a doctor. Noelle also suspected he was even more in need of holiday spirit than a physical therapist. She believed in modern medicine, but also had faith in the power of hope.

Anyway, she figured Dakota would be tougher to deal with than Saul. Aside from their brief conversation at the door, he'd said little to her. He was eating quickly, likely determined to get the food down as fast as possible and leave.

"Sweetheart, I picked up the mail in town," Jordan told his wife. "We got a letter from the Christmas Ranch Homes Tour committee, giving us the dates for the tour. With Daniel on the way and winter settling in early, I'd completely forgotten we were asked to be part of it this year."

A harassed expression crossed Paige's face. "Me, too. But we can't pull out since they probably have most of the publicity in place."

"You're going to be part of the Christmas Ranch Homes Tour?" Noelle asked.

Excitement bubbled in her. The tour raised money for the local museum and the community center. People bought tickets and visited ranch homes on the tour, enjoying snacks and decorations. It was great fun.

Margaret Bannerman had always wanted to be included, but the Blue Banner ranch house wasn't architecturally distinctive. In contrast, the Soaring Hawk was a grand combination of different styles—a great big birthday cake of a house that begged to be looked at and appreciated.

"Yes," Paige said, sounding vexed. "And I haven't done a thing to get ready. I haven't even bought a single new decoration. We got some last year for the house, but nowhere near enough."

Paige and Anna Beth looked at each other and Noelle felt a wistful pang. The two women had become close. Now that her sister was married and had another family, she was naturally forming strong ties with them as well.

"I can lend a hand with baking cookies and making snacks, but decorating isn't my thing," Anna Beth said.

"I'll take charge if you'd like," Noelle offered, trying not to seem overly eager.

"This is your vacation," Paige objected. "Mom says you need to rest and I agree."

"Christmas *is* restful. You know how I feel about the holidays." Noelle had been born in December and named in honor of the season. But unlike some children, she'd never minded sharing her birthday with the festive rush.

"You might have to shop in Bozeman or Helena for everything," Paige said. "Maybe even go to Billings."

"That's okay. I'll check in Shelton first. But if necessary, I can return my car to the rental agency in Bozeman and exchange it for an SUV, which I should have gotten to begin with. That way I'll have room to carry lights and all the other stuff. I'll make more than one trip if needed. I just don't want to step on anybody's toes."

"I don't mind," Anna Beth said firmly.

The others chimed in with their agreement. Saul added that Noelle could have free rein to do whatever she wanted and that the ranch hands could be asked to lend a hand whenever they were available.

Noelle already had a vision of how she wanted everything to look, and not just the house. The barns and fences nearby should also be lighted and decorated with colorful, oversize Christmas wreaths and ornaments.

Then there would be the baking and candy making. She wasn't much of a cook, but she could bake like a pro. The ranch homes tour meant a public reception on four different nights during the holiday season, over the last two weekends before Christmas. Shelton was known for its holiday traditions. Weather permitting, visitors came from Helena, Bozeman, Great Falls and other locations to take part in the tour and various festivities.

None of the events could compete with the popularity of Shelton Rodeo Daze week in June each year, but they were better in Noelle's opinion. Aside from the hazards of slippery ice, injuries were unlikely. She couldn't say the same about bull and bronco riding.

"Dakota, it would be good if you could help Noelle with the decorating," Saul suggested. "Supporting the community is important. To start, why don't you go into Shelton this afternoon with her to look for holiday stuff?"

Noelle winced. She hoped to get Dakota in the spirit, but she didn't think his "bah, humbug" attitude would contribute much to preparing for the tour.

"Since when did you start to believe in supporting the community?" Dakota retorted. "Or Christmas?"

"We all make mistakes, son."

"I'm not—" Dakota stopped abruptly and stood up. "Fine. Noelle, let me know when you're ready to go into town."

The silence that fell was palpable and Noelle ducked her head. Her sister might have married into a lovely family, but they had their share of problems. As if in response to the awkward atmosphere, a loud wail came from the baby monitor. Daniel had woken up and wanted somebody *now*.

"I'll check him," Noelle said.

Before Paige could protest, she jumped out of her chair and hurried across the house to the sunroom, which had been dedicated to her niece and nephew. Not that Daniel was big enough to require an entire room. His needs were mostly a bassinet with a colorful mobile.

"Hey, little guy," she murmured.

Daniel blinked. She wasn't his mama and his little face crumpled into another wail.

"It's okay—I'm Aunt Noelle. You're going to discover that aunts are terrific to have around. We love to spoil our nieces and nephews and we hate saying no."

She checked his diaper. It was wet and she changed him, talking all the while. Then she cuddled him in her arms, ignoring the familiar ache in her heart and chest. The funny thing was, she hadn't thought much about having children until losing her baby. Becoming a mother was something she'd figured would happen someday. Now "someday" might never come since a higher rate of infertility followed an ectopic pregnancy, along with the chance of reoccurrence.

Noelle sat with Daniel in the rocking chair and sang a folk song she'd learned while in the Himalayas. He quieted and watched her with seeming fascination until his eyelids drooped and his breathing evened back into sleep.

"You have a way with babies," whispered her sister as she tiptoed into the room carrying the baby monitor.

"Just lucky, I think," Noelle said softly. "Did you finish eating?"

"Yes, thanks to you. I don't know how many meals I've needed to reheat since he was born. Or just ate cold. Jordan fusses about me doing that, but he's no better. Especially at night. As soon as Daniel cries or a sound comes from Mishka's room, he's up like a shot."

"I'll be glad when it's the weekend and Mishka isn't in school. How is she adjusting to no longer being an only child? She seemed to dote on Daniel the other evening."

Paige grinned. "She loves being a big sister. There was a two-day school closure because of the storm, so she got unexpected time with all of us after her online classes. She was disappointed to go back today. I don't blame her, it was nice being tucked up in front of the fireplace, drinking warm cider and listening to the wind blow. Except for Dakota. He worked the whole time, checking on the ranch buildings and horses. Mostly he's working hard at avoiding Saul. This was the first time he's come to the house since before the storm broke."

"Dakota hasn't been back in Montana for long. Didn't your husband take a while to develop a relationship with his grandfather?"

"Yes. It just means so much to Jordan having his brother home, though not the way it happened. All we know is that there was an explosion. Despite Jordan being a former SEAL, too, everything is classified, so we don't have a clue how to help."

Noelle continued rocking Daniel. "Recovery takes time. Dakota's entire image of himself has been upended."

"The scars aren't that bad."

"I'm guessing he isn't bothered by the scars on his face," Noelle said in a cautious tone. "At the moment, I'd advise you not to do anything except be welcoming and available, the way you'd be with anyone else."

"But you'll still help with his rehab?"

"Only if he's willing. He doesn't want a

doctor and I can't blame him. People who've gone through major medical treatment sometimes avoid doctors because we're a reminder of something they'd rather forget. As for the rest? He doesn't seem the type to readily confide his feelings. He might have to work through this by himself."

The irony of her advice struck Noelle because she was trying to deal with her own loss alone. Maybe if this was any other time of year she'd feel more comfortable telling the family, but she didn't want to throw a shadow on their celebrations.

Meanwhile, she'd be the best aunt in the world.

Paige sighed. "All right. Are you sure you want to take charge of getting ready for the tour? You're lovely to offer, but Jordan and I got ourselves into the situation. We'd been fixing up the house along with Anna Beth and Saul, so when the committee asked, we were excited at the chance to show the place to everyone."

"I'll love doing it. You know how I feel about Christmas. And with Thanksgiving falling so early this year, there are several extra days to prepare, along with an added weekend." Noelle got up and shifted Daniel into her sister's arms.

Paige kissed her son's forehead. "It still isn't much time. We should have started buying decorations back in August when they began arriving in stores, but getting ready for Daniel distracted us."

"You were distracted for a great reason. I'm sure there are plenty of holiday supplies left. I'll figure it out. But now I should go speak to Dakota."

Noelle asked her brother-in-law for a measuring tape and put it in her coat pocket to use later. Outside the air was crisp, the sky clear, and the mountains to the west rose in layer upon layer of white and blues and purples. Smoke rose from a stovepipe on the bunkhouse, curling upward in a spiral, and there were smaller curls of white, streaming out with each breath from the horses.

She sighed with pleasure and crossed to the fence to watch the equine herd, healthy and happy in their woolly winter coats. The paddock sloped away from the barn and looked as if it would drain well, but the snow was still crisply frozen and the scene was a Christmas card come to life.

"I apologize for leaving that way," Dakota said from behind her.

Noelle turned her head to look at him. "No need. Your relationship with Saul is none of my business."

"Nevertheless, it was wrong to put you in the middle. Just be cautious when you help with the exercises for his hip. He has a sharp tongue."

She shrugged. "I can look out for myself."

"Fair enough. Is now a good time to go into town?"

"I don't want to put you out."

Dakota smiled suddenly, chasing some of the darkness from his face and reminding her of the boy she'd once known. "That's okay. There's an order waiting at the feed and seed store. I was going to send someone to pick it up, but I can just get it myself."

"That's good." Noelle was relieved he'd found a reason to make the trip useful.

The feed and seed store was their first stop. While the ranch's supplies were loaded into the back of the truck, they looked at the small display of decorations and gifts inside the store—all very agriculture oriented.

"This is really cool." Dakota picked up a toy and checked it over. "Looks like an ancient tractor my dad owned. It must have dated back to the 1920s. Those old machines were built to last."

"Is it still at the Circle M?"

"I don't know. The place was deserted for years, but my brothers and I own the place now. I should ask Jordan more. To be honest, I haven't been there since I was a boy. This is only the second time I've been in Montana since I enlisted. The previous trip was just a quick stop to see Jordan and Paige."

"You didn't return when you acquired the Circle M?"

Dakota shrugged. "That was all done long distance. After that, we had an estate agent look after the property. Jordan has now put the land back into production and enlarged the Soaring Hawk's herd."

Though he returned the toy to its shelf, Noelle noticed his gaze lingered on it for a moment. She pretended to evaluate the limited selection of decorations until he went out to check on the supplies being loaded, then swiftly bought the tractor and had it put in a bag. She could always give the toy to her niece or nephew.

Or to Dakota.

She had a feeling that toys hadn't been a

big part of his childhood after going to live with Saul and sometimes big kids needed toys, too.

Dakota was less interested at the hardware store and the Bibs 'n' Bobs shop, though the selections were more extensive.

"Maybe you should look for the kind of light strings used on commercial buildings instead," he finally suggested in a low voice. "They'll last longer."

"Good idea."

Though Dakota was being cordial, Noelle doubted he had changed his mind about the holidays. So on the drive back to the Soaring Hawk she quietly took out her phone and began making notes. Her excitement was growing with all the possibilities.

At the main ranch he parked by a building marked Supply Shed and a couple of ranch hands came over to help unload the contents of the pickup.

Noelle waited until the work was done, then looked at Dakota. "I was wondering about the old homestead house." She gestured to the original home built by the Hawkins family. It stood on a knoll dotted with tall sycamore trees and was as picturesque as the one they'd built in the 1920s, except a little smaller. "Do you know if it's still habitable? It could be decorated as well for the ranch home tour."

He shrugged. "I'm not sure what's going on with it now, but my great-something grandmother refused to move to the new house, staying in the old homestead cabin until she passed away. Initially the family kept it in repair after she was gone, thinking their younger son would live there when he got married."

"What happened to that plan?"

"Korea. Wars have taken a toll on families in Shelton. We can look at the house if you want. I poked around as a kid, but don't remember much. It was more to defy Saul than anything else, not that he ever knew."

Noelle was delighted. "I'd love to."

CHAPTER FIVE

DAKOTA DIDN'T WANT to understand why Noelle's smile made him feel warmer.

She was different than he would have expected. The little girl who'd kept her head down studying in high school was now a woman who must have practiced medicine in some rough situations, but still seemed to view the world with appreciation. He'd yet to spot a trace of cynicism in her, which was astonishing.

"What type of locations are you sent to for your work?" he asked as they walked toward the old homestead cabin. The name was misleading. It was a large two-story home that could have remained in use with reasonable updates. He wasn't sure why past generations had built the new place. This one had plenty of space and was in its own way quite charming.

"I've mostly gone to spots where there's

been a natural disaster, though I've also been in a few war zones."

"Difficult either way, I guess."

Noelle shrugged and he guessed she didn't like talking about her work. He was the same, but from a different perspective. Navy SEALs weren't allowed to reveal anything about classified missions and a good number of their medals were private because they'd been awarded for those actions.

"Wait a minute," he advised, testing the porch steps.

Everything seemed solid. Storm shutters covered the windows and the air inside was cold and stale, but the basic structure was remarkably sound. Come to think of it, he remembered his grandfather putting on a new roof when he was a kid and doing other maintenance work. Even at the time he'd wondered how Saul could care more about a building and a ranch than his own family.

They went inside.

"Look at that fireplace," Noelle exclaimed when they entered the kitchen.

It was huge, one of the old pioneer fireplaces used for cooking meals and heating the home. Constructed of native stone, it dominated the better part of a wall.

"I bet this was a one-room cabin in the beginning," she said, running her fingers across the stones. "Then they expanded and made the first section into a kitchen."

"I suppose."

She tried the old faucet over the farm sink, shaking her head as the pipes clunked and groaned without result. "Maybe the water is turned off. The plumbing must be antiquated. Wanna take a look at the bathrooms?" Noelle asked, a mischievous look on her face. "Any bets on whether they have those huge claw-foot bathtubs, or do you remember?"

"Not really." Dakota gave her a strained grin. How anyone could get excited about an ancient house and its outdated fixtures was a mystery.

NOELLE EXPLORED WITH growing enthusiasm, though Dakota held her back at several points while he ensured the stairs and flooring were sound. His leg plainly bothered him going up and down the two different staircases, but he approached the task with grim efficiency; it was easy to imagine him scouting an enemy's location with equal diligence.

For most of the bottom floor, the wood beams overhead had been left exposed, giving a rustic vibe. It would be perfect for old-fashioned decorating. She could look for electric "candles" and battery-powered lanterns. All sorts of things.

"You can't seriously consider doing both houses," Dakota said, sounding exasperated when she explained a few of her ideas.

"I'm very serious. I could decorate the main house on a more modern style, and this one in Victorian. Frontier Victorian, that is. Fires could be lit. Retro is very 'in' these days—I should be able to order what I need from the internet or find stuff in Bozeman. Use your imagination," she coaxed.

"I don't have an imagination. Anyway, I doubt the wiring is safe. And I wouldn't count on the condition of the three chimneys, either."

"An electrician could check the wiring and electricity might not even be needed. A lot of battery lights are available these days, or I could look into renting a generator and run extension cords. As for the chimneys, I'll contact the stove store in Shelton. They do inspections and repairs."

"And maybe you could just donate the money you'd spend to the community center or museum and have done with it."

Sheesh.

The ranch home tour was about more than raising money. Like all Shelton holiday events, the tour represented Christmas cheer and solidarity with the community. Aside from common work days, socializing was difficult for ranchers, but this provided a chance to offer hospitality without the pressure of getting calves branded or the haying done first. There were commercial benefits, too, for homes offering bed-and-breakfast services.

"Stop being a scrooge," Nicole scolded. "My parents decorate for Christmas, even though they aren't part of the tour. And I'm sure Paige and Jordan plan to decorate more in the future when they aren't busy with a new baby. This will just mean they have what they need for next year."

Dakota held up his hands in a mock gesture of surrender. "Fine."

"What is it with you and Christmas, anyway?" she asked. "Most people have reasons for disliking a holiday."

"I just don't see the point."

Hmm. Noelle wasn't sure she believed him. "Well, I can manage the decorating on my own. You don't have to help me."

He shrugged. "My grandfather disagrees."

"I was there. It was nice of you to go into

Shelton with me, but Saul didn't order you to participate."

"With Saul, a suggestion is the same as an order. I'm here to prove myself as a rancher. I didn't have any idea I'd end up on a decorating committee."

Apparently, changing his attitude was going to be an even bigger challenge than Noelle had thought, but that was all right. She liked challenges.

As they walked back to the main house, a small figure flew toward them, one of the family's dogs following close behind.

"Aunt Noelle, Aunt Noelle," Mishka cried. "I *missed* you."

Noelle caught her niece, staggering a little under her enthusiastic onslaught. Mishka was small for a five-year-old, but she was still nearly forty pounds of excited energy.

"How could you miss me?" Noelle teased. "We saw each other just days ago."

Mishka hugged her neck. "You were gone since Mama and Daddy got married. For-*ev*er."

To a child her age, the time between visits would seem even longer than for an adult. Kids changed quickly, and for Noelle, the occasional video call wasn't an adequate way to watch it happen.

"Are you going to give your uncle Dakota a hug?" Noelle asked.

"Course."

Dakota's face softened as he lifted Mishka from Noelle's arms. He might have been badly injured a few months ago, but he was still strong. "Hey, kiddo."

Mishka kissed his cheek. "I love you, Uncle Dakota."

"I love you, too."

"Your ouchies are mad," Mishka said, peering intently at the healed lacerations on the side of her uncle's face. "Do they hurt?"

Noelle sucked in a breath, hoping he wouldn't overreact to the innocent question. She'd noticed Dakota's facial scars had darkened, a temporary reaction to the cold air, but wouldn't have risked saying anything. One thing she knew for sure, he was lucky—he could have had nerve damage or lost an eye.

"They don't hurt much anymore," he assured her.

"Goodie. Mama says butterfly kisses make ouchies better. I want you to get all better." She kissed the scars, one by one. Dakota not only didn't mind, he seemed to appreciate her concern.

In an effort to conceal her emotions, Noelle crouched to give the dog's neck a proper rub. She got teary-eyed too easily these days.

Some people were better with children than adults, accepting their artless affection at face value, while questioning the motives of everyone else. If she'd said anything about Dakota's scars herself, he wouldn't have reacted well.

As for butterfly kisses?

Noelle's heart turned over. Mishka had gone through surgeries to correct both a congenital heart defect and problems with her leg. So even though she was just five years old, she understood pain and the struggle to recover. Maybe that explained Dakota's acceptance.

"Did you have a good time at Grandma's?" Noelle asked her niece when she straightened.

"Uh huh. Grandpa let me help in the barn. I cleaned two whole stalls. All by myself."

"Wow. You're a great helper."

Margaret Bannerman took Mishka to school every day and picked her up, usually bringing her back to the Blue Banner for an hour or two. She wanted as much time as possible with her granddaughter, and it was especially helpful to Paige with Daniel being a newborn. Still, apparently the setup had prompted a minor power tussle between their mother and Anna Beth, who seemed to have boundless energy and a determination to embrace her new role in the family as a wife and grandmother.

"Jordan and Anna Beth have been pals since he enlisted, but he's also become a surrogate son to her," Paige had explained.

Noelle had laughed, thinking the whole thing was charming. And the more family support her sister and brother-in-law received with raising Mishka and Daniel and any other children who came along, the better. Besides, it was clear Anna Beth and Margaret had become friends—if also cordial rivals when it came to sharing grandchildren.

Mishka wiggled and Dakota set her down. "I hafta give the dogs their treats," she said.

"We can't let them go hungry," he agreed.

"Uh-uh." She turned and ran back to the main house. Now that the problems with her leg had been resolved, she seemed to run everywhere. A pack of Australian shepherds and Aussie collies burst from the house to greet her, along with her mother and Margaret Bannerman.

"Mishka is some kid," Dakota murmured.

"She sure is." Noelle took out the heavy steel tape measure she'd borrowed earlier. "Do you want to help me measure the barns and paddock fences? I need to get an idea of how many Christmas lights will be needed."

"Building records should be in the ranch office. They would be easier and faster than measuring. I'll go look for them."

Noelle stared at his departing back and decided he was just trying to get away from her, so she caught up and pretended it was his idea that she come along. While he frowned, he didn't tell her to go away.

The office walls were hung with historic photos of the Soaring Hawk and the door was open to the foreman's quarters, where the bed appeared to have been made with military precision. Noelle glanced away, not wanting him to think she was prying. Yet she was curious.

She'd encountered the military, both in wars zones and when they were deployed to help during disasters, but Navy SEALs had a mystique of their own. Some of their larger-than-life aura might have been magnified in movies and by the media, but she suspected a lot of it was true, probably making any physical limitations harder for Dakota to accept. In all likelihood, his doctors had said he should be able to manage regular activities. Except he wasn't accustomed to "regular."

Dakota stroked the cat sleeping on the desk, then opened a drawer in the filing cabinet. The feline rolled onto his back, a purr rumbling as if trying to get more of Dakota's attention. Noelle reached over and petted the cat's white tummy, half expecting him to see the caress as an invitation to play. Instead, his purr grew louder.

"I looked through the files last night and saw something about ranch construction," Dakota explained as he rummaged. "Yeah, here it is."

Noelle opened the folder without expecting much. Most of the Soaring Hawk buildings were at least a hundred years old and the documentation would be long gone.

"Coffee?" Dakota asked.

"No. If I drink any this late, I won't sleep tonight."

"You could probably use the rest."

"Gee, thanks," she returned in a dry tone.

He cleared his throat. "I didn't mean anything by that. You were yawning earlier is all."

Hmmm.

"True enough. I'm still trying to catch up on my sleep."

"Hasn't the idea of 'catching up' on sleep been debunked?"

Noelle cocked her head. It almost sounded like a question someone asked a doctor, but she wasn't going to fool herself that Dakota was suddenly comfortable with her profession.

"That depends. Some researchers call it sleep debt, which means I'm so deep in hock by now, I'd have to turn into Rip Van Winkle to make up for what I owe."

Dakota's mouth curved. "You should have taken your vacation in a tropical locale, where you could snooze in a hammock by the beach instead of stringing Christmas lights."

"Nah." Actually, Noelle wasn't technically on vacation. The head of the relief organization had taken one look at her team after they returned and said they *had* to take a break. "I haven't been home since Paige and Jordan got married. And then just for a couple of days."

"About that—I hope Paige understands why Wyatt and I couldn't get here for the ceremony. We both felt bad about missing it."

"Of course she does. I barely got to the

wedding myself. I heard they were getting married when I was in Indonesia following that terrible tidal wave. Luckily a new medical team arrived and relieved us. Sometimes there isn't any extra help available." Noelle hesitated. "We were all sorry to hear about Wyatt losing his wife. How are he and your niece doing?"

Concern filled Dakota's face. "As well as can be expected. That's what people say, right? The truth is, Amy was everything to him and he's just putting one foot in front of the other for his daughter's sake. At least the Navy base where he's stationed has childcare options available. Christie is just eighteen-months old and he hates leaving her while he's on duty, but what choice does he have?"

"It's difficult being a single parent."

"I can't even imagine what he's gone through."

The cat on the desk stepped onto Noelle's lap as she began looking through the contents of the folder. He meowed loudly and she paused for a moment to give him more affection.

"That's Buddy," Dakota commented, probably relieved to talk about something less personal. "Formally known as Frances. I'm told he's become more people oriented lately."

"Hello, Buddy." Noelle scratched under the tuxedo's chin and his large paws began kneading her leg. He was magnificent, with long tufts of fur extending from his ears and between his toes. Paige had told her about the mama cat and five adolescents that Jordan had originally adopted. They were all exceptionally large, suggesting a Maine coon was in their background, along with the Siamese genes they could see in the mother's fur and hear in her voice.

Noelle looked back at the folder of information. As expected, the ranch's building documentation was slim. She found the plans for adding a business office and storage area off the foreman's quarters. Not a surprise, they'd just been completed the previous spring. But there was little else. One fun item was an old drawing of the main house, possibly rendered by the architect.

To be polite, she recorded a few details, along with starting a list of features to measure and count around the Soaring Hawk. Her imagination had been captured by the idea of decorating the old homestead "cabin" along with the main ranch house. It would be unique to have the two homes on the tour, each reflecting a different era. Maybe she could even find a Victorian outfit and dress the part.

She cast a glance at Dakota from under her eyelashes, imagining him in a Victorian suit and top hat. The old saying, the clothes make the man, would be the reverse in his case; his trim physique would definitely make the clothes.

"Thanks," Noelle said finally, handing the folder back to Dakota and returning Buddy to the desk. He yawned and stretched out again. "I'll leave you to work now."

She went outside, enjoying the crisp, cold air. The sun was already dropping toward the western mountains, casting long shadows across the ranch center. Evergreens on the crest of the hills were painted with light. If the sky didn't cloud up, it would turn pink and gold when dusk approached.

First she counted the windows on the main house, then did the same with the original homestead. Weeds were sticking up around the porch and base of the building and would need to be cut. But it looked as if the "yard" had been mowed before the first snowfall. Her brother-in-law had probably cut every inch of grass to put up for winter stores.

She was measuring the horse barn when Dakota emerged from the ranch office. He frowned and headed toward her.

"Didn't you get what you needed from the file?" he called.

"Oh, well, the material is mostly about the new construction off your quarters."

"You should have told me. I'll pull the tape—just tell me what you want measured."

The process went faster with Dakota's assistance and Noelle soon had the dimensions and counts she desired. Tomorrow she'd drive to Bozeman and start getting the decorations. The closer to Christmas it got, the less selection would be available, but she also didn't want to be away on the weekend when her niece would be home all day from school.

The crunch of approaching footsteps made her turn and she smiled at her mother. "Hi, Mom. Have you heard that I'm in charge of holiday decorations on the Soaring Hawk and other prep for the ranch home tour?"

"I did, but you don't know about the phone call I just got." Margaret's eyes danced with pleasure. "They want the Blue Banner to be on the tour as well. The Soaring Hawk is the only ranch they asked on this end of the county and they realized it's best to have a second place down here for visitors. They apologized for the late notice, but I don't care. Looks like we're both going to be busy."

"That's great." Noelle was sure once the committee saw how amazing the Blue Banner's decorations looked inside and out, they were going to kick themselves for not inviting the Bannermans years ago. "Mom, this is Dakota Maxwell, Jordan's brother."

"Hello, ma'am," Dakota said, returning the steel tape measure to Noelle. "Thank you for the food you sent the other night."

"Please call me Margaret. I just wish you could have eaten with us. You'll come for Thanksgiving, I hope. The more, the merrier. We eat early so family traveling from a distance has time to relax after the meal and still drive home if needed."

He shrugged. "I appreciate the invitation, but I'll have to see. I have responsibilities here."

Noelle gave her mother a shake of the head to stop her from declaring that he *had* to come. Margaret knew his relationship with Saul was otrained, but she also believed shared meals helped mend fences. When it came to Dakota, Noelle wasn't so certain, especially after hearing him snap at his grandfather.

Saul didn't have a reputation for community involvement and she couldn't recall ever seeing him at holiday events when she was a girl. He seemed reformed now, but who could blame Dakota for being skeptical? It was surprising to her, as well, though she figured her sister was largely responsible for Saul's improved attitude. That is, Paige and Anna Beth both.

"Noelle, when will you be home?" Margaret asked, breaking into her thoughts.

"In about an hour. I have something to do first. Oh, and I'm driving into Bozeman tomorrow to shop for decorations. So I'll be leaving early."

"All right." Margaret gave them both a smile and headed for her truck.

"Something to do. More measuring?" Dakota asked.

"Not at the moment. I'm going to see if your grandfather has the energy to do his exercises. My hope is that he has paperwork from the orthopedist to show what is and isn't advised. Otherwise it'll have to wait until I can speak with his surgeon."

"Just remember my warning." Dakota turned on his heel and walked away.

Wonderful. Two prickly men to navigate.

It was lucky she liked to test herself, because they were going to push back in every way possible.

"ARE YOU HELPING my grandson with his therapy?" Saul asked as Noelle read through the description of exercises he was supposed to be doing. They were standard, straightforward motions, intended to strengthen his muscles and increase flexibility.

She gave him a stern look. "That's between us."

"Dakota could have died when he was injured. You're a doctor and I want to know. I'm his grandfather."

Saul's Australian shepherd crowded next to him in response to his unhappy tone. Noelle had already seen how devoted he was to his owner, following him from room to room, as watchful as any trained service animal.

"I'm not his doctor or yours. I'm simply a concerned bystander with specialized knowledge."

Saul snorted as he rubbed his dog's neck. "Fine. What silly things do you want me to do?"

"Have you done any of these exercises today?" The instruction sheets were pristine, so she doubted he'd looked at them more than once or twice. Or ever.

He shifted, looking grumpy. "They're boring. I'd rather spend the time with my family."

Noelle put the sheaf of papers to one side. Perhaps Saul was trying to make up for the decades he'd spent as a miserly sourpuss, pushing everyone away.

She gave the dog a pet while picking her words. "Is there something in particular worrying you about your health? Something you haven't told anyone?"

"Nothing like that," he returned firmly. "With Jordan, Paige and the kids living here, I feel twenty years younger. And Anna Beth, naturally. Who could have imagined a fine woman like that marrying me at this point in my life? I just didn't bounce back from the surgery the way I hoped. Kinda discouraging."

"From what Paige has told me, you've done remarkably well. But taking better care of yourself could mean you'll have more time with your family," Noelle said. "Frankly, I know people older than you in much better shape, including my grandmother. She walks all over town and even leads a tai chi class at her retirement community."

"What's her secret?"

"My educated guess is eating right, staying active and being just as obstinate as you are right now. You have obstinacy down pat, so you've aced a third of the formula. Work harder on healthy eating and physical fitness, and you might be around to watch Mishka and Daniel graduate high school. Don't think I didn't notice you ignored the vegetables and salad at lunch."

He chuckled. "You remind me of my wife. She would have scolded me about eating healthier if you hadn't been there. Anna Beth and Paige both."

Noelle was starting to understand what her sister saw in Saul. They'd become friends while Paige was leading a volunteer project that reached out to older members of the community who didn't have family in the area. Her lively emails describing their first encounters and growing closeness had kept Noelle thoroughly entertained.

"Okay, let's start with leg lifts," she told him. "You can do that, right?"

He made a face and demonstrated.

Together they went through the various exercises, Noelle doing them along with Saul to encourage him. She was pleased to see him making a genuine effort. Hip replacement surgery had come a long way, but it required work from the patient for the best outcome.

"The doc says I might be able to ride a horse again," he mentioned as they finished side stretches. "But she won't give me the go-ahead for a while. Better be soon, I need to teach Anna Beth how to ride."

"How does Anna Beth feel about that?"

"My wife is a tough retired marine who's nervous around horses. I love to tease her about it. *Hah.* How can anyone be nervous of a horse?" Saul slapped his knee with a grin.

"That's easy." Noelle pulled up her sleeve and showed him the faded scar on the inside of her upper arm. "I was kicked by a frightened stallion when I was younger than Mishka. Lodi didn't intend to hurt me, but his intentions didn't matter. It took weeks for my heart to stop pounding around horses."

"I suppose, but horses were my only friends for a whole bunch of years. Besides, when me and Anna Beth decided to get married, I agreed to have my hip replaced and she said she'd learn to ride a horse. You still ride, don't you?"

Noelle nodded, recalling the sturdy mountain ponies that had taken them from one shattered village to another in Nepal. "I rode the day after they stitched me up. I just think it would help to understand how Anna Beth feels. Horses are large animals, especially to somebody who didn't grow up around them. It can be hard getting past that."

"She's city folk. They don't know what they're missing."

"City folk would probably say the same about you." Noelle consulted the list of exercises again. "Looks like we've done all of these."

"I suppose you're gonna come back and make me do them over again tomorrow," Saul grumbled, not sounding too unhappy at the prospect, though the light exercises had brought a sheen of perspiration to his face.

She fixed him with a serious look. "Yes, *early* in the morning because I'm driving into Bozeman to shop for decorations. But you should be doing these two or three times a day, along with walking. I can't emphasize enough that you have to do your part to get better. I've treated too many people who didn't have that chance. Don't blow it by being a stubborn, uncooperative old coot."

Instead of scowling, he grinned. A thoroughly charming grin that lit up his face. "You *do* bring Anna Beth to mind. She doesn't mince words, either. That's one of the things I love about her. But you're a doctor—what about your bedside manner?"

"You aren't my patient. Besides, sometimes doctors have to be blunt to make their point."

"I suppose that's right."

Noelle took the rolled towel Saul had used under his knees and set it on the dresser. She thought about everything that had happened that day and turned around.

"Saul, I don't understand something. You asked Dakota to help me with the holiday decorating, which has nothing to do with ranching or showing he can run the Soaring Hawk. You must know that as a former Navy SEAL, he's a highly capable individual, so what do you *really* want from him?"

A crafty look entered the old man's dark brown eyes, so much like his middle grandson. "Maybe I'll explain when we get to know each other better. Anyhow, being a SEAL isn't the same as ranching."

Noelle let out a resigned sigh. She was getting the distinct impression that there were secrets all around her. Not necessarily *bad* secrets, just things that weren't being said.

CHAPTER SIX

THE NEXT MORNING Noelle got out of bed at five o'clock, though her body wanted to stay longer. It was frustrating to be this tired because on other trips home she'd had no trouble adjusting to ranch life.

Not that the family was pushing her to get up when they did, today or any day, but she'd reserved a large SUV with the rental agency and hoped to be in Bozeman when the stores opened.

Her mother had almost decided to go with her, then changed her mind; she didn't want to cancel on taking Mishka to school since her granddaughter had an early dismissal today.

"Anyway," Margaret said as the family ate breakfast, "I'll still have to drive to Bozeman next week to shop for Thanksgiving lunch."

"I can do it for you," Shane offered. He was the youngest Bannerman son, born a year before Noelle.

"You can go with me. The only time I sent one of you boys with a shopping list, you came home with cans of palm hearts instead of water chestnuts, and curry powder instead of the poultry seasonings I wanted. Fortunately I found sage and thyme in the back of the cupboard, or the turkey stuffing would have been terrible that year. Do you know how bland stuffing is without the herbs?"

"Mom, they were out of the stuff you wanted," Elijah protested. He was the eldest and did little cooking except on a barbecue grill, where he was a master of everything from hot dogs to shish kebobs. "And Noelle had mentioned she loved curry."

"Curry powder might be great in curry, but it isn't a replacement for poultry seasoning. I distinctly remember telling you both to call me if there was a problem."

Noelle ducked her head to hide a smile. The Great-Poultry-Seasoning-Versus-Curry-Powder debate had been raging for years. Shopping for the holiday meal was a cherished ritual for her mom and the only reason Margaret hadn't gone that time was because she'd caught a cold and however mild, hadn't wanted to pass her germs to anyone else.

Elijah leaned forward. "Mom, you really can't blame—"

"I'd better get moving," Noelle interrupted, though she enjoyed the friendly wrangling. "I should be back by dark."

"All right, dear. Your father put an emergency pack in your trunk, so try and remember to transfer it to the SUV when you switch vehicles. Also, there's a container of coffee and I packed a small lunch. Both are by the door," Margaret explained.

"Thanks."

The coffee was in a half-gallon insulated container, and the small lunch was enough to feed several hungry people. Noelle appreciated her mother's gesture, though she'd planned to eat pizza at a place near the college. In the field they mostly ate freeze-dried emergency provisions and she'd been craving true pizzeria pizza. Maybe she could still get some and not confess.

It was still before dawn when Noelle drove into the Soaring Hawk, but except for the dark homestead on the knoll, the main house and other immediate buildings were ablaze with lights. In her mind she could already see how the homestead would look decorated with battery candles and lamps. She'd researched various retro-style battery and solar-powered lights the evening before and ordered what she wanted. The path up to the house would also have to be lit for safety, but that shouldn't be a problem.

Dakota walked toward her from the ranch office. "Apparently I'm driving into Bozeman with you," he said with a wry expression on his face.

"That isn't necessary. I can manage on my own."

"My grandfather insists. He spoke to me again last night. He wants everything to be put on the ranch accounts. Also for me to be fully involved. He's assigned 'joining in' as one of my responsibilities as foreman."

Noelle wasn't sure she was ready for that many hours alone with Dakota, but it would be a chance for them to get better acquainted and encourage yuletide cheer.

"I'll talk to him," she said, also suspicious of Saul Hawkins's motives. "He's expecting me."

"I heard you were doing a second physical therapy session this morning. How many times did he bite your head off yesterday?"

"My head is obviously intact."

"Hi, Aunt Noelle," a voice interrupted.

Mishka dashed from the house and flung herself at Noelle.

"Hey, sweetie, you need a coat."

"I'm not cold. We get out of class early today. Does Grandma 'member?"

"She remembers. She's picking you up at eleven from school."

"Okay."

Mishka hugged Dakota in turn and he told her to go back inside to wait for her grandmother. An awkward silence fell when the door closed behind her.

Noelle had worked with people from varying cultures around the world; she could surely handle a bad-tempered Navy SEAL. Besides, the way his face looked whenever he was talking to Mishka... Noelle's heart turned over. He was one of the most striking men she'd ever met, but the warm tenderness he revealed to his niece was even more compelling than his looks.

She told herself to forget it. She'd lost a baby and gotten divorced in the last year; the next few weeks were supposed to be about getting her head and emotions sorted out. Anyway, while she might be attracted to Dakota, she wasn't ready for romance, even presuming he found her attractive in return.

"I was going to buy the decorations as a gift for my sister and Jordan," she murmured finally. "I'll explain to your grandfather."

"That isn't necessary," Dakota said, surprising her. "I'm sorry if I sounded unhappy about going with you. It's just that I have a new ranch hand starting today. She should be here at eight. If you can wait until then, I'll be able to show her the bunkhouse and give her instructions on what to do while I'm gone. We could be on the road by nine at the latest."

It wasn't the early start Noelle had wanted, but she was willing to be flexible.

"Sure." She hurried inside the house.

"Hey, sis," Paige said, coming from the direction of the kitchen. Now that Daniel's colic was mostly gone, she looked much more rested. "Saul is waiting for you. We really appreciate your offering to help."

"I'll keep working with him while I'm here, but that's only until January eighth. And he needs to do the exercises multiple times a day, along with walking. I'd prefer seeing him do both without urging. It might make a difference if the family takes turns walking or exercising with him. At least part of the time." Noelle dropped her voice. "I think what he hates is feeling bored and alone."

Paige blinked. "Why didn't we think of that?"

"You've had a new baby and other things to keep you occupied. Maybe you could make it a family fitness project. Then he wouldn't feel singled out."

"I'll speak to Jordan and Anna Beth."

The exercise session went well and Noelle was able to ask Saul several questions about the old homestead building.

"I've had it checked and repaired regularly, so it's structurally sound," he told her. "Great-Grandma Ehawee lived to be a hundred and six and wouldn't budge from the place. My grandfather was handy and put in the plumbing. Then when we finally got electricity this far from town, he installed wiring in both houses."

Noelle nodded. She'd lived without either on many of her assignments and clean running water was what she'd missed the most. "Ehawee is a beautiful name," she mused.

"It means Laughing Maiden. She was Assiniboine. They're North American plains people. I take after her, the same with Dakota and Wyatt. You like Dakota, don't you?" he asked when they'd finished the workout.

Noelle gave Saul a shrewd look, remembering his comment about having a doctor in the family. It wouldn't be wise to encourage him. "I like most people. I'll see you later this afternoon or tomorrow. Promise you'll eat a few vegetables today. And maybe a piece of fruit."

"I promise. I'm a reformed man. I want to see my great-grandchildren grow up."

"I'll believe that when I see it. Don't forget, Paige has been emailing me stories about you for years."

Saul's chuckle followed her out the door.

An unfamiliar green truck was parked near the ranch office and Noelle saw Dakota talking to a young woman. The new ranch hand, presumably. Noelle waved to him, then went to her small rental to wait. The sun coming through the glass had heated the interior, so rather than take her coat off, she ran the windows down and put her head back with a yawn.

BLAIR WASN'T SURE if Alex knew she'd gotten a job on the Soaring Hawk, but he should know soon enough.

She left a suitcase of clothes in the bunkhouse and paid close attention as Dakota showed her around the main ranch, introducing her to several employees. She was acquainted with most of them.

"The Soaring Hawk is part of the Christmas Ranch Homes Tour this year," he explained, "so you'll probably be asked to assist with decorating. Mrs. Maxwell's sister Noelle Bannerman is in charge."

"I see."

"Most of us will be involved," Dakota added. "In fact, I'm driving to Bozeman today with Dr. Bannerman to assist with shopping for the, uh, Christmas stuff."

Stuff?

That said a lot. He obviously wasn't thrilled at the prospect of being involved with the tour. Still, it reassured Blair that she wasn't going to be singled out to work on the preparations, either as a woman or as the most recently hired employee.

"The horses are spending days in the paddock now that the temperature is above zero, which means the manure needs to be removed," Dakota continued. "Feed has already been put out for them, but keep watch in case the supply gets low. There are heaters to keep the water troughs from freezing, but check them as well. Speak to Melody James for any questions while I'm gone."

Blair nodded. "When I'm done, is it okay if I haul a load of hay and straw over in case another storm moves in? I noticed the stack of bales for both is getting low in the horse barn. I've driven the make and model of the ranch's tractors, so using them isn't a problem."

"That's fine. The most important thing is keeping the horses warm enough and fed. If the wind comes up, I want them back in the barn."

Just then Alex walked a pair of horses out to the paddock; he carefully didn't look at her and Blair sighed.

She'd been considering the best way to handle things, so maybe for the moment, she would act as if he was no more than a fellow employee. It was the unfortunate truth, even though his high school senior ring still hung from a chain around her neck in place of an engagement ring.

After what he'd said to her yesterday, she was surprised he hadn't asked for it back.

Blair stiffened her spine. She'd cried buckets over that ring and didn't intend to cry any more. She was giving Alex a last chance for her own peace of mind. He'd gone through something terrible, but he hadn't let her share even a tiny piece of it with him. She didn't want a fair weather marriage; she wanted something that could get through both the good *and* the bad. What would he have done if they were already married, demanded a divorce?

"Any questions?" Dakota asked, pulling her from the unpleasant thought.

"No. I'm ready to work."

She'd arrived dressed for the messiest jobs possible and shoveling the paddock qualified. Even when it was still freezing, the sun could heat dark patches of ground and melt the snow around it.

"Then I'll let you get to it."

Blair appreciated him not telling her where to find a shovel, pitchfork and wheelbarrow; he'd already shown her the different outbuildings and she'd noted what was stored in each.

Her new boss went into the ranch office and she promptly headed for the horse barn. Alex brushed by her without a word, leading another pair of horses. She resisted doing anything childish, like sticking out her tongue at his back.

The next few weeks weren't going to be easy.

"NOELLE," DAKOTA CALLED, suspecting she'd fallen asleep in the car while waiting for him. She jumped and shot upward.

"Ready?" she asked.

"Yeah." He moved the passenger seat back as far as it would go and got in. The small compact wasn't built for a tall man with long legs.

His irritation with Saul rose again. He shouldn't be shopping; he should be working. But maybe this was another way the old man was suggesting his grandson wasn't up to the physical demands of ranching. Dakota did his best not to limp when his grandfather might see him, but Saul was fully aware of his injuries.

He'd have to look for a way to show he was sufficiently fit for the job.

"The SUV I'm getting will be roomier," Noelle said as she drove toward the highway. "There's coffee in the backseat if you want a cup."

He glanced into the rear. "That's a big container. Did you know I'd be coming along?"

"No, my mother made it. There are also blankets and other supplies in the trunk in the unlikely scenario we break down or something else happens. My parents believe in preparedness."

"Better to be safe than sorry. How did the exercise session go with Saul?"

"That's between Saul and myself. I *will* say he's an interesting guy."

Interesting?

"Are we talking about the same Saul Hawkins? The one who either growled yes or no through meals or said nothing when I was a kid? He used to mutter 'silence is golden' and he took it to an extreme."

Though Noelle was focused on the road ahead, he could tell she was exasperated.

"What *is* it between the two of you?" she asked. "He and Jordan seem to have worked things out."

"I'm sure your sister has already told you everything about the Maxwell brothers' childhood."

Noelle cast Dakota a quick look. "Actually, hardly anything. Paige is discreet. If she thinks something is private between Jordan and the rest of you, she isn't going to tell anyone else. But everybody knew the relationship was difficult. Beyond that, I'm in the dark."

Difficult?

Dakota ground his teeth.

"Difficult doesn't begin to cover it. Saul kept us from seeing Dad. Wouldn't let us near him and got the judge to agree. No phone calls, no visitation, not even *supervised* visits. For a while I'd see Dad's truck most weekdays, down the block from where the bus picked us up after school. He'd just sit there, trying to get a glimpse of his sons. I tried talking to him once, but he said they'd throw him in jail if we were seen together. I didn't dare tell anyone he was watching for us, not even Jordan or Wyatt."

"That must have been hard."

"Yeah. I'm not denying my father had a problem, but if we'd been at home, we might have stopped him from drinking. We could have helped on the ranch and encouraged him to do his wood carving or the other things he enjoyed. He only drank because he missed Mom so much."

Noelle tapped the steering wheel, the motion drawing Dakota's gaze. She had nice hands with long slender fingers and neatly trimmed nails. He didn't see a tan line on her left hand from a wedding ring recently removed, though maybe she hadn't worn one. A ring wouldn't have been practical while working in the situations she'd been in, any more than perfume would have been.

Dakota inhaled deeply, catching a wisp of the peachy fragrance she favored. Nice that she didn't wear too much of the stuff, instead it was faint and seductive.

Seductive?

Where had that come from?

"You know, it wasn't your responsibility to stop your father from drinking," Noelle said finally, throwing a cold damper on his thoughts. "Adults are supposed to take care of children, not the other way around."

"Except I *could* have helped. Dad and I were really close. I'm not saying that he loved Jordan and Wyatt any less, but we understood each other. If I'd had enough time with him, maybe it would have made a difference."

Dakota stirred angrily, banging his knee against the gear shift and sending a jolt of pain through his leg. He tried to ignore the throb, along with the concern that he might do real damage if he wasn't careful. It was unlikely, but unlikely could happen.

"Would driving be easier for you?" Noelle asked. "There's more room on this side and it's an automatic."

"I'm fine."

Despite his assurance, she pulled off the highway and parked. "Let me take a look."

"I'm wearing the same kind of jeans as before."

"There's no harm in me doing a brief check the way I did the other night."

Dakota stopped protesting, remembering the relief he'd felt when she'd massaged his healing knee the first time. He swung his legs from the car as Noelle came around the vehicle. She eased her fingers beneath the cuff of his jeans and he told himself not to expect too much. The swelling wasn't as bad, so she was able to slide his jeans above the knee, revealing the maze of scars.

"I'm almost afraid to ask, but are *you* doing everything the orthopedist told you to do?" she questioned. "Exercises to strengthen your muscles and keep the joint flexible?"

"When I have time. I've got other priorities."

"They should be one of your *top* priorities. I can tell most of the swelling is down. That's good. But it's also true you haven't had enough time to overwork yourself today."

Noelle started to massage his leg and awareness shot through Dakota, putting him on edge. She was a kind, smart, desirable woman, but he didn't have time for dating or romance. He had to focus on proving himself to Saul while regaining the full use of his leg…which also meant she was right about the exercises. He needed to do exactly what the Navy docs had ordered if he was going to get back to where he had to be physically.

No excuses, just do what was required. He could lock the door to his quarters to keep anyone from walking in and seeing him— someone like Saul.

"I suppose as a crusading doctor, you're going to offer to assist with my physical therapy, the way you offered to help Saul," he said, unable to keep the cynicism from his voice. "Dr. Bannerman to the rescue."

Noelle looked up. By rights she should have been insulted by his tone, instead she looked sad. "Doctors can only do so much. I'm in Montana to see my family. And to be frank, my entire team has a touch of PTSD, including me. So we're all on leave, work-

ing on recovery. It isn't unusual for first re-
sponders."

"Sorry."

"I understand. You're angry and I'm an
easy target."

Dakota sighed. Her golden-brown eyes
seemed to see more than he wanted anybody
to see. He'd even told her something about
his father that he'd never admitted to another
person.

"It isn't you," he said finally. "I'm sure the
Navy doctors would say I have PTSD, too,
but it's more than that. I'm angry because my
career is over. Breaking my leg this badly
means I can't do the job I'm best trained
for—helping people. Not that ranching isn't
important, but I was making life-and-death
decisions out there. Now I'm deciding who
gets to shovel manure from the barn and paddock or ride fence lines."

"Life-and-death decisions are made on
ranches," Noelle said. "Ranch hands can be
injured and the right choices need to be made.
Harsh winters mean animals starve if feed
isn't put out, yet distributing hay and protein
cake before and during a storm can be a risk
to you and your employees. The scale might
seem different, but every life is important."

NOELLE UNDERSTOOD SOME of what Dakota felt. He had highly specialized training as a Navy SEAL and had lived a life on the edge, while her specialty was emergency medical care in field conditions. His particular skills were quite different than hers, but they both seemed to feel out of place in Montana. It wasn't that Shelton couldn't use more doctors, but there were places in the world with no doctors at all. On the other hand, she also wasn't setting up a practice in those places, just going there in emergencies.

She'd never thought she *would* stop doing relief work, but the divorce on top of losing the baby had pulled her up short. Steffen wanted to believe the ectopic pregnancy was her fault, but maybe he'd also wanted an excuse to get out of the marriage. The possibility stung, even though they'd been wrong for each other from the beginning.

Now she needed to reassess her life. Maybe she would continue doing emergency medicine, and maybe she'd apply her knowledge in a new direction. She didn't know. But she had choices, while Dakota hadn't been given one when he was discharged from the service.

"Noelle?" Dakota's voice filtered into her tangled thoughts and she looked at him.

"Sorry, I got distracted."

"Maybe I should drive so you can get some rest."

"Only if you want to. I was merely thinking, not about to fall asleep. How does your leg feel?" she asked.

"I'm fine."

She stood up. "Okay. Give me a minute."

Noelle collected snow in a plastic bag and wrapped it in a cloth to put on Dakota's knee. He grimaced, but accepted the cold pack. When she was back in the car, she poured them both a travel cup of coffee.

"Great brew," he said after his first sip.

"Mom doesn't use flavorings," Noelle said as she drove back onto the road. "She orders a selection of coffee beans and has a special blend she's developed."

"That's dedication. Just like what you're doing with the decorations for the tour."

"I can't compare to my mother on that score, either," Noelle said, shaking her head. "Last night she laid out sheets of drafting paper and sketched where she wants everything put up, down to the ribbon and color. She already has a menu for the visitors and wants to coordinate with Paige, Anna Beth and me to be sure there aren't too many duplicates. Who knows what I'll discover when I get home. She may have decided to put reindeer horns on the horses and hire a brass band."

"Is it a contest?"

Noelle grinned. "Nah, she wants to be a big success so they'll ask again next year. Some of the ranching families have been in Shelton County for over a hundred and forty years, but we only got here in 1953. We're the new kids on the block. Mom thinks this means we really belong now."

"Seriously?"

She shook her head with another grin. "*No*. Honestly, I thought you were the Maxwell brother with the best sense of humor. My mother simply likes decorating and having people enjoy her efforts. She also loves entertaining, so the tour is perfect for her. Not that I'd expect Mr. Ebenezer Scrooge Maxwell to understand."

Dakota settled deeper into the car seat. "Scrooge or not, I'm here, aren't I?"

"Yeah, and soooo happy about it, too."

"I'll survive."

A glance told her the tense lines in his face had eased. "That's good. Can you keep something to yourself?"

He rolled his eyes. "My whole career has been about confidentiality." Despite his words, he sounded vaguely uneasy, as if she was planning to spring an emotional trap on him.

"In that case, my mom sent a picnic, but as an alternative, is there any chance I can interest you in a never-to-be-mentioned-pizza? You'd have to keep the food she made for me and never *ever* admit it wasn't consumed in Bozeman. Unless she asks directly. I'd never lie to Mom or ask you to lie, either."

Another glance showed Dakota smiling. "You're hungry for Italian?"

"They give us something called pizza in our emergency rations. Cardboard would taste better. In medical school I practically lived on pizza and loved every bite. But Mom, bless her heart, is determined to feed me home-cooked meals."

"I'm familiar with field rations. A pizza sounds good."

"Great. My half will have pepperoni and all the veggies they can fit on it, including artichoke hearts," she said promptly.

"You've given this some consideration."

"It used to be my standard order. That way I could assure my parents that I was eating my vegetables."

"You were young when you went away to school. A child prodigy."

"I wouldn't say that. More a case of being determined to get a head start on the life I wanted."

"Don't you feel as if you missed out on your childhood?"

She shrugged. "Now and then. But nobody could have persuaded me to do anything different."

While the road ahead appeared dry, Noelle kept a close eye out for ice in the shade, or areas where the snow had compressed into a slick patch. Years had passed since she'd driven much in Montana. Or anywhere. The rare times she was in the states, she'd worked at a medical clinic down the street from her small studio apartment, which had helped with payments on her school loans. She had seen no need to own a car, even for the relatively short time she and Steffen were married.

Field vehicles were different. She'd driven Jeeps, Land Rovers, trucks…anything necessary to get into an area and carry supplies.

Dakota was quiet, letting her concentrate, yet his tension seemed to rise again as the minutes passed.

"Is my driving making you nervous?" she asked wryly.

"No, just thinking about everything I want to get done. Will there be room for a few cans of paint?" he asked. "If not, I can go into Shelton for it."

"I'm sure they could be tucked in corners, but this isn't a good time of year to paint. Outside, at least. Much too cold."

"Yeah, but if you're determined to include the old homestead cabin as part of the tour, that large downstairs bathroom should be put into working order. The paint isn't just dark, it's peeling in long shreds off the walls. Propane heaters can be used to heat the interior. I've checked and a functional water line still goes to the house. It can be turned on and I'll repair any problems I find with the plumbing."

"Oh."

Pleasure filled Noelle.

Dakota might be bah humbugging out loud, but he was also doing something meaningful to help.

"THEY HAVE A good variety here," Dakota said as they looked at the selection of wreaths in a warehouse store in Bozeman.

"Do you think that one is big enough to

have a showy impact on the end of the barns?'" Noelle asked, gesturing to the sample wreath which had been assembled and hung from a post above them.

Dakota nodded. "Sure. It's almost as tall as you are."

"Great." She consulted the notes she'd made on her phone. "We need at least three of the super-size wreaths. And I think four of the thirty-two inch and a dozen of the twenty-four inch."

"Just tell me which ones to load."

He stacked the boxes she wanted on their flatbed cart, then grinned as Noelle leaned deep over a bin of fresh evergreen wreaths and inhaled.

"You're like a cat going after catnip," he joked.

She straightened. "I love the scent of evergreen. Even sticky pine sap doesn't bother me. But as my parents always say, artificial wreaths and trees can be reused and are less of a fire hazard. Oh, before I forget, I want trees on the porches of both houses as well as inside. And by the horse barn."

"How about artificial trees inside, and real ones outside?" Dakota suggested. "Unless we get a warm Chinook wind off the Rockies, they should hold for a couple of weeks, especially if they're only lit during the tours. The trees can be cut on Soaring Hawk property."

"That's a good compromise. I'm also hoping to get fresh evergreen swags and garland from the church youth group, right before the tours. They make them to raise money."

Dakota resisted temptation for a moment, but reached up and plucked a pine needle caught in her hair. "You have a stowaway." He showed it to her.

"Oh." She laughed. "When you said stowaway, I thought you meant a spider."

"You don't like spiders?"

"They're fine if we're a mile or two apart, though I've had to get used to them in some of the places I've worked."

A strained expression flickered in her eyes and he was reminded of when they'd stopped on the road and she'd become distracted while rubbing his knee. "Hey, what's up? I'm safe to talk to, in case I haven't mentioned it already." He gave her a lopsided grin. "After all, I've been privy to dozens of classified secrets that even Santa and his reindeer couldn't drag out of me."

His effort at making a Christmas-related joke prompted a smile. "Santa and his reindeer, huh? I just…" She sighed. "I haven't told anyone, but I've been giving my career some thought lately. Evaluating my choices. Not about being a doctor, just about where I'm practicing medicine. I'm not saying I'm giving up relief work, but I've never really considered other options."

"Surely that's normal for anyone in your situation."

"I suppose." Noelle put her chin up. "Look, let's add Christmas trees to the cart and then make our next stop a hardware store for the paint."

"What about light strings? They have quite a selection here," Dakota said, accepting the change of subject. Obviously she had said as much as she intended to say.

"I want to see other options first."

"Sounds like a plan."

NOELLE COULDN'T BELIEVE she'd admitted to Dakota that she had questions about continuing to work in international aid, but she wasn't worried he'd say something out of turn to the family.

And it had been a relief to voice some of her doubts out loud.

At the hardware store he went to the paint

department while she checked their stock of Christmas lights.

"Find anything you like?" Dakota asked, coming over when he'd finished.

"I like all of them, I just don't think they'd work on fences and rooflines."

"Not even these?" He picked up a package that had plastic "tractor" light covers for the individual globes, his expression reminding her of when he'd examined the toy tractor in Shelton—a blend of pleasure and nostalgia. And maybe a hint of wistfulness, like a child hoping for a treat. He'd probably be surprised to know he was revealing so much.

"You obviously have farm equipment on your mind," Noelle said in a teasing tone. "Novelty lights won't show up well at a distance, but I'll get a few strings."

"Don't overlook this one." Dakota held up another package, this time with grinning orange Jack O Lantern light covers.

She laughed. "I think that's a leftover from Halloween."

"Hey, I'm just trying to be sure you don't miss any possibilities."

"Your help is duly noted. But what about that string?" Noelle gestured to a light set with red hearts which had been tucked behind the box with Jack O Lanterns.

His slow smile made her tingle. "The kissing holiday? Doesn't that apply year round?" He leaned closer and brushed a feathery kiss across her lips. "Just practicing for mistletoe time," he whispered.

She wanted to fan herself. There was something utterly appealing about a man with a sense of humor.

"I'm surprised you need practice," Noelle managed to say without sounding as breathless as she felt.

"Just when it comes to mistletoe. Though I must admit, kissing under mistletoe is the one aspect of Christmas I've enjoyed."

She gave him a long look. "At least that gives me something to work with. You know, in getting you to appreciate the holiday."

Sadness flickered in his dark eyes and was gone just as quickly. "I'm afraid you're out of luck if that's what you're hoping."

Noelle wished she hadn't said anything. Still, with someone like Dakota, there was no telling what might make him uptight and she couldn't walk on verbal eggshells every minute.

She started loading the cart, but at the cash

register she insisted on paying for the novelty lights herself, saying they weren't really for the tour. And they weren't. She wanted to decorate a tree for Mishka and Daniel, along with putting one up in the ranch office for Dakota. There wasn't any way she could make up for his unhappy childhood, but sharing holiday cheer was a small step in the right direction.

Out in the SUV, Dakota consulted his phone. "I've been thinking we should check at a specialty lighting store for the heavy duty light strings you need. There's one up the street that seems promising. Their website says they stock decorations for businesses."

"Great. Let's go," Noelle agreed.

She'd wondered how successful the shopping trip would be since Dakota had been ordered to go with her, but it was turning out to be a lot of fun.

As for his kiss? It was going to make sleeping difficult tonight, even though she knew it didn't mean anything.

At least, she didn't think it did.

CHAPTER SEVEN

ALEX'S NERVES WERE frayed from trying to ignore Blair all day.

How could she have gotten a job on the Soaring Hawk? He'd been trying to do the right thing by avoiding her. Why couldn't she understand?

For most of the morning she worked on the paddock by the horse barn where he was mucking stalls. So practically every time he came out with a wheelbarrow of straw and manure, he couldn't escape seeing her.

Luckily she was done by early afternoon and he hadn't seen her in over an hour.

But now the sound of a tractor motor came from outside the barn, along with Rod Gaffney's voice, who had attended high school with them and knew they'd planned to get married someday. "Hey, Blair, you're a treat for sore eyes."

Alex heard her laugh.

"Really? You just saw me a couple of hours ago."

"Yeah, and you get prettier every time."

Alex's fingers clenched the pitchfork as the flirtatious exchange continued for a minute, then Blair sent Rodney along, saying she had work to do and so did he.

Soon she backed a flatbed trailer through the open double doors, stacked with both straw and hay.

"Uh, I'll unload the bales," Alex said.

"Not your responsibility," she replied, giving him a cool look as she stepped down from the tractor seat. "Stop bothering me—I'm busy."

That was rich, considering her presence on the ranch was already scrambling his brain like an egg in a frying pan. Besides, he'd only said one thing. The rest of the time he'd pretended she wasn't there. "Why did you apply to be a cowhand at the Soaring Hawk?" he demanded.

Blair grabbed one of the bales and swung it into place. "Same as you. I wanted the job."

Alex opened his mouth to say she could always work on her uncle's ranch, but then she'd just repeat that he could be working for his father.

"But you're into computers now. You didn't stay with ranch management."

"Is *that* what bothers you? Me switching to computer science?" she asked as if she couldn't believe her ears. "Grow up. You kicked me out of your life, and also out of the life we planned together. You gave up any right to make comments about what I studied in college. Now go away. Surely you have something to do that doesn't involve annoying me."

Alex went back to work, pretending she wasn't shifting heavy bales into place, moving them higher and higher up a staggered stack against the back wall. He'd planned to fetch the hay and straw himself, but she'd gotten to the task ahead of him. Now he felt like an absolute heel for letting her do it alone.

Blair was still moving the bales when he left to dump the last load on the compost heap. He was rolling the wheelbarrow back toward the barn when he saw a silvery-blue SUV drive up to the storage shed built off the ranch office.

Someone *else* to face?

He was tired, just at the thought. He'd expected life on the Soaring Hawk to be quiet, without people always coming and going.

Maybe it would settle down after the holidays. Ranchers didn't have time to get together for most of the year.

Alex tightened the knit scarf around his throat and went over to the SUV. "What can I do to help?" he asked as the foreman and Noelle Bannerman began unloading bags and boxes from the car. Being good at his job meant not hiding from anything that needed doing.

"That's nice of you," Noelle said. "These go in the storeroom for now. Put Christmas lights on the left, wreaths and trees on the right."

"Those are humongous light strings."

"I know, a thousand bulbs each. We went to a specialty store that Dakota found. The staff was very knowledgeable."

Alex liked her. The first night she'd mentioned knowing his parents, but not as if they were close friends, so maybe she didn't know much about the accident. Anyhow, she didn't live in Montana. The other ranch hands had mentioned she was a doctor with an aid organization.

Someone reached past Alex into the SUV. It was Blair, doing her bit. He should have expected that.

"Hello, Dr. Bannerman," she said, plainly giving him the cold shoulder. "I'm Blair Darby. Your mom and dad talk about you all the time at the ranching association meetings. And a few months ago I saw a news program about the earthquakes in Nepal. The one when you were interviewed. It made everyone in Shelton proud that you were one of the doctors helping out."

"Call me Noelle," she urged. "To be honest, I barely remember that interview. We were busy and someone stuck a microphone and camera in my face."

"Yeah, it was cool when you told them to stop talking and start working."

Noelle shook her head. "I should have been more diplomatic."

"Nah." Blair grabbed a big container of light strings. "I bet they were jealous because you were the news and they were just filming it."

"Somebody needs to report on what's happening," Noelle said seriously. "Our donations go up each time we're in a story. We couldn't keep going without folks seeing and caring about what we do."

"I guess. What's Nepal like?" Blair asked

as they moved back and forth from the SUV to the storeroom.

"Beautiful. I absolutely fell in love with both the place and its people. But I've treasured every country and continent I've seen. Each is unique and there's so much to appreciate about the people who live there."

"That's awesome. I haven't gotten too far from Shelton since I was little. Well, except around Montana and the surrounding states."

Noelle nodded. "I've enjoyed the chance to travel, but Montana is special. We have Yellowstone to the south and Glacier National Park to the north, along with dozens of other great things to see and do. Not that I'm biased about my home state, you understand."

Blair giggled. "Of course not. But we do really have great stuff here, like the Continental Divide."

"Right. As stunning as the Himalayas are, the Rockies are just as beautiful."

They went on discussing the scenic wonders of home and very quickly the SUV was emptied.

Alex looked at the foreman and wondered if they were thinking the same thing. Blair and Dr. Bannerman were like beautiful, colorful butterflies, while he was more of a

162 THE SEAL'S CHRISTMAS DILEMMA

worker bee. People enjoyed butterflies, but they didn't think much about bees unless they got stung.

Before the accident Alex had enjoyed sitting back and listening to Blair while she teased and laughed with their friends. *She* was the reason they'd been voted Homecoming King and Queen in their senior year. Nowadays he wondered why she had fallen in love with him in the first place. He was just a quiet, average guy, not especially clever or good-looking, even before the accident.

As for Dakota?

The older cowhands claimed he used to be wild in high school, so maybe he wasn't a worker bee, either. He'd played awesome pranks around Shelton. He must have taken after his father—Evan Maxwell had pulled epic practical jokes that people still talked about. Sharing stories about the Soaring Hawk was a thing in Shelton, and especially ones about Sourpuss Saul Hawkins. Alex wouldn't have dared apply for a job at the ranch if he hadn't been desperate.

But it turned out that Mr. Hawkins wasn't a bad guy.

"Thanks for the help," Noelle said when they finished. "Please spread the word around the ranch that anyone who doesn't have plans for Thanksgiving is invited to the Blue Banner. Festivities start at eleven."

"This morning Dakota told me that we all have the day off," Blair said. "I think everyone has family in the area, but I'll let the crew know, just in case. I'm sure they'll appreciate it."

She cast Alex a sideways glance and he could tell she wasn't nearly as cheerful as she sounded. In fact, if looks could kill, he'd probably drop dead on the spot.

He left, hoping to avoid another discussion with her. Not that they'd discussed much earlier, but Blair had made it clear she was still upset.

Okay, he *was* bothered that she'd switched to studying computers. But she'd been majoring in ranch management as part of their overall plan to convert the Sunny Crest to an organic beef ranch, so it was silly of him to think she would continue after he stopped seeing her.

Alex had a sudden dismal suspicion that he'd made a mistake by cutting Blair out of his life, but he didn't know how to go back to where they'd been. After all, she might be trying to reconcile out of a sense of duty. He wasn't even sure how well he knew her any longer. She was different than before the accident.

But then, so was he.

NOELLE COLLECTED THE box of food her mother had made for the trip into Bozeman and handed it to Dakota. She thought about commenting on Blair's frosty attitude toward Alex, but it wasn't her business and she didn't want to create a problem for the young woman.

"Are you all right?" Dakota asked in a low tone before she could say anything.

"All right?"

"About what Blair said—that everyone was proud of the work you were doing in Nepal. I realize I'm overstepping here, but any decision you make about your career should be based on what's right for you, not what other people expect. You'll be needed wherever you decide to practice medicine."

Noelle's stomach had undeniably churned at the younger woman's comments. After all, if everybody was so proud of what she'd done, how could she consider stopping? But she was touched by Dakota's concern and perceptiveness.

"You aren't overstepping. I'm the one who

decided to tell you how I felt. And I appreciate what you're saying," she said.

Dakota seemed to hesitate. "About what happened at the hardware store—"

"I know, you were just practicing for mistletoe," she said swiftly. She didn't want to hear him apologize for kissing her. "Thanks for coming to Bozeman with me."

"Don't tell anyone, but I enjoyed it."

She nodded and went up to the main house for a quick visit with the family. Saul looked tired, yet bright-eyed as he declared that he'd taken Mishka for a walk earlier, along with a few of the ranch dogs. He'd also done another set of exercises and promised to do more that evening.

In the kitchen, both Paige and Anna Beth hugged her.

"Whatever you did, it really got my husband motivated," Anna Beth declared. There was a hint of pride in the way she said *husband* that made Noelle suppress a smile. She knew it was a first marriage for the retired marine, who'd made her career a priority over a spouse and children.

"My pleasure," she assured Anna Beth. "But it's later than I told my mother I'd be gone. I should get going."

Paige walked her out to the SUV. "I'm embarrassed you figured Saul out so quickly. You're amazing."

"Just doing my job," Noelle said, keeping her tone light. It was a nice reminder that she *could* make a difference wherever she practiced medicine. And as Dakota had said, doctors were needed everywhere.

DAKOTA WAS UP at four o'clock on Thanksgiving morning to clean the barn and let the horses into the paddock.

Jordan came out and insisted on working with him until it was time to leave for the family gathering at the Blue Banner.

"You need to get ready to go," Dakota kept saying.

"Hey, I was doing your job a month ago," Jordan said. "Aren't I qualified to work alongside my brother?"

"Don't be ridiculous."

"Maybe you don't trust me because I've made my peace with Saul."

Dakota sighed. He didn't know *how* Jordan had made peace with their grandfather—enough that he was even living with the old guy—but he accepted it. "I don't care what your relationship is with Saul, just don't expect me to do the same."

"Maybe if you sat down with him and talked for a while, you might see that he's trying to change. Besides, I thought you'd stopped being angry about the past."

"Coming back has resurrected a few issues. I'll survive."

"Are those issues *just* from coming back?"

Though it was cold in the barn, the heavy work had raised beads of sweat on Dakota's face. He stopped and wiped his forehead. Curiously, he wished Noelle was here. She pushed just as hard as his brother on certain questions, but it felt different with her. Noelle didn't have a stake in him reconciling with Saul, and when they talked about post-traumatic stress, he knew it was something they were both dealing with in their own way.

She also had a way of drawing him out of himself and making him see what was possible, rather than just the past. Maybe it was the Christmas spirit she was so enthusiastic about sharing.

He didn't know what had possessed him to kiss her on their shopping trip. And though he'd tried to discuss it with her, she'd brushed it off.

"Dakota?" Jordan prompted.

"I can't talk about the mission, as you well know," Dakota said finally. "Even if I wanted to, which I don't. But I wouldn't mind knowing why Saul suddenly thinks community involvement is so important. He wasn't even civil to people when we were kids."

Jordan pitched a load of fresh straw in a stall. "If fault needs to be laid, you can drop it at my door. I was having trouble finding employees and Paige kept telling me that getting involved with the ranching community might help. She said everyone needed to understand I was in charge and that Saul wouldn't be part of employee management."

"I understand why potential employees could have a hard time believing he wouldn't interfere."

Some of Dakota's clearest childhood memories were of his grandfather barking orders and bullying folks. It was tactic he'd always despised.

"Saul doesn't get involved in running the ranch now, even when he has the opportunity," Jordan said. "We discuss what's going on, but he's left the decision-making in my hands. I'm trying to learn from that and do the same with you. That's why I've been spending so much time at Mom and Dad's old ranch since you got here, working to get things in better shape. If I'm not at the Soaring Hawk, I can't stick my nose into how you run the place. You deserve the same chance I got."

Dakota had wondered what his brother was doing with his days. He thought about asking if their father's tractor was still on the property, but that could wait for another time. "How does Saul's interest in community involvement figure into all of this?"

"Paige urged me to attend a ranching association meeting. I didn't expect much from talking to the group, but the next thing I know, a few dozen ranchers and cowhands arrive to help brand and vaccinate the spring calves. I had several job applicants by the end of the work day. Saul has become a firm convert of mutual support between neighbors. Folks actually seem to enjoy his company."

"Surely he can't brand cattle any longer."

"We don't know what's possible now that he's had his hip replaced, but he's willing to send paid employees and go himself to show solidarity." Jordan looked at his watch. "Time for me to get going. We'll bring you food from the meal. Don't object—my mother-in-law will insist. Margaret is determined."

"You seem to admire her."

Jordan's smile was as happy as Dakota had ever seen it. "Margaret and Scott are amazing. Paige had decided she didn't expect to get married when she adopted Mishka, and her parents loved having them live at the Blue Banner. They could have resented me for up-ending everything. Instead, they treat me as a son. I couldn't have gotten luckier with my in-laws."

A whole lot luckier than Dad, Dakota thought. Saul had been a nightmare as a father-in-law, disowning his daughter, refusing to have contact with her and bad-mouthing the marriage to the few people who would listen.

"Uh, that's great," Dakota said, not wanting to bring up the past—specters from the past were all around him, they didn't need to be roused more than they already were.

"Yeah." Jordan put his pitchfork on the tool rack. "I'll see you tonight. The Bannermans play games, go for rides, all sorts of things. They're very social."

"I'm happy for you."

"They want you to be part of the family, too," Jordan said. "The same with Wyatt."

"That's nice of them. Maybe after I've been in Montana longer." Dakota didn't enjoy prevaricating, but it was plain that becoming part of the Bannerman clan entailed accepting Saul along with it; he still wasn't sure that was possible.

He continued working for another couple of hours after Jordan and the others left for the Blue Banner, though there was little to do around the main ranch. He and his brother had groomed the horses and taken them outside, cleaned the stalls, put fresh straw down and stocked the feed bags.

Maybe he could ride fence lines. He'd kept several employees busy with that particular task, so it shouldn't be needed, yet his instincts were telling him to get out on the range and check the herds.

The cowhands had been released at noon the day before in order to allow extra time with their families. They must have wondered if he'd require them to work on Thanksgiving, but even if Dakota hadn't wanted a polite excuse to duck the gathering at the Blue Banner, he would have given everyone the day off. While holidays had little meaning for him, they were important to a lot of people.

He noticed one of the ranch's working dogs,

Pepper, sitting and watching him. Pepper was a young, energetic border collie and Australian shepherd mix that his brother called an Aussie collie. She was an attractive animal, with blue merle markings along with a white chest and patches of solid black.

"Hey, Pepper."

The dog wriggled with visible excitement.

"Come here, girl." Dakota slapped his hand on his leg and the Aussie collie dashed over. It was nice that she was friendly. Jordan had mentioned Pepper wasn't bonding with the other residents on the Soaring Hawk.

"Are you lonely?" he asked the animal. It didn't seem odd to speak to her. After all, he talked to horses.

As Pepper let out a small yip, Dakota realized he was grinning at the dog.

"Shall I brush you, too?"

She seemed to understand when he held up one of the brushes they used for the horses, dancing back and forth excitedly. He led her to the porch and sat on the lowest step.

He patiently worked the brush through every inch of Pepper's coat. She stood with equal patience, making a huffing sound he recognized as pleasure. Somebody on the ranch had to be grooming her regularly and he wondered why she hadn't become attached to them. She was an appreciative, friendly animal.

Dakota was concentrating so hard, he didn't notice a vehicle arriving until Pepper let out another yip. He looked up. To his surprise, he saw the SUV Noelle had rented.

"Hi," she called as she got out.

"Why aren't you with your family?"

She shrugged. "I needed a little peace and quiet, so I brought you something to eat. Ooh, what a lovely dog. I don't remember seeing her before."

"Jordan says she's a loner."

Noelle laughed. "Yeah, a real loner."

Dakota looked down. Pepper's jaw was resting on his thigh, gaze fixed on his face, even though he'd finished working on her coat. "She just wanted to be brushed."

NOELLE DIDN'T ARGUE the point, but she thought Pepper had chosen Dakota to be her best friend.

"The food is still warm if you want it now," she said.

Dakota looked ready to refuse, then she heard his stomach growl. "Um, all right."

He mumbled something about cleaning up.

By the time she had unpacked the containers in the office, he came from his quarters in a clean shirt and pair of jeans.

"Will you have some pie, at least?" he asked, gesturing to the two uncut pies she'd put on the broad desk.

"Maybe a sliver," she said, rubbing Buddy's nose. He'd been disgruntled at losing his usual sleeping space, but his mood had improved when she fed him a scrap of turkey. "Mom is fussing that I should eat more, but I haven't been hungry. I'll wait until you have some."

Dakota poured two cups of coffee and pushed one to her side of the desk. "I noticed you didn't have much pizza the other day, even though you claimed to be craving it."

Noelle would normally avoid the sensitive subject, but she felt safe with Dakota. "I have appetite issues after an emergency assignment. They go away."

"You're talking about the earthquakes."

Noelle nodded. Perhaps with Dakota she didn't have to pretend something she didn't feel and she'd already admitted to him that she had post-traumatic stress. "It was terrible. You can only do so much to help and it's never enough."

Dakota sipped from his mug, looking as if

he was trying to find the right words. "Sounds like survivor's guilt, to be honest."

"It goes with working in a disaster area."

"It goes with a lot of things. I lost two men on my last mission."

Noelle didn't say anything for a long moment. "I can't imagine how hard that must be."

He cleared his throat. "You seem to have a special feeling for the people in Nepal"

She nodded. "Even in the face of so much devastation, their spirituality awes me. I love the prayer flags they hang to spread blessings in the wind. The flags are everywhere. I wanted to put ones up to honor the patients we couldn't save, but I didn't know if it was appropriate and there was never enough time to ask. Or put them up, for that matter."

"Love is a blessing," Dakota murmured, then looked surprised. "My mother used to say that. Surely it's okay to hang them in respectful memory. You could do it here."

The possibility intrigued Noelle. "That's a good idea. Prayer flags are supposed to be hung in high places in the morning, on a sunny and windy day."

"Enough wind is rarely an issue around here. Maybe we could do it when we cut the fresh trees for the tour."

"I'd like that. I was told the blessings aren't just for Nepal—they're for the whole world. It's a beautiful thought."

Noelle petted Buddy and sipped coffee while Dakota ate and they talked about the Himalayas. In her mind though, she kept going back to what he'd said on the way to Bozeman—*I can't do the job I'm best trained for—helping people.* He'd wanted to return to active duty, so being medically discharged must have come as a terrible blow. And now she'd learned others had been killed on the mission that ended his career.

"Paige mentioned your parents are throwing you a birthday party a week from tomorrow," Dakota said as he finished. "I told her I'd come."

Noelle blinked. "Um, that's nice. To be honest, I'm trying to talk them out of a party. Not that it will do any good. Mom is determined to go ahead."

"You're too young to be bothered by a birthday coming around."

DAKOTA SPOTTED A flash of sadness in Noelle's eyes that vanished as swiftly as it had appeared.

"It isn't an age thing—I'd rather just focus

on the holidays," she said. "A birthday party seems trivial after being in a place devastated by an earthquake and the aftershocks."

"Some would say the same about Christmas decorations."

"Except decorating for the tour isn't about one person," Noelle insisted. "It raises money for a purpose and makes people feel better. The spirit of Christmas is more than a catchphrase to me. I've seen the power of hope and love, over and over."

Dakota could tell that she meant it and wondered if he should write his own special wish on a flag to hang in the wind—then nearly choked on the sentimental thought. He regarded Noelle with a wary eye. He'd seen how his brother had changed due to Paige's influence and wondered if he was headed the same direction.

He shifted in the chair, wishing his thoughts didn't keep returning to relationships, family or romantic. Focusing on establishing himself on the ranch was his priority and he needed to remember that.

"How about that pie?" he asked, preferring to think about something else. "Pumpkin or apple or both?"

"Pumpkin."

He served two slices onto plates and handed one to her.

Normally, he enjoyed quiet time on the ranch, but it seemed almost too quiet today and he found himself wishing his family, especially his energetic niece, was around. Spending time with Mishka and his new nephew was even making him think about having a family of his own someday—another reason to wonder about Noelle's influence— though it was more a case of thinking what it would be like to be a father and husband. On one side his eldest brother seemed utterly happy and content, while his younger brother adored his eighteen-month-old daughter, but at the same time was grieving deeply for the wife he'd lost.

When Noelle was finished eating, she set her empty plate aside and rubbed Buddy's tummy some more.

"How about going for a ride after we're done?" Dakota suggested, his instincts still telling him to get out and check the ranch. "The horses can use the exercise. I'll check the cattle and you can tell me more about the Himalayas. Unless you need to get back to the Blue Banner."

Noelle brightened. "A ride would be nice.

I don't need to go back for a while. I love my family, but it's chaotic at home with so many people. My grandmother, aunts and uncles and cousins and their kids are there, along with everybody else. And of course, the adults want to commiserate with me about my divorce and say angry things about my ex. It's their way of being supportive."

Curious.

The flash of sadness in her eyes deepened at the mention of her divorce. Could she still be in love with her ex-husband?

"You don't have angry things to say about your ex?"

"We just didn't work out. My career is mostly to blame. Steffen was an engineer with the same aid organization, but after we got married, he thought we should stop doing international relief and get better-paying jobs here in the states."

"Oh." Dakota would have commented that Noelle's ex sounded selfish, but she'd said she didn't want to engage in negative talk. Maybe there was more to the divorce, or maybe she felt the healthiest route was letting go.

He stood up. "I'll put the leftovers in the fridge and then we'll saddle up."

A short time later they were riding west on

Tucker and Stormy, Pepper racing ahead of them. Noelle moved easily with the mare and the tension in her face gradually eased. She had a way with animals—the gentle, instinctive way she'd communicated with Stormy when they were saddling their mounts had spoken volumes.

Like him, she'd seen some of the harsher aspects of life. What amazed him was her ability to continue finding pleasure in simple joys, like cats and horses and colorful strings of Christmas lights. The sweet way she'd given Buddy her undivided attention had made him envious of the feline.

"Perfect day for a ride," she said as they headed up the broad valley. The sun was out and the air brisk, rather than frigid.

"It is." He noticed that for someone who hadn't ridden in a while, she sat well in the saddle.

"Mmm. My parents think it's going to be a hard winter. Their motto in life is 'prepare for the worst and hope for the best.'"

"Wise people."

Dakota gave Noelle another long glance, frustrated by how much she fascinated him. She was different from anyone he'd ever known, embracing the holidays in a way he'd never seen and possessing a natural optimism that took his breath away. Yet he suspected the grief shadowing her eyes wasn't solely for the lives she hadn't been able to save.

He'd first noticed it in her face the day Mishka had run to greet them when they were coming from the old homestead cabin—a wistful melancholy before the emotion vanished.

Whether it was related to her career or divorce or another issue, something was definitely going on underneath that she still wanted to keep private.

CHAPTER EIGHT

A MEASURE OF Noelle's cares fell away under the steady, even pace of the mare she was riding.

Unlike some days on the eastern edge of the Rockies, the wind was light, barely a breeze. A fair amount of snow still frosted the landscape and the sky above was a brilliant blue, the sun just an hour past its highest point. The Rocky Mountains rose above the waves of hills ahead, crisply outlined in the clear air, the snow-capped sentinels of the state.

Home.

Her heart often longed for Montana and she especially enjoyed riding in the winter. It wasn't hot and the horses were eager for activity since they weren't ridden as much this time of year.

Doctor or not, she was a rancher's daughter, so it was instinctive to check the fences they were passing, along with the condition of the cattle. They were in good shape and ought to be in a desirable weight range for spring calving, provided enough food could be distributed to eat during storms and those storms didn't last too long.

In bad weather the cattle huddled at windbreaks, but right now they were scattered, digging through the small amount of remaining snow to find what calories could be gained from the yellow grass beneath. A few had found dry patches and lay contentedly chewing their cud.

A cow bawling in one of the fields caught their attention and they rode over to find her leg caught in the blue polypropylene twine used to bind hay bales. It was tangled with a fallen tree. She was fighting to free herself and complaining just as hard.

"I'll take care of it," Dakota said when Noelle dismounted.

"No law says I can't lend a hand if needed."

He didn't protest. Pepper shifted into position, barking at the cow as though telling her to stop making such a fuss. The animal quieted, keeping a resentful watch on the dog. A strain of wild independence was desirable in a range animal, but it made them trickier to handle.

"Be sure to leave her a clean avenue of escape," Dakota said as Noelle came over.

"You think I'm getting in the path of eight hundred pounds of irate cow?" she asked in a dry tone. "Not likely."

Noelle almost laughed at the chagrin on his face. She moved around him for a better view of where the twine was caught on the animal's leg. At least it wasn't wire, which would have been more damaging. The cow didn't seem injured, simply offended that she couldn't escape the pesky twine.

Dakota drew a large chalk X on her rump for temporary identification and began cutting the twine. When she was free, she bolted away with a last indignant complaint. Within seconds she was mingling with the rest of the herd and searching for food.

"There might be a few bruises," Noelle said, "but she doesn't seem to have any trouble running. No limp or hesitation in her gait."

"Yeah. If she had an open wound I'd move her to the main ranch to treat and watch for infection. Instead, I'll ride out and check on her over the next few days." He frowned as he gathered the blue twine. "The new rule is for the ranch hands to collect and dispose of this stuff."

"It's being recycled in some areas."

"I can look into that as well." He gave her a glance. She was patting Pepper, whose tail wagged with happy abandon. "You have an instinct for animals. Did you think about going into veterinary medicine?"

Noelle shrugged. "I considered it briefly. Why do you ask?"

Dakota shifted his feet and seemed uneasy. "Because in my own awkward way, I'm trying to say it's fine to talk to me as much as you need. About your career or your latest relief assignment. Whatever. I may be a grouch, but who better to understand what it was like for you?"

Noelle's heart melted a little. His concern was endearing.

He must see them as kindred spirits, as if she was a fellow soldier who might need to talk about a traumatic experience. But how could she explain that her emotional struggle wasn't entirely about treating the injured in Nepal or her career? It was intimate in a way he probably wouldn't want to hear, no matter what he'd said.

"I'm sorry I called you a scrooge and a grouch. I've decided you're just…misunderstood."

His low chuckle surprised her. "Misunderstood? Like you misunderstood me arguing with my grandfather?"

"Families are complicated."

"True. I guess that's why you're out riding with me, instead of doing something with them."

Noelle shrugged as she tipped her head back and inhaled the crisp air. "Right now I'm exactly where I want to be. It's so beautiful and peaceful here. I really need to get home more often. I'm in touch with myself in Montana—it makes me feel truly alive in a way I don't feel in other places."

DAKOTA KNEW WHAT Noelle meant. He would never be happy about the reason he'd needed to leave the Navy, but he was learning the cadence of the ranch again. There was something reassuring about following the traditions that generations of ranchers had cherished.

He remembered an old rancher saying it wasn't one thing that kept him going day after day, it was a thousand little things. The scent of a spring rain. Watching a hungry calf nurse and its mother's low, contented moo.

Long grass rippling in the wind. Seeing new life come into the world.

Dakota got it. Perhaps as time went by he'd rediscover what Noelle felt—that sense of truly feeling alive. He even had a sense of it now. A little flicker of hope that things were looking up.

"Why don't we ride over that hill and find out what's there?" she suggested.

"Maybe another day. Your family is going to feel abandoned if we stay out too long."

"I suppose you're right, though not about my family. They're all doing their own thing. Some will be out riding like us or chatting in the kitchen. The kids enjoy board games and will have talked a few of the adults into participating. I'm sure my brothers are tossing a football around and looking forward to watching the game on TV, while Nana Harriet is probably taking a nap."

"Sounds nice. Almost like a holiday movie come to life," Dakota said. "But that doesn't mean they won't miss you."

Noelle shrugged. "Mom and Paige knew where I was going and the rest will assume I'm just doing something with somebody else. I don't get home for Thanksgiving that often, so I'm not part of the usual pattern of activity."

Dakota thought Noelle's absence must be missed, no matter what she said. She glowed with warmth and color, like a tree burnished gold and red by autumn. Her ready smile had to be as healing as the medical care she offered in the midst of disaster. How her husband could have wanted to end the marriage was beyond him.

They turned the horses back toward the Soaring Hawk.

"When you started out, did you realize you wouldn't be able to see your family as much?" he asked.

"I knew it in my head, but it got real the first Christmas I spent sloshing around a flood zone, doused in mosquito repellant. Actually, it was earlier than that. Medical interns and residents tend to work holidays, at least in emergency medicine."

"Did you help Saul with his exercises today?"

"Absolutely. Our bodies don't give us time off, just because it's Thanksgiving. Keeping in mind what you said on our trip to Bozeman, I'll even lend a hand with your exercises. Not as a doctor. As a friend." The offer seemed offhand, but Dakota wasn't fooled.

Noelle had an impulse to heal people, no matter what she was going through personally.

He did remember his behavior on their trip, along with the things she'd confided to him—and he especially remembered their kiss. Flatly refusing her offer seemed rude.

"I guess it would be good to have you watch me do a set and see if I'm doing anything wrong."

"Sure, whatever you want."

The surprise on her face mirrored Dakota's own feelings. Maybe he didn't mind her offering an opinion about his rehab because he knew she wasn't judging him in any way. Dakota felt on edge with both Saul and his brother. He understood why he wasn't comfortable with his grandfather; the reasons were less clear with Jordan.

Or maybe not.

When Jordan had returned, the Soaring Hawk was falling apart. No employees. Nobody willing to take a job from anyone connected to Sourpuss Hawkins. But Jordan had held the ranch together, turning everything around, and now Dakota didn't know *how* he was supposed to prove himself with that as a standard of comparison. There were no major hurdles left beyond the usual challenges of running a cattle ranch.

Dakota recalled his earlier thoughts about Saul showing approval when he won at the rodeo as a kid. Competing might be a way to make his efforts stand out to his grandfather. Also, the expertise needed for the rodeo was applicable to his work on the Soaring Hawk. So practicing for competition was the same as polishing his ranching skills, which were rusty after years away from the ranch. There was no rush, either. He didn't have to make a final decision until Shelton Rodeo Daze week.

"What complicated thoughts are running around your brain?" Noelle asked lightly.

"Nothing too deep. Just thinking about my grandfather."

"I imagine anything to do with Saul Hawkins is *very* deep and complicated."

"You're right. I've never understood him, but he never understood me, either, so maybe we're even."

Dakota urged Tucker forward. Pepper was still filled with energy, racing around in happy abandon. Her paws had to be cold in the snow, but she didn't seem to notice.

The only good thing about finding the cow

caught in the poly twine was thinking his instincts had been on-target about needing to check the ranch. Most people would see it as pure coincidence, but Dakota had relied on his instincts to stay alive as a Navy SEAL and it seemed reasonable to believe those same instincts could help him run the Soaring Hawk more effectively.

ALEX GATHERED A load of firewood and went inside the house. He sniffed the air, surprised he couldn't smell roasting turkey.

"Mom, aren't we having turkey?" he asked, putting the logs into the wood rack.

He'd spent the morning helping his father with ranch chores—the ranch hands had left that morning to be with their own families. He and his dad had eaten a light lunch and gone out again to finish. Traditionally the family didn't have their Thanksgiving meal until five o'clock or later, but while he didn't know much about cooking, he knew it was late to shove a turkey in the oven. Even a small one.

His mother shrugged. "We're eating at the Canary Diamond this year. Sarah said it was their turn to host, so she's doing the turkey, ham, stuffing and candied yams. I've made desserts, mashed potatoes, salad and a green bean casserole. Also my deluxe cranberry sauce."

Alex looked at her in dismay. "We can't eat there."

"We always used to share holiday meals with the O'Briens," she retorted. "You know that."

"Not since..." He stopped. "I don't want to go."

A clunk sounded as his father dropped a second armload of firewood in the rack. "The O'Briens are friends and we're no longer excluding them from our lives because of how you've treated their niece. They've generously chosen to overlook it themselves."

Alex's jaw dropped. "I haven't treated Blair badly. I just didn't think staying together was fair to her after I got hurt. I've been trying to do the right thing."

His father let out a disgusted snort. "Believe what you want. But as for breaking up, did you ever tell her that? Seems to me you just left her hanging in the wind."

Alex clenched his jaw. He was already wondering if ending his relationship with Blair had been a mistake, but even his parents seemed to think he'd messed up. Not that he was surprised they disapproved. They adored Blair. And his dad was right, he'd never actually told Blair that they were over until she'd shown up at the Soaring Hawk. Even then he'd been a little vague.

"Take those pies out to the truck, along with the other food," his mother said briskly. "We're eating with the O'Briens and that's final. You say you want to be treated the same as before the accident? Well, you're getting what you asked for."

Even if he could have gained his father's support, neither one of them would cross Donna Sorenson when she spoke in that tone of voice.

Grumbling under his breath, Alex carried the food to the pickup, reminded of other trips to the Canary Diamond before life had gotten turned upside down. He still vividly remembered the first time he'd seen Blair after her mother left her in Montana.

Eight years old. Defiant, angry and the prettiest girl he could have imagined with her dark brown hair and blue eyes. They'd instantly become friends and by the time he was thirteen, he'd realized he was in love, though he thought it had taken longer for Blair to feel the same way.

Now he had to listen to the other cowhands at the Soaring Hawk flirt with her. He wanted to confront Blair about it, but there was no guarantee their discussion would stay private. The last thing he needed was having word get back to the foreman about them arguing. He was already out on a limb the way he'd let it slip that he wasn't happy about the chance of her working at the Soaring Hawk.

Alex squirmed as he remembered Dakota's cool remark that the foreman made hiring decisions.

It had reminded him of the difference between being an employee or the son of the ranch owner. Not that Dakota wasn't a great boss. He worked harder than anyone else and he was fair. His expectations were high, but that was a good thing.

"Oops, I almost forgot this," his mother said, coming down the front steps with a large pastry box.

He peeked inside and saw she'd made her sweet potato cheesecake. Despite his dismay about having to see Blair, his mouth watered. Mom made the best cheesecake.

"Don't worry, son," she said. "I have a second one in the fridge. You can take it to eat at the Soaring Hawk. There's plenty to share."

"Thanks, Mom. Everyone shares there," he said, which was true, except for booze. Alcohol wasn't frowned on at the ranch, but it wasn't encouraged, either. No surprise, everyone knew that Dakota's father had messed up his life with drinking.

His mom nodded. "That's nice. I have other treats to send, too."

"They feed us really good, Mom. Mrs. Hawkins is a decent cook. The food's simple, but tasty."

"I'm sure she does a fine job, but I'm practicing for the Christmas Bake-Off. I've decided to start entering again."

Alex stayed silent as they drove to the Canary Diamond. He *did* want to be treated the same as before, though it was disconcerting to realize "the same" included his parents getting upset with him and insisting he do something he didn't want to do. Maybe they'd gotten upset at other times and just hadn't let it show.

As for the Christmas Bake-Off? His mom had always entered until the accident, often winning prizes for her cheesecake and other specialties. Was he the reason she'd stopped? It was true that he'd refused to attend any of the holiday events in Shelton. Maybe they hadn't wanted to leave him behind. He felt lousy at the possibility. He'd been so busy thinking about his own life getting turned upside down, he hadn't given much thought to how it had affected everyone else.

At the neighboring ranch, dogs raced to the truck, barking in happy welcome. Alex recognized most of them from when he and Blair had been together.

Mr. and Mrs. O'Brien gave him a friendly greeting, along with their five sons. There was a woman he didn't know who smiled and shook his hand—she turned out to be Davie's new wife, Stephanie, who was from Medicine Hat up in Canada. Davie was the eldest and everybody was calling him David now. Jeanette Rayburn, who'd been a fellow student in high school, was there, too. She and Noah O'Brien were getting married soon.

It bothered Alex, as if the world had passed him by.

He bent to pet the eager tricolored Australian shepherds. At least the dogs were the same, greeting him as an old pal. Only Fletch, Blair's dog, didn't seem interested in affection.

"Hey, Fletch," Alex called.

The German shepherd turned and went

into the house, a pointed snub. They'd been pals once upon a time, but Fletch was smart and adored Blair. He had to sense the situation had changed.

Blair came out and hugged Alex's parents. "Happy Thanksgiving," she said without looking at him.

"Happy Thanksgiving," chorused a round of voices.

"Mom, I'm starving. When are we eating?" complained Cort. He was Blair's youngest cousin, born after she'd come to live at the Canary Diamond.

"At five o'clock, as usual. There are stacks of appetizers until then. Let's help Donna get everything into the house."

Alex caught hold of Blair's hand before she could follow the others. "This wasn't my idea," he told her.

"No, it was mine."

He stared. "You asked your aunt and uncle to invite us?"

"I made the suggestion. The Sorenson and O'Brien families have been getting together on the holidays for over two decades. It isn't fair that our problems are keeping everyone else from enjoying themselves. You can just pretend I'm not here."

"That isn't what I want, Blair."

"You've done a good imitation of it over the last two and a half years. You didn't even know about David getting married."

"Because nobody told me."

Blair gave him an icy look. "Did you *want* to hear about us?"

Alex gulped, embarrassed. All right, he hadn't wanted to hear about the O'Briens because it meant hearing about Blair. He'd read her social media postings for a while after the accident, stopping finally because it made him miserable to see her comments about switching to computer science or going to the movies with friends. But surely his mom and dad could have mentioned Davie getting married and about Noah being engaged.

"I would have wanted to hear about that," he muttered.

"Your parents can't read your mind. I'm sure they don't know what is and isn't okay to talk about. Since I'm off-limits, they must have figured anything connected to me is off-limits, too."

He hated seeing the angry hurt in her eyes. "Blair, please understand. I just didn't want you hanging around because you thought it was what you're supposed to do. Or because of an idealistic notion you had about love. Like the stuff you said about your mom getting so confused over some guy and ending up in jail."

SOMETHING DEEP INSIDE Blair froze as if exposed to the coldest of Montana winter storms.

No one outside of the O'Brien family knew about her mom and how she'd gotten into trouble. Blair had confided in Alex because she trusted him and now he was using it against her.

"Is that honestly what you think I've been doing?" she asked, feeling as if she could shatter at any moment. "My fiancé is in the hospital and when he wakes up, I no longer love him in a healthy way, but compulsively. Or else I just want to stay with him out of a misplaced sense of duty. On the other hand, I'm also not allowed to pick another college major because of the plans we made—plans that you no longer seem to want anything to do with. How is that fair to me or even make sense?"

Alex's face turned red. "I didn't say you shouldn't have picked another major."

"Pretty darned close. I saw your expression when I mentioned computer science. Now,

I could have explained that I'd realized it was possible to make a good second income working from the Sunny Crest after we got married, which would help support the ranch. More and more companies allow employees to work remotely now. But we *couldn't* talk about anything. You wouldn't take my calls or let me visit."

"Because you're beautiful and smart and talented, and now I look like this," he blurted, gesturing to his face and neck, though most of his scars were covered by a high turtleneck sweater.

Blair would never minimize what had happened to Alex, but she didn't see his scars, she saw *him*. And even if she was furious for what he'd said about her mother, it had nothing to do with how he looked.

She crossed her arms over her stomach. "So, the truth comes out. It's all about appearances. Which means if *I'd* been in that truck when it crashed, you would have expected to break up because I didn't look the same as when we fell in love. Not too promising for when I started getting wrinkles, either. This seems to be a lucky escape for both of us."

Alex's eyes widened. "That isn't what I meant."

"That's how it sounds. Whatever you may think, believing in marriage and commitment and standing by someone through thick and thin is a good thing, Alex. Although, ironically, right now I'm wondering what I ever saw in you." She pulled the chain with his class ring from around her neck and lobbed it at him. "Make up your mind who and where you want to be. Just don't expect the rest of us to stop living while you're figuring it out."

Turning, she then walked up the stairs. She'd promised herself that she would never give that ring back to him unless he asked. Well, there were more ways than one of asking.

Yet her heart was curiously silent, the pain blunted by disappointment and shock. Aunt Sarah was right, they might have grown too far apart in the time since the accident.

The Alex she'd known would never have brought up her mother that way. He would have remembered how deeply she'd been hurt when Renee abandoned her.

On Sunday, Noelle drove back from church, humming "Jingle Bells." Now that they were past Thanksgiving, the Christmas season had officially started. There had been the traditional holiday hymn sing before the service and a potluck afterward, with everyone bringing their extra special dishes. And, tonight, the first of the weekly Park Caroler events would take place.

Before leaving, she told the youth group she wanted to buy lengths of the fresh evergreen garland they made each year as a fund-raiser. It was for the porches on the two houses and she also needed evergreen swags for the fence posts. The numbers involved made their eyes widen with delight.

She changed her clothes and hurried over to the Soaring Hawk. Driving in, she saw more lights had been strung on the fences. The decorating wasn't complete by any means and she was convinced that more supplies would be needed to have the right impact. The ranch center was huge and there were several barns and outbuildings, along with the two houses.

"Hi, Noelle," Blair Darby said, coming from the bunkhouse dining hall.

"Hi. Have you seen Dakota?"

The ranch hand shook her head. "He rode out an hour ago and said he'd be back later. He's probably checking the cow that got tangled with the baling twine. We've offered to go for him since he marked her with chalk, but he prefers checking on her himself. Or maybe he just wants to be sure we have the evening free to see the Park Carolers. He's really nice about that kind of thing."

"I'll go look for him."

Noelle saddled Stormy and rode up the valley, but when she got to the little-used paddock on the far side of the equipment barn, she saw Dakota riding Tucker in a fast circle. He threw a rope at a barrel in the middle of the space, the loop expertly dropping over it.

Impressive.

"Good afternoon," she called.

He flipped the rope off the barrel and looped it into a coil before urging Tucker to the fence. "I didn't think you'd be over today."

"I said I wouldn't come this morning, but the decorating is ongoing. When Saul gets back from the church I also need to work with him. And, uh…"

"Me?" he asked.

"If that's what you still want."

In the two days since Thanksgiving, she'd been watching while he did sets of exercises advised by the Navy doctors and then massaging his leg afterward. Massage was the only aspect of physical therapy where Noelle had experience; she was a firm believer that it helped to both heal and reduce pain. Dakota could probably benefit from a full body massage as well. Limping took a toll, the same with riding a horse.

Noelle sighed recalling his confident movements around the paddock. She was drawn to him…disconcertingly so. But it was more than a physical attraction. He was strong and decent and so very sweet with Mishka he nearly made her cry.

"I'm doing everything the Navy docs told me to do," Dakota said, "so another round of exercises will be fine. But don't you want to go for a ride first? You've taken the time to saddle Stormy and I still haven't checked on that cow."

"Sure."

As they rode west, Dakota gestured to the hazy sky. "The weatherperson isn't predicting snow, but I have to wonder."

Noelle tried to ignore her response to being so close to Dakota and tipped her head back, breathing deeply. Her mother used to call her a human weather barometer, but her instincts were rusty after being in so many different countries with varying climate patterns.

"It feels like when we used to get a light snowfall overnight," she said finally. "You know, clear at dusk, clear the next morning, but you wake up to an inch or two of fluffy new white on the ground."

"I remember that happening before my mom died. It wasn't enough to keep us home from school or even to delay opening."

"A good many schools don't have weather closures any longer—they just do classes online. Mishka's teacher had online sessions during the last storm, quite a feat with kindergartners."

"No more snow days?" Dakota looked mock appalled. "How can they do that to kids?"

Noelle grinned. "It's the face of the future. Mom told me the Shelton Rodeo Daze committee helped get internet to all the outlying homes where children live. They also have loaner computers available to students during the winter. The service isn't always reliable, especially in the outer reaches of the county, but improving."

"Then the ranching association is responsible for the end of snow days in Shelton. How could they afford it?"

She shrugged. "The rodeo. A major rodeo champion lives here now, which changed everything. Josh McKeon is well-known in both Canada and the United States, though he's retired from competition. He owns a rodeo training facility on what used to be called the Galloping G Ranch."

"I've heard his name. Doesn't he represent a Western wear clothing company?"

"That's right. You'll meet Josh and his wife before long. Paige and Kelly are friends and their kids have playdates. Anyhow, as Mom tells it, Josh competed in Shelton Rodeo Daze the summer he retired and suddenly our little rodeo became a huge deal in the rodeo world."

Dakota lifted his eyebrows. "You don't sound convinced that's a great thing."

"Local people don't attend as much because it's so crowded with visitors and contestants. Still, how can we object? The week is a bigger moneymaker than ever and local businesses have also benefited. Money raised by the rodeo has traditionally supported emergency services in the area, but the committee announced last year that they would be able to expand to another community improvement project—helping schools and teachers."

He nodded. "Supporting kids is a good choice. How do you know about everything going on around here if you can't get home very often?"

"Email with the family. We also call whenever possible, though during my last assignment we could only talk once a week on the team's satellite phone. And then just for a minute or two."

"Would you have had time to talk to them more often?"

Noelle shrugged wryly. "Probably not. Oh, look, there's the cow you marked. She seems to be doing well." The cow snorted at two other cows who were near the spot where she was foraging and they hastily moved away from her. "And she seems to be the boss of the pasture."

"That's probably why she was so indignant about being trapped by the baling twine."

"Yup."

DAKOTA WONDERED IF Noelle had just wanted to change the subject. Her assignment in the Himalayas seemed to have had a significant impact on her. She would say so much, then shut down about it.

"By the way," he said, "I happen to know you went shopping last Monday *and* Tuesday, even though you unloaded all the decorations you'd purchased while I was out riding fence lines."

"How do you know that?"

"I saw the storeroom was filled floor to ceiling. Did you think I wouldn't notice?"

Noelle pursed her lips. "Nothing ulterior is involved. I went Monday with Mom when she got everything for the Thanksgiving meal. It was a personal day we wanted to spend together, but I didn't see any reason not to buy more decorations while we were there. Then I went into town again Tuesday on the spur of the moment. Regardless, you don't have time for trips to Bozeman and I didn't want to go this weekend. Shopping is too busy right after Thanksgiving."

"Saul wants me involved in the preparations."

"You *are* involved. There's lots more decorating you can help with if you don't have something else more urgent. Oh, and the chimneys on the homestead house passed inspection. I'm going to start building fires in the fireplaces to get everything drier in there."

"About that, I spoke with the representative from the stove store when he came out." Dakota gave her a stern look. "As foreman, it would have been nice to know the inspector was coming. So from now on, *include* me. I don't need to be protected and it's what Saul expects."

"I wasn't protecting you. But I'd prefer your being involved because you want to be, instead of being ordered to help."

To Dakota's surprise, while he still didn't see the point of decorating, he genuinely wanted to help Noelle. She had a unique, generous spirit and he was concerned about her, particularly now that he knew more about her time in Nepal. She was in Montana to rest, yet she'd taken responsibility for the ranch home tour and was helping both Saul and him with therapy. Who knew what else she'd end up doing?

"I'm fine with participating," he said firmly. "I'm even enjoying it to a certain degree. Give me the receipts and I'll arrange for reimbursement. Saul and Jordan budgeted a healthy amount for various supplies and decorations."

Noelle gave him an exasperated look. "All right. In the spirit of full disclosure, I'm going to Bozeman again tomorrow. Primarily to look for Christmas gifts."

"I'll need to go if you're purchasing more decorations for the tour."

"But it's mostly gift shopping for my family," she protested. "You know, store after store, indecision, having to choose between this and that."

Dakota rode closer. "Are you saying you wouldn't enjoy my company?"

"No, but maybe you wouldn't enjoy mine."

DAKOTA'S GAZE FLICKED across Noelle's mouth and her pulse skidded out of control as she remembered their kiss on their previous shopping trip to Bozeman. Even more, his faintly teasing tone sent shivers to the base of her stomach.

The old Dakota, with his sense of humor and devilry, was starting to assert itself.

"I think I can survive more time together with you," he drawled. "In fact, I can't think of another way I'd rather spend tomorrow."

She let out a shaky breath, wondering how he'd turned tables on her so quickly. Granted, she wasn't terribly experienced with casual flirtation, but this was utterly ridiculous.

CHAPTER NINE

"THAT'S THE LAST exercise in the set," Noelle told Saul.

After riding with Dakota, she'd gone into the house to do exercises with his grandfather. Saul had put out a good effort. Already he seemed to have more color in his face and better mobility, though she didn't want to comment on the possibility in case he took it as an "I told you so." People had their pride.

"Anna Beth thinks my balance has improved since you started helping me," he said as if he'd read her mind. "So don't worry— I'll keep working at it. You couldn't have given me a better reason to take care of myself than seeing Mishka and Daniel graduate high school. I want to do better and see them graduate college."

Noelle rolled the yoga mat she'd borrowed from her mother and put it in the corner. "That's what my grandmother is planning. I think she's given up hope on the rest of us giving her great-grandchildren, so her hopes are set on Mishka and Daniel."

"I enjoy your grandmother. She reminds me of Anna Beth."

Noelle thought it was a fair comparison. Both women were forthright, capable and talented. And unlike some people in Nana Harriet's generation, she'd embraced modern technology. Email and video calls were her favorites, followed by Wi-Fi enabled digital photo frames. Whenever possible Noelle sent her and the family pictures of Atlanta and her team. She'd even gotten a few of the countryside as she was leaving Nepal.

"You seem to be a long way away," Saul said, breaking into her memories.

"Just thinking about my last assignment and the photos I sent the family."

"I've seen 'em. Real interesting, I just can't understand the bits of worn fabric hanging in the background, from fences and the like."

"Those are prayer flags and I love them," Noelle said firmly. "They start out in specific colors. As they fade, the Nepali believe the blessings are spread by the wind and elements to the world, so the weathering is a good thing."

Saul didn't look convinced.

"Dakota has offered to put some up with me," Noelle added. "Higher in the mountains on a windy day."

The elderly man brightened. "He has?"

She nodded, wondering if she should have kept her mouth shut. Dakota's work as a Navy SEAL had been filled with secrets. She just didn't know how much he was willing to share in his private life.

"Yes. Tell me something," Noelle said slowly, "you obviously want to reconcile with your grandsons. Why not extend that to your son-in-law?"

Saul scowled, but his fierce expression swiftly faded into sadness. "I wronged the boys and I wronged Evan. I'm trying to make it up to my grandsons, but I don't know how to make it up to Evan."

"Then you know where he is?"

Saul seemed to squirm. "Might. I hear things."

"Then you *might* want to consider getting in touch. I can't speak for Jordan or Dakota, but surely it would give them some peace to know what happened to their father. And maybe knowing he's welcome is all that Evan Maxwell needs to come back again."

"I'll think about it."

Noelle left Saul stewing on the possibility, wondering if she'd said too much. Or not enough. She didn't think it was right to reveal that Dakota's biggest issue with his grandfather seemed to be that he'd kept Evan from seeing his sons. So all she could do was urge Saul to get his son-in-law in contact with the family, assuming Evan was willing.

A part of her enjoyed Saul; another part was still unsure about him. After all, his ogrish reputation had alarmed generations of children, herself among them. Her sister certainly believed Saul was a reformed character, and his wife was a treasure. Maybe the right person could change someone for the better. For the sake of everyone involved, Noelle hoped that was the case.

She shared a pot of tea with Paige and Anna Beth, then headed outside to work on the decorations. Her eyes narrowed when she saw Dakota and another employee on the horse barn, stringing Christmas lights across the peak of the roof. Dakota wasn't wearing safety gear—not even a rope—maneuvering around up there as if he was invincible.

She didn't dare call out for fear of startling him. But she was furious. Too many people got hurt by refusing to take reasonable precautions.

In her coat pocket, her fingers closed around the packages she'd gotten at a medical supply store in Bozeman, though her chances were slim of convincing him to use a supportive sleeve over his knee. He'd probably consider it a sign of going backward in his recovery, even if worn under his jeans.

Noelle watched, her heart pumping hard until Dakota and the other employee finally descended safely from the barn.

"You look upset," Dakota said walking over to her.

"Why would I be upset? I love seeing people hang off the ridge of a roof without any safety precautions," she couldn't resist retorting, though it wasn't her place to tell him he was being reckless.

He shrugged. "It was just a few minutes and I can't ask the cowhands to do anything I wouldn't do."

"You can hit the ground in nothing flat and your cowhand was wearing a harness and safety line." She tried to calm down. "Are you going into town tonight for the Park Carolers? It's the first official event of the season."

"I have work to do. Besides, as I recall, there's carol singing in the park every Sunday night, up until Christmas. Plenty of opportunity. But I'm definitely coming to your birthday party on Friday."

"It's a different group that sings each Sunday. Tonight the high school choir will be performing. They usually don't request donations, but the school is raising money for new band uniforms, so folks will turn out in big numbers to support them."

Dakota extracted a twenty dollar bill from his wallet. "Put this in the donation bucket for me. I'm going to go work on the bathroom in the old homestead."

Noelle looked at the crisp bill in her hand and scrunched her nose. City hall kept an online calendar of all the holiday activities in town and she wanted to be part of every one possible. The only thing she didn't want to go to was her own birthday party and *that* seemed to be the only gathering Dakota planned to attend.

"Noelle, where do you want these giant wreaths?" Eduardo Reyes asked.

She shoved the twenty in her pocket. "Is it possible to put one above the main door of the horse barn, and another on the east end so people can see it from a distance while driving into the main ranch? And I'd love to have the third on the calving barn, all lit up."

"No problem. We've run extension cords up the corners and under the eaves so they won't show as much. Oh, and in case you're interested, there are outlets at the entrance to the ranch road. When Jordan was the foreman he had lights installed over the sign for the ranch and made sure there were outlets available. So we can put lights up and extend them on the fences coming in several hundred feet. Just let us know what you want."

"Great. I appreciate you thinking about that."

"The decorating is loads of fun. Dakota keeps doing some of the stuff we'd usually handle, so it's nice to—" The young ranch hand stopped and looked abashed. He'd probably realized it might sound as if he was criticizing his new boss. "That is, we have time. We aren't too busy. It's our lightest time of the year."

"I still appreciate the work. You're all doing a marvelous job. Are you coming over to the Blue Banner on Friday night?"

"For your birthday? *Yes, ma'am.*"

"It's mostly just a holiday gathering," Noelle said hastily. "No gifts or anything, and no need to dress up."

"Do I at least get to give you a birthday kiss?" Eduardo asked with a cheeky grin.

She laughed. "I'll think about it."

Noelle wondered why the light exchange with Eduardo didn't bother her, but the same discussion would make her pulse pound with anticipation if Dakota was involved.

Sighing, she went up to the old house to check on the progress there. She'd had a vision of everyone decorating together, perhaps with a CD player belting out Christmas music and thermoses of wassail being shared. But Dakota was getting the job done with a minimum of fuss, which was more realistic, if less fun.

Somebody had been busy at the old homestead house. The storm shutters were open, the porch was clean and the ragged weeds cut down. Inside, the floors shone with the satin glow of wood worn smooth by years of use, accompanied by the scent of lemon and beeswax.

She headed to the back and found Dakota installing new fixtures in the bathroom. The walls were a fresh white matching the sink and claw-foot bathtub and the floor, which was laid with white hexagonal tiles.

"Curtains covered that when we were in here before," she said, admiring the stained-glass window with an ornate pattern of frosted glass, accented by amber and teal. "It's beautiful."

"The curtains are in the junk pile," Dakota said, tightening something beneath the pedestal sink. "The fabric fell apart when they were taken down. I don't know why someone would need curtains in here, anyway. Nobody can see through the stained glass."

"They might reduce drafts, but what a shame to cover that gorgeous design." Noelle ran her fingers over the mahogany frame on the door, matching the frame around the window. "The house isn't in bad shape aside from some cosmetic issues. If the wiring is safe, someone could still live here."

"I've checked and the wiring isn't too bad. I wouldn't move in without a better heating system, but I'm impressed with what I've seen."

She cocked her head. "You can do plumbing, electrical work, run a ranch...is there anything you can't do?"

Dakota looked embarrassed. "It's no big deal. A couple of my men bought fixer-upper houses and I helped get them in shape. I learned a lot, but I'm not a certified electrician and I don't know if you can get one to inspect before the tour. Electricians in Shelton must be very busy."

"Someone will be here on Monday. My dad is calling in a favor with a friend."

"Helps to have contacts."

"Uh, yeah. And if everything is okay, I'm going to use some special light globes I ordered. They're supposed to look like a flickering gas flame. Look, I'm leaving early, but I'll be back later."

His eyebrow went up. "That isn't necessary— I can manage to exercise by myself tonight."

Noelle rolled her eyes. "Fine, I'll give you these now." She held out the neoprene knee sleeves she'd bought. "I got two different sizes. Instructions on how to wear them are included. I've been looking for the right time to talk to you, but a right time obviously isn't going to happen."

If possible, Dakota's eyes grew darker. "No."

"At least wear one when you're riding."

"No."

"My dad used a special brace for months after he popped his knee out," she argued. "It was the kind that some rodeo contestants use to reduce injuries. I didn't get one of those for you because I knew how you'd feel about it, but I thought a knee sleeve wouldn't even show under your jeans. Especially when you're wearing leather chaps. And it might stabilize the joint a little while you're rebuilding strength."

DAKOTA GLARED AT the two packages.

The Navy doctors had recommended he wear a brace—he'd cooperated until they decided to discharge him. After that, the brace had gone in the trash.

"Look, I'm just trying to be a friend," Noelle said. "My *own* knees hurt from our two horseback rides. I'm not accustomed to riding any longer, so I'm going to get a pair of knee sleeves in town for myself."

"Use these."

She laughed. "How big do you think my legs are? They'd fall right off."

Dakota looked down at Noelle's slim legs, outlined by snug, worn denim. She was considerably smaller than him. And far more shapely.

"You're an amazing guy, with mad skills," she added. "A lot of people couldn't come close to being as active as you are at this point in recovery, but you're working on a ranch, doing everything your employees are doing and more. That's remarkable."

Dakota clenched his fingers. It was true that over the last few days he'd considered wrapping his knee with some type of sports tape, and a knee sleeve would be easier. But he'd had a gut reaction seeing them in her hand—a stab of wounded ego. She was a beautiful woman and more and more he wanted her to see him as a man, not as a patient. At the same time, she'd just called him amazing.

What was it about Noelle that made him so ambivalent? One minute he felt okay about her massaging his leg, the next he hated the idea of her seeing him as damaged.

"I'll pay you back."

She shook her head, her shimmering hair tinged with different colors by the light coming through the stained-glass windows. The soft length tempted him. His life had held harsh realities for almost as long as he could remember, but Noelle reminded him that strength wasn't only found in muscles and a cold focus on succeeding.

As a matter of fact, her brand of resilient strength might be the one that mattered most.

"Dakota, you're helping with the decorating, even though you aren't fond of Christmas, going over and above what Saul asked you to do. Can't you accept a small token in the spirit intended?"

"Aunt Noelle, Uncle Dakota, where are you?" sang a child's voice before he could answer.

Dakota locked gazes with Noelle another long moment, then he took the packages and shoved them deep into his coat pocket. Other than his two brothers, he wasn't used to people doing something for him unless they had an ulterior motive. But while he was still figuring Noelle out, he was convinced she had good intentions. And she'd picked the one option he'd consider for his knee—something that wouldn't be obvious to anyone. He didn't know how many times he'd seen Saul watching him with an assessing expression in his eyes.

His grandfather could claim he was concerned, but that didn't mean he wasn't looking for signs of fallibility. Being able to say his grandson wasn't physically up to ranching might be an excuse for getting out of their agreement.

Earning a portion of the ranch was becoming especially important to Dakota, over and above knowing what it had meant to their mother. Jordan now had a family, and at some point their brother Wyatt would probably return. Wyatt said he was never getting married again, but he still had a daughter to raise. Dakota wanted to be sure his brothers had access to the prime Soaring Hawk ranchland for their sakes, even more than for his own interests.

"Uncle Dakota?" his niece called again.

"We're in here."

Mishka ran into the large bathroom. "May I help?" she asked. "Mama says you're making everything pretty for company."

"Sure. You can put the handles on the faucet."

He showed her how to get the porcelain swing handle correctly threaded and watched as she concentrated, turning until it was tight. Then she did the second one without assistance.

"Good job, kiddo."

The compliment was met by a hug. Affection from his niece was easy to accept. She was guileless and filled with love for the world.

"Hey, everyone." It was his sister-in-law. "I'm impressed. This place is looking great."

Noelle nodded. "Except there's no furniture. Mom is letting me borrow some of her folding tables and chairs. They'll have to do.

It doesn't make sense to buy antiques for the tour."

"Saul says you can use whatever you want from the main house attic. There's a bunch of stuff up there. I've explored, but haven't had time for digging in and checking everything. Too much else to do."

"That'll be fun."

Dakota saw the delight in Noelle's golden-brown eyes and knew he'd have to help bring down anything she wanted from the main house. He wouldn't mind if his grandfather wasn't involved, but avoiding Saul might be impossible if they were in the same building for very long.

"Oh, and we appreciate your looking at Rod Gaffney's leg yesterday," Paige added. "Rod says the antibiotics are already working. He wants you to know he'll go into the clinic for a follow-up exam."

"I also treated one of my father's ranch hands. I'll call the clinic tomorrow and explain how it happened. They probably won't mind, especially with this being Thanksgiving weekend."

Dakota remembered what Noelle had said about not wanting the local physicians to think she was competing with them. It must he difficult for her to get a real break from work in a place where everyone knew she was a doctor.

But Gaffney's injury frustrated Dakota in more than one way. As foreman, he should have been told the cowhand had snagged his leg on barbed wire. He would have insisted Rodney visit the clinic immediately, rather than waiting until the wound was infected. When Dakota finally found out, he'd told Gaffney to call for an urgent appointment. Instead the cowhand had gone to Noelle.

Paige held an arm out to her daughter. "Come along, Mishka, we need to get ready to see the Park Carolers."

"Okay."

Mishka kissed both Dakota and her aunt before leaving with her mother, face alight with anticipation.

"About Rod Gaffney," he said when he and Noelle were alone. "I'm sorry you were dragged into that."

"Nobody drags me into anything. After all, I survived growing up as the perpetual class nerd. And it wasn't any picnic being years younger than the average college and medical student, either."

Dakota couldn't resist laughing at her mischievous expression. "He still should have told me about cutting his leg when it happened. It was an injury on the job and I'm the foreman, but I didn't even know he was hurt until he limped into the dining hall yesterday morning with an infection."

The warmth of Noelle's smile caused him to smile back. "Dakota, even though you're still recovering from your injuries, you want everyone to see you as invulnerable. The Navy SEAL who can handle anything. That might be intimidating, especially to the younger ranch hands. Basically, you don't want to look incapable in front of your employees, and they don't want to look weak in front of you."

"He was injured, that doesn't mean he's—" Dakota stopped abruptly.

He didn't see an "I told you so" in Noelle's eyes; she wasn't that kind of person, but he understood her point. The ranch hands might be taking their lead from him.

"I'll talk to them," he said. "Alex Sorenson mentioned wanting to prove himself. He could be even more determined than the others to conceal an injury or illness."

"I'm sure they'd appreciate clarification.

Having a new foreman can be stressful. Most of them had gotten used to your brother and now you've taken over." Noelle looked at her phone. "Oops, I'd better get going, too. I don't want to be late for the Park Carolers."

"I'll see you tomorrow," he said before she could leave. "Remember, we're going to Bozeman for shopping."

"You really want to come when I'll be selecting family gifts?"

"Sure. I need to get presents, too."

"Oh. Okay. I'll be here early in the morning, weather permitting."

With another smile Noelle was gone and Dakota hated that it suddenly felt colder and darker in the empty house, but he was glad she hadn't asked him again to go to the Christmas event. For some reason, saying no to her was harder than refusing his sister-in-law and brother.

It was even harder than saying no to his niece.

Before leaving for Bozeman the next day, Noelle phoned the medical clinic in Shelton and spoke with the senior Dr. Wycoff, explaining that she'd treated two cowhands over the weekend.

"Truly, I'm not trying to poach your patients," she said. "It just seemed better to treat them than have you come into the clinic during the holiday break."

"You know we wouldn't worry about that, Noelle," Dr. Wycoff scolded. He'd been the town's only doctor when she was a child, though his daughter had since joined the practice. "We're busy and appreciate the backup, so feel free. And any time you want to come work with us, we'd love to have you. Cheyenne and I have talked about this several times. We'd be happy to offer a full partnership or whatever arrangement you'd prefer."

"Right now I'm just on a break, but I'll give it some thought. In the meantime, I don't want to keep you."

"We haven't opened the doors yet, but it'll be a mad rush once we do. So pleased to hear from you, Noelle. I'm sure we'll see you at some of the holiday events."

"Absolutely. Merry Christmas."

"Merry Christmas."

She disconnected and leaned against the SUV. She'd always known the Shelton medical clinic would welcome her. The town could use several more doctors and the senior Dr. Wycoff would want to retire at some point. But she wasn't sure if having an open invitation complicated an already difficult decision about her career.

"You look as if you're contemplating the fate of the world," Dakota said as he walked over. "Or are you concerned about the weather?"

She shook her head. A few light flecks of snow were still falling, but the sky was clearing and there wasn't enough accumulation to warrant postponing the trip. The light dusting of snow overnight mostly made the existing snow look whiter and more Christmassy.

"We're fine," she said. "The rental has snow tires. I also checked on road conditions and there aren't any warnings. An aunt who lives there texted that Bozeman only got a minor flurry last night, with nothing sticking to the streets."

"Sounds good."

The trip went quickly and when they entered Bozeman, Noelle was pleased to see the town was now fully decked for Christmas. Houses were decorated even more than usual and the shopping areas were bright with holiday cheer.

"I almost wish it was still cloudy," she said, maneuvering into a parking spot near her favorite shopping area.

"Winter is dreary enough, but you want things dark and gloomy, too?"

"Cloudy days aren't gloomy when Christmas lights are glowing. It makes me happy and cozy to see them, but some stores don't bother to turn their outdoor lights on when it's sunny, figuring they don't show very much."

"Aren't you seeing enough holiday lights at the Soaring Hawk?"

Noelle glanced at Dakota. Despite what he'd said about the weather, he wasn't in a bah humbug mood. She'd put a Christmas CD on the car player—a jazzy instrumental version of traditional carols—and he'd tapped his foot along to the music as they talked about where to shop and what other decorations were needed. He'd even suggested they buy more of the giant Christmas ball ornaments they'd purchased on their first trip.

"I can never see enough Christmas lights," she said firmly. "Or Christmas trees and wreaths. Or decorations."

"Obviously. But it reminds me of something I wanted to talk with you about."

"That sounds ominous. Let me have more coffee first."

He poured her another cup from the thermos her mother had sent.

"Saul wasn't happy that I didn't attend the Park Carolers last night," Dakota explained. "He says I'm still not showing enough community spirit."

Noelle made a face. "You can't force someone to have community spirit. You're helping to prepare for the tour, which he knows. I also told him that you'd fixed up the bathroom in the old house without me asking you to *and* sent money to put in the band uniform donation box. I thought he was pleased."

"Apparently not enough. So for the various community Christmas events, I'd like to suggest we go together. If that's all right. Or I could meet you and your family. I'm not a hypocrite and won't pretend I'm okay with spending time with my grandfather."

She put her free hand over her heart. "A woman's dream escort."

"It doesn't have to be like we're dating."

"Meaning no kisses or expectations," she said wryly. "Make-believe dating for appearances."

A slow smile filled Dakota's face. "I'm not opposed to kissing. Expectations are another matter. I can't think about the future until everything is settled with my grandfather, but that isn't a problem, right?"

"Um, right. Except I thought you were concerned about the ranch hands seeing us together."

"Only in my quarters in the evening, right after I started as foreman. As for the rest? Even if we're headed in different directions in our lives, that doesn't mean we can't be friends."

The butterflies in Noelle's stomach jumped even higher. She'd never known a man like Dakota and he was amazing with Mishka. It was logical to assume that he hoped to get married and have a family someday, so maybe his assumption about them being headed in "different directions" was for the best. After all, she couldn't simply announce that she might not be able to have children. It would sound too much as if she *was* thinking about the future.

"What do you think?" he prompted.

A part of her said no, yet how else was she supposed to help him find his holiday spirit?

"Um, sure," she said. "The more the merrier."

"Great. You're looking festive today. How did you find red jeans?"

The swift change of subject made her blink. "Online. But I didn't bring a lot of clothes, so I'm going to look for a few things here in Bozeman. Mom and Paige will lend me whatever I need, but I want some festive sweatshirts."

And maybe a Victorian dress, she thought as they put their cups in the holders and got out of the SUV. She remembered a vintage clothing shop from when she was in college. Perhaps they'd have something she liked.

Playing dress-up had never interested her as a child, but now she wanted to give it a shot. Greeting people at the homestead house would be fun with her hair swept up and wearing rich velvet or satin. Perhaps she could add elegant gloves and a cameo at her throat. The possibilities were endless. Once again she mused that the picture would be even more complete if Dakota was there wearing a period suit.

The fact that most of her images for the tour included Dakota bothered her, but how else was she going to share the holiday with him? It was sad to think of those Christmases after his mother died and he was living at the Soaring Hawk with Saul. Noelle was sure they hadn't involved any yuletide joy.

The stores were crowded with holiday shoppers, but she soon found gifts for Mishka and Daniel, as well as for her father and brothers. They made several trips back to the SUV to leave parcels. Her biggest disappointment was that the vintage clothing store she remembered had become a frozen yogurt shop, though the peppermint-and-chocolate-swirl cone she got was compensation.

"Want some?" she asked Dakota as they went back onto the street. He hadn't gotten a cone, giving her an are-you-serious look when she bought one for herself.

"No, thanks. It's cold out here."

"Okay."

Noelle ate the frozen treat in record time. Secretly, she admitted to herself that next time she'd have a hot chocolate.

She wiped her face with a napkin. "Did I miss anything?"

Dakota took the napkin and wiped a spot on her chin, but his gaze was fixed on her mouth. He bent and gave her another kiss, one she couldn't resist returning.

"I said I wasn't opposed to kissing," he whispered against her lips.

"With no expectations," she managed to add in a light tone as she stepped back. "I presume that means no analysis or need for future discussions."

"It seems best for both of us."

Noelle supposed that was true. They could share a holiday flirtation that was harmless unless she let her heart become involved. Except her heart *was* becoming involved whether she wanted it to be or not.

They continued walking down the street.

"Oh, look," she said to Dakota, grabbing his hand to pull him into a shop.

It had a wide selection of high-end snow globes, something both her mother and sister loved, along with music boxes and other fun items. An arched entryway led to a children's toy area.

Dakota stepped away as one of the snow globes on display caught her attention. Inside was a lighted house and barn that looked like the Soaring Hawk main ranch in miniature. There were even a paddock and horses. A Christmas tree with lights shone through the front windows and lighted wreaths hung on the front door and barn. She looked at the description; the music box in the base played six holiday tunes, each of which she loved.

"That's my favorite," said the salesperson.

"Designed locally by a new artist. Turn it on, the snow swirls automatically and the music box has a great sound."

Noelle slid the switch and "I'll be Home for Christmas" rang out, making her smile. She put the display model back on the shelf. "This is just right for my sister. I'll take one."

"Good timing, we only have two left in stock. Shall I wrap the box?"

Noelle laughed. "Not a chance. Wrapping is half the fun. Will you put it behind the counter for me while I keep looking?"

"No problem. I understand how you feel about wrapping. It doesn't matter how many packages I wrap here at work, I still love playing Christmas music and drinking eggnog while I find new ways to make a gift look just the way I want. Isn't Christmas the best?"

"Yes," Noelle agreed, knowing she'd met a fellow Christmas lover like herself.

She continued browsing and found another snow globe, ideal for her mother and designed by the same artist. All that remained was choosing something for her grandmother.

And Dakota.

She went to the toy area and summoned a smile for him. "Have you decided?"

"Still debating. Do you think Daniel would prefer a buffalo or a moose?" He showed her each of the stuffed animals in turn. "They both have a label saying they're safe for infants."

"Either would make him happy at his age," she said, charmed he was taking his selection so seriously. "But the moose is softer and easier for little hands to grab."

He promptly tucked the large moose under his arm. "Makes sense. How about one of those for Mishka?" he asked, gesturing to a group of colorful dragons on a shelf, each with a sweet, goofy grin.

"Get one clutching a crystal. She loves crystals. Her bedroom is full of rainbows when the sun rises."

"That's good to know."

Dakota looked between the various figures as if deciding the fate of the world and a treacherous longing grew inside Noelle. What would it be like to be the focus of so much attention?

Of *his* attention?

CHAPTER TEN

BY LATE THE following Thursday afternoon, Blair decided she'd overreacted to Alex's behavior on Thanksgiving, but she was still glad she had returned his class ring.

If everything was over between them, it was over.

She went into the dining hall's mud porch, stomping her feet and brushing snow from her hair. Luckily this wasn't a major storm; less than an inch was predicted, so no need to put down feed for the cattle. Earlier in the day they'd even laughed, saying nature was just frosting the landscape for Dr. Bannerman's benefit. Noelle really had a thing for the holidays.

"Hey, Blair. You sure look extra pretty today," Eduardo said with a big smile.

"Aw, you say the sweetest things."

Behind Eduardo she saw Alex roll his eyes. Well, tough for him. It was nice to be reminded she was an attractive woman. Rod and Eduardo were good guys and under different circumstances she might have dated either of them.

"It smells great in here. What's for dinner?" she asked.

"Anna Beth's lemon barbecue meatloaf and baked potatoes." Eduardo patted his tummy. "Her meatloaf is amazing. Even better than my father makes—just don't tell Dad I said so."

"I'm not promising anything," Blair teased.

She didn't think Mr. Reyes had any concerns about his reputation as a cook. The Reyeses were a cool couple. They owned a small ranch which Mrs. Reyes ran, while Mr. Reyes managed the popular deli in Shelton's grocery store.

"You won't promise, not even for me?" Eduardo teased, a twinkle in his eyes.

"Not even for you. It's too useful having embarrassing information available for leverage."

He chuckled. "I asked Anna Beth if she'd give Dad her meatloaf recipe, but she told me it's a secret known only to the Marines. I may sneak a piece home for him to sample. I'm sure he can figure out how to make something similar."

"Anna Beth probably doesn't have a recipe. Aunt Sarah uses them for baking, but not for regular cooking. I don't have a talent for baking *or* cooking. Maybe that's why I'm not married yet," she said, the irony in her voice aimed directly at Alex.

"Come on, you don't believe that old-fashioned stuff about a wife having to do the cooking," Eduardo protested. "Look at my folks. Mom can barely make a cup of coffee and Dad doesn't like ranch work."

"Then there must be another reason I'm still single."

Alex abruptly grabbed his coat and stomped out of the dining hall.

"Don't let him get to you," Eduardo said. "He's had a burr under his saddle, ever since you started working here."

"That was my plan. It seems to be backfiring."

"You could always marry me instead," Eduardo suggested with another cute smile.

Blair laughed. "I'll keep your offer in mind."

She went into the kitchen to make a cup of tea.

Working on the Soaring Hawk was pleasant, though she missed her family. It was funny. She'd hated Montana when her mother dumped her with Aunt Sarah and Uncle Will. They had always lived in the city and suddenly she'd landed in a place where she didn't fit and couldn't imagine *ever* fitting. Besides, it had smelled funny with all that fresh air. Now she couldn't imagine living anywhere else.

Alex had become her first friend in Montana. Her *best* friend. Which meant she hadn't lost just her fiancé in the accident, she'd lost her buddy.

On the other hand, while the Soaring Hawk foreman didn't show favoritism, it was pretty clear how much Alex and Dakota had in common. There were times when everyone knew they'd been talking, and not about ranch business—if only Alex would talk to *her* that way.

Blair's eyes burned as she looked out the window at the Christmas lights, gleaming in the dusk through the falling snow. It was beautiful and the decorations were getting prettier by the day. But the sight didn't make her feel better. For the first time she was seriously contemplating a future without Alex.

"Chin up, Blair."

She turned and saw Melody James. Like

the other hands, she knew about Blair's history with Alex. "I'm okay."

"Of course, you are. Dakota showed me the website mock-ups you designed for the Soaring Hawk. They look good, though I'm not sold on the design with the blinking features and banners running across the screen."

"I'm not, either," Blair admitted. "But some people want the bells and whistles, so I offered several options. I'm just waiting for Dakota and the owners to pick which design they want, then I'll do the rest."

"Do you really believe having a website makes a difference?"

"Sure. The future is here. Most businesses need an online presence, and being active on social media also helps."

"Dakota showed me your own website the other day. You seem to have quite a few clients. That must be what you do in the break room after everyone else goes to bed."

Blair shrugged. She'd told Dakota about her freelance business when showing him the designs she had created for the Soaring Hawk. He'd said he didn't care what she did on her own time as long as she was able to handle her regular responsibilities.

"Isn't our flaky internet service a problem?" Melody asked.

Blair made a face. "It can be, but I'm managing all right. If necessary, I'll get a satellite phone and connect that way."

"Good idea." Melody poured a cup of coffee from the large pot that was kept available day and night.

The other ranch hands came into the kitchen and started taking food from the oven and top of the stove, along with getting plates and silverware. Anna Beth fixed their chow, but they were expected to serve themselves and clean up afterward. If they didn't keep the kitchen in good order, they heard about it from her. Blair put her cup down and grabbed the salad and sour cream from the refrigerator.

Nobody was going to wait for Alex. If he was too stubborn to eat with the rest of them, he'd just have to accept potluck when he decided to return.

ALEX WENT INTO the horse barn. It was too cold to stay outside and he didn't want to go back and listen to Blair and Eduardo tease each other.

He'd felt like a crumb ever since saying such stupid things to Blair about her mother.

The betrayal in her eyes had brought him up short. How could he have done that?

Bingo, a brown gelding, put his head over the stall gate and nickered for attention. Alex rubbed his nose, wishing he could get along with people the way he got along with horses. They didn't look at him funny or get hurt feelings.

Or throw rings in his face.

Uh, well, maybe he'd deserved that part.

The barn door opened and Alex looked up, hoping it wasn't Blair. Instead he saw Dakota come down the center aisle with one of the ranch dogs.

"Is there a problem, Alex?"

"No, sir. Just checking."

"You checked on them an hour ago."

Alex turned back to Bingo. "I like being here. Horses are easier than people. I don't disappoint them."

"You haven't disappointed me."

Alex lifted his shoulders with pride. "Thank you, sir. It's just that my parents want—"

He stopped. The situation with his mom and dad couldn't seem that bad to Dakota. After all, everybody knew Dakota's mom died when he was a kid and his father ended up with a drinking problem before running off and never coming back.

"What do your parents want?" Dakota prompted.

Alex looked at the scars on the side of the foreman's face. They were more visible than his own, but Dakota didn't try to cover his scars or duck his head or anything. Now it was like no one hardly even noticed them. It made Alex wish he'd done the same thing from the beginning.

"For one, a few months ago Mom got really pushy about me having more plastic surgery or laser treatments, like she could erase what happened in the accident," Alex said. "But nothing is ever going to make me look the way I did before."

Dakota patted Pepper, the Aussie collie who followed him everywhere. "I suppose families naturally want to fix things that can't be fixed. They worry you're in pain and that can bother them more than it does you."

Alex wondered if Dakota's brother and grandfather wanted to fix something for him. He knew there was a bunch of stuff going on in the Maxwell and Hawkins families, stuff that started before he'd even been born. But he couldn't see anyone pushing a guy like Dakota to do anything.

"You were a Navy SEAL. It's like, the most awesome thing in the world. Surely you don't need to prove yourself to anybody," he said slowly.

Dakota shook his head. "That's where you're wrong. I have to show my grandfather that I can run this ranch, even though my knee is still healing from a bad injury. I could have lost my leg, so I'm lucky. I can do what I need to do, but I'd find a way to do that, no matter how it had turned out."

Alex frowned in thought. "Everyone says I was lucky, too. I didn't get any deep burns over my joints or major muscles or anything."

Even as he said the words, the realization that he *was* lucky hit home for the first time. The doctors and other burn patients had told him he was fortunate, which he'd known in his head, but had never quite put together with how he felt. He should have paid more attention and let it sink in. The accident wasn't his fault, but he kept thinking that he could have avoided it somehow. Then he'd wonder, what if it *had* been his fault? How much worse would he feel, or would it make any difference since he was already blaming himself?

"You've also moved out on your own, getting a job here," Dakota said. There was never any judgment or criticism in his voice, which was one of the great parts about talking to him.

"I wanted to show I could do the work, no matter what I looked like or what had happened."

"You've done that."

"I'll do whatever you need," Alex said stoutly. "My dad calls ranching a 24/7 life. You either love it or leave."

"That's right."

Dakota didn't say anything about going into the Navy, but everybody knew the Maxwell brothers had enlisted in order to get away from the Soaring Hawk. The weird part was Jordan and Dakota coming back and things being so different. Maybe Dakota and Jordan returned because Saul Hawkins had changed. He seemed to be a pretty decent guy now. He came down every day and walked up and down the length of the barn, all the while talking about horses. Alex had learned a lot from Mr. Hawkins.

He'd put his hand on Alex's arm and point

out the features that made the best stock horses—strong backs and powerful hindquarters, medium-length legs, a light, quick gait and the way the animal's neck came forward from the shoulders. Then he'd say the most important things were their intelligence and agility.

"The right horse can practically read your mind if they trust you," Mr. Hawkins said almost every time they talked. He'd also declared that there weren't any bad horses, just some that didn't get treated right, and that they all deserved a chance somewhere.

Alex's dad was a good rancher, but he bought yearlings rather than breeding them himself. It was easier to understand now why a few hadn't worked out as well. Cattle were Jeff Sorenson's first interest and he used ATVs a lot of the time while dealing with them, rather than riding horses the way folks did on the Soaring Hawk.

Alex was glad that a local rancher was giving homes to old horses and ones that other ranchers had given up on. Josh and Kelly McKeon had even *paid* for horses like that. People questioned it and joked they were running an equine sanctuary. Once Alex had questioned it, too, but now he realized it was important.

Alex rubbed Bingo's nose again. It was odd the way things were turning out. He still wanted to be a rancher and raise organic cattle. But being at the Soaring Hawk was showing him that he might want to work more with horses than his father did. He'd have to talk to his dad about where the Sunny Crest was going.

He blinked, realizing that going home was starting to seem possible. Maybe he'd never needed to show anything to his father, just to himself.

"Um, have you always loved horses?" he asked Dakota.

"I SURE HAVE. I missed them when I was in the Navy."

Dakota was pleased with Alex's meticulous attention in the horse barn, but he wanted to get the young cowhand involved in other responsibilities to keep him fresh. Besides, rotating the work assignments would help the employees understand that every task was meaningful. He didn't want them to start believing one job had priority or status over another.

There was nothing glamorous about scooping horse manure from a stall, but it was essential.

Horses weren't just vital to the Soaring Hawk's operations, they also represented an investment in the future. Jordan had sold several weanlings late in the summer, and the upcoming foals were generating even more interest with horse buyers. Getting the website active should help. Dakota doubted Saul would understand the importance of a website, but he had to think beyond the bargain he'd made with his grandfather. A ranch had a bottom line, like any other business, and diversifying was a sound strategy.

"Dakota?"

"Here."

Noelle walked over and smiled at them both. "Hi, Alex. Dakota, I don't want to interrupt anything, but I'm going up to look around your grandfather's attic. How do you want me to tag the items to be moved to the other house?"

"There's no need to tag stuff. I'll go with you." The offer seemed to surprise her, but he'd also surprised himself. "Is there anything else, Alex?"

Alex shook his head, looking slightly less

troubled than when they'd first started chatting. Dakota was sorry the kid was struggling so much. Though the scars on his own face didn't bother him, Noelle had mentioned how grueling burn treatment could be for a patient. Maybe that was why he'd mentioned his knee and that he needed to show he could run the ranch, to help Alex not feel alone.

None of it was a secret, yet Dakota doubted he would have said anything without Noelle's influence. She had an innate kindness and concern for others that pushed him to be better himself.

He automatically tensed as they went inside the main house. In the past the place had been dark, full of shadows, old smells and the memory of his mom's passing, but it really *was* different now than when he was a child. The off-white paint had lightened the atmosphere and evergreen garland entwined with white lights draped the doorways and banisters. A tall Christmas tree stood in the foyer, and other decorated trees were in the parlor to the left and the formal living room to the right. The entire house was filled with light and color and the fragrance of spice and baking.

If the ghosts of his childhood were haunting such cheerful surroundings, he wouldn't know how to summon them. This was a place for the living.

Dakota looked at the twinkling star on the tree in the foyer, reaching up to the second floor level. "I'm not an expert with felines, but isn't there a problem with the cats climbing this? I've seen them run up and down the stacks of hay bales, so I can't imagine them resisting something that looks like a real tree."

"Oh, yes. Marmalade and Lady G raced each other to the top as soon as we put it up," Noelle said. "In case you don't know, Marmalade is Anna Beth's cat and Lady G is devoted to Jordan. If you look closely, fishing line is attached to the banister in several spots, holding the tree in place. We also didn't use ornaments that break easily."

He sniffed. "Do I smell orange and lemon along with everything else?"

"We sprayed the lower branches with citrus oil, which cats don't like. It seems to be keeping them away, though they're also miffed that the tree nearly fell over with them in it. Cats are proud and don't enjoy looking ridiculous. Lady G actually hisses at the tree when she goes up and down the staircase. I think she blames it for her loss of dignity."

Buddy was the only cat Dakota knew much about. The large tuxedo feline hung out in the office, mostly sleeping on the desk. While Buddy enjoyed petting and neck scratches, he spent the majority of his waking hours pursuing his pest control duties. The other cats—their original numbers increased by adoption and strays finding their way to the ranch—remained mostly in the barns. They weren't unfriendly, but they'd formed a community among themselves and seemed self-sufficient aside from the basics of food, water and clean litter boxes.

He'd seen Pepper sleeping with them, though less often lately. The young cow dog had decided she'd rather stretch out in front of the heating unit in his quarters. Who could blame her? She had a thick coat, but it was cold this time of year. The ranch hands towel-dried the dogs after they'd been out working, but the warmth had to appeal, nonetheless.

Pepper also seemed to worry whenever Dakota woke up from reliving his last mission in his sleep, jumping on the bed and licking his face. Her affection helped pull him more quickly away from the disturbing images.

Memories of what had happened after the explosion were returning, including the way his team had gotten him out and onto a chopper. Remembering was tough, because it also meant remembering how two of his men had died. But he was proud of them all, knowing how well they'd done their jobs.

"Are you okay?" Noelle asked softly.

Dakota realized he'd stopped in his tracks, halfway up the staircase. "No problem."

He stroked Pepper, who had followed them into the house, and her tail wagged furiously. It would seem he'd been adopted by the intelligent Aussie collie, which was oddly flattering.

The three of them continued to the third floor attic and Dakota was glad his grandfather hadn't made an appearance. He knew Anna Beth and Saul now lived on the ground level because of his hip, so running into him upstairs was unlikely.

"This is wonderful," Noelle said as she turned on the attic lights. An ancient ceiling fan began to lazily turn, circulating the air.

The open space was the length and width of the entire house, though the ceiling was sloped beneath the roofline. The attic's contents looked like a massive collection of junk to Dakota, but clearly Noelle saw more to the jumble.

"Everything is cleaner than I expected." It seemed a neutral thing to say.

"Anna Beth and Paige have vacuumed and dusted up here," she explained, "but they haven't had time to go through all this stuff."

Dakota smiled at Noelle's anticipation. "You must be a treasure hunter at heart."

"Treasure *lover*, maybe."

As they explored, they discovered broken furniture had been stored on the west end of the attic, while items that must have come from the homestead house were on the east. Antique trunks, a rocking chair, sturdy chairs with arms, writing tables and other pieces were crowded together, along with cardboard boxes marked with labels such as Kitchen and Parlor and Miscellaneous.

"They must have brought everything over from the house and just left it up here as is after your great-great-grandmother Ehawee passed away," Noelle said, running her fingers across an old table.

"I don't suppose any of it is valuable. Why bother?"

"Family history has value. Saul told me Ehawee refused to leave the old house. She would have used this table thousands of times. Maybe her husband made it for her after they got married. Can't you feel the positive energy?"

"Not really. Does positive energy go along with Christmas spirit?"

"Of course."

NOELLE WASN'T SURE she was making progress with Dakota when it came to a yuletide attitude. Still, sometimes people started changing on the inside and it took a while to see it on the surface. He participated in her decorating efforts and he'd seemed to enjoy their shopping trips together—*really* enjoyed them, considering their never-to-be-discussed kisses.

"Isn't there *anything* you're sentimental about?" she asked.

"I guess it would be nice to have my father's gold pocket watch. It came down through the family from my great-something-grandfather. There was a circular pattern etched into the gold, like feathers, I think."

"That sounds nice," Noelle murmured, suddenly knowing what to get Dakota for Christmas in addition to the toy tractor. She couldn't replace his father's watch, but could look for a similar timepiece to help him remember and become a keepsake to pass down himself someday.

Footsteps sounded on the stairs and she saw her sister appear with Daniel cuddled against her in a baby sling.

"Hi, Noelle. I wanted to see how you were doing."

"Mostly we've debated the sentimental value of old belongings."

"You can't put a price on sentiment," Paige said with a nod of agreement. "But I confess, Anna Beth and I also found a Stickley writing table up here. It's worth a fair amount and is absolutely gorgeous. We put it in the library. I love thinking about what letters were written there—back when people wrote letters instead of texting and emailing."

"I know what you mean."

Noelle was disappointed by the first trunk she opened; it was empty. But her excitement rose as she opened another containing clothes. She lifted a layered evening dress from the 1920s, dripping with fringe and sequins. The flowing hem dropped on one side in an asymmetrical sweep that matched the line of fringe above.

"I can't imagine anyone wearing *that* on the Soaring Hawk," Paige marveled.

"I know. And here's a man's suit that looks like something from a gangster movie."

Paige turned to her brother-in-law. "Dakota, would you mind holding Daniel while we look at the clothes?"

"Sure. Just promise you won't ask me to try on anything," he said as he took the baby.

"We promise."

Noelle stayed focused on the trunk; she had enough heart pangs without watching Dakota and Daniel together. The dresses and suits inside all seemed to be from the twenties.

"These are fabulous, but I was hoping to see clothes from an earlier period," she said.

"I think there are more in the old wardrobe." Paige pointed across the attic.

Noelle jumped up and opened the wardrobe. Inside there was an assortment of men's suits and women's dresses, still from the 1920s, and all unsuited to ranch life. For a while she and her sister held the dresses to themselves, admiring the extravagant gowns. They were beautiful, if not what she'd hoped to discover.

She glanced back and saw Dakota had Daniel on his shoulder, patting the baby and looking utterly at ease with the task. Her stomach swooped. Maybe it was her imagination, but she thought he was starting to see the possibilities of having his own family.

Noelle pulled her gaze away from him. "Um, Paige, do you know if Saul's grandparents had a major social life back in the twenties? These are party and dinner clothes, not something you'd use for cooking or mucking stalls."

"They might have. That's when his grandparents built the new house. The ranch was booming so they weren't worried about taking out a large mortgage, then the Great Depression hit and they nearly lost the Soaring Hawk. Saul grew up on stories about how hard they worked to keep the ranch."

"That could explain why they packed all this stuff away. No parties or dressy dinners, no need for silk and beaded fringe. Or reminders of money spent that they couldn't get back."

"What did you hope to find?"

"Victorian outfits. I want to dress up for the tour, but the vintage clothing store I remembered in Bozeman was closed and I didn't want to take the time to look for another."

Paige cocked her head. "An Edwardian

costume would work. Remember the renewed interest in the Titanic when the hundredth anniversary of the sinking rolled around?"

"Vaguely."

"Leo Striker—the history teacher at the high school—has an ancestor who survived the sinking. Richard Carson."

"I've heard stories about Mr. Carson. He started the bank. A branch of the family still runs it."

"That's right. Shelton had a parade and parties to welcome him home. Leo thought it would be fun and educational to revisit the period and wrote a play about Richard's life. The drama department might have some of the costumes left from the production. You could talk to the school about borrowing what you need."

Noelle was thrilled. Edwardian-style clothing would still have the historic ambiance she wanted and it was so romantic in style. "I'll do that. And come to think of it, I've seen Edwardian-type clothes online, probably because there have been so many movies and television programs set in the era," she said.

A whimper from Daniel caught their attention.

"Paige, your son needs a diaper change," Dakota said calmly. "Or he's hungry. Or both."

"Parenthood calls." Paige went over and put Daniel back into the baby sling. "You're good with kids. What about having a family of your own?"

He grinned. "The thought has crossed my mind a time or two, especially after meeting your two."

"Good. I'd love to have a bunch of cousins growing up together here." Daniel cried harder and she patted his bottom. "Gotta go. Anyhow, you can get more done without us here."

When she had descended the attic staircase, Dakota hiked an eyebrow at Noelle. "All right, what do you want moved to the other house? I'll have to take care of it after the weekend is over—I'm giving the hands some extra time off."

She wanted to answer *everything*, but that wasn't practical. "The trunks. I'll empty them tonight or tomorrow morning. Also any of the chairs and tables that aren't broken. The two cherry bedsteads and dressers would be nice for a couple of the downstairs rooms in the back." She swallowed as she looked at the antique cradle; it was especially difficult after hearing Dakota casually mention his growing interest in having a family. "Also the cradle. We won't need much more. I'm blocking off the staircases, so nothing needs to go upstairs."

Dakota looked around the attic. "I don't see mattresses for the beds, which is probably a good thing. They wouldn't be worth much after all this time."

"That's okay—I can borrow air mattresses from my folks. They have a stack for when family is visiting. The mattresses won't show—I'll make up the beds with old quilts and use ruffled dust skirts. I just want to create an impression of what the house might have looked like, but it doesn't have to look fully occupied."

She went over to a box marked Dishes. Inside was blue-and-white china, probably over a hundred years old. It would look lovely in the old farmhouse kitchen hutch that was standing against one of the attic walls, but she didn't want to ask Dakota and his crew to do too much. At least she could set the table.

"Noelle?" Dakota prompted.

"Just seeing what's here," she said and closed the box, too aware that everything moved over to the old house would have to be moved back. Leaving furniture and other items in the untended aging building wasn't a good idea.

She looked at Dakota, imagining him in an Edwardian suit. He'd look amazing. But then, he also looked amazing in jeans, boots and a worn work shirt.

Noelle sighed.

She needed to remember her divorce was only a few months old and that she had entirely too many things to sort out to consider the possibility of a future with any man, much less someone like Dakota Maxwell.

CHAPTER ELEVEN

"IT'S MOSTLY A holiday party," Noelle kept re-minding guests on Friday evening as they wished her a happy birthday.

It didn't make any difference. Her parents were too busy telling everyone how pleased they were to be celebrating their eldest daughter's special day.

The early December birthday party had been a long tradition in the Bannerman family, serving also as her mother's deadline for getting the ranch decorated. Noelle had loved having Christmas lights and trees for her birthday decor. She'd always had a new red velvet dress to wear and it was the only time during the school year when her head wasn't buried in books. Well, she'd studied in front of the Christmas tree every night, sometimes sleeping there, wrapped in the cheer of the holiday.

Dakota stood by the fireplace. While he wasn't being antisocial, he didn't look comfortable. Then his grandfather had gone over to him, putting Noelle on edge as she anticipated an argument. Saul had done most of the talking, Dakota listening expressionless, before Anna Beth directed her husband to another group.

Because of the crowd milling around the large house, Noelle hadn't found a chance to say more than hello to Dakota, yet whenever she looked at him, he seemed to be focused in her direction. Maybe that was to be expected. He was no longer acquainted with anyone in the area except for his brother and grandfather and she liked thinking they'd become friends.

Their discussions had mostly stayed impersonal since the afternoon when she'd given him the knee sleeves. Well...except for the trip to Bozeman when they'd kissed again. And she couldn't forget that he'd suggested the possibility of more kissing on their "dates" to Christmas events.

Maybe she should be insulted that he wanted to attend the town festivities with her as a way to avoid his grandfather. But she understood the desire not to feel hypocritical. Besides, they got along well most of the time.

She also felt ridiculous for thinking about him so much.

"Are you happy, Aunt Noelle?" Mishka asked, hugging her waist.

"Of course I'm happy." Noelle leaned over and kissed her niece. The five-year-old wore a green gown with a red satin sash and she positively glowed. "You're beautiful, sweetie. I love your dress. It's so Christmassy."

Mishka beamed. "Mama and Papa got it special for me to wear at your party. But they…" Her face scrunched in thought. "They think you don't like your birthday anymore. Why?"

A blend of humor and sadness fought inside Noelle. The family must have guessed more from her protests over the party than she'd intended. In turn, her niece must have overheard the adults speculating about it. Kids were so open—if they wanted to know something, they asked.

A few nearby guests looked over with concerned expressions, apparently catching part of what Mishka had said.

"I'm having a great time," she replied carefully. "But when people grow up, they sometimes enjoy celebrating other days even more than their own birthdays. It's nothing for you to worry about. For me, Christmas is so much more important."

Yet when Noelle thought about the reason she'd resisted having a party, tears threatened. She had tried not to think about the baby's due date, but there was no escaping it would have been around her birthday.

"Noelle, sorry to interrupt." It was Dakota. "But I have some decorating committee business. You promised to show me around the Blue Banner so I could get a better idea of how your mom does things and what her other plans might be."

"Um, *right*. We should do that now."

"Can I go, too?" Mishka asked.

"Not tonight, kiddo," Dakota said. Just then her sister waved Mishka over. "Come on, Noelle, let's get our coats."

Grateful for the excuse to temporarily escape, she fetched her coat from the entryway closet and slipped on a pair of boots, then led Dakota to the room where her mother had laid out her guests' winter wear. Soon they were outside in the crisp, quiet night air, stars blazing across the sky. Some constellations were brighter than others, including Orion, the first star cluster she'd ever learned to identify.

"We never talked about me showing you my mom's decorations," she said softly.

"Yeah, but you seemed upset. And I didn't think you'd want anyone else to know."

Noelle swallowed another surge of emotion. Dakota's perceptiveness no longer surprised her. "I appreciate that."

Beyond the barns lay the Blue Banner's home orchard, the trees strung with twinkling white lights, while the fences were lit by multicolored strings. The frozen ground crunched beneath their feet as they walked.

"Why put Christmas lights out here when they can't be seen that well from the house?" Dakota asked.

"There will be hayrides later. Dad decorates the tractor and drives down here along the orchard to one of the pastures before circling back to load a new group. He and my brothers take turns at the wheel. I told him he shouldn't go to so much trouble this year, but he insisted."

"Remember the summer hayrides with the Shelton Youth Ranching Association?"

Noelle smiled wryly. "I never went on one of those. It was an activity for couples and I was too busy studying to have a boyfriend.

Either way, boys my age didn't know me because they were still in junior high, while my fellow classmates in high school were too much older to pay attention to me."

Dakota drew her arm under his, pulling her closer as they strolled. "I'm sorry you missed out. For what it's worth, you're no longer overlooked. In fact, you've caught my attention completely."

Warmth captured Noelle, but it wasn't embarrassment.

"Being unable to participate could be why Dad started doing hayrides at my birthday parties," she said. "To sort of compensate for me not fitting in with the crowd."

"I was the same age as the other kids, but I didn't fit in well, either."

"As I recall, you were the ringleader of mischief," Noelle said in a dry tone.

"Ugly rumors, never proven." He winked at her, something she couldn't have imagined him doing a few weeks earlier.

"Yeah, right. Do you want to see our horses? We don't have any that compete with the Soaring Hawk's purebreds, but they're primarily descended from mares and stallions the family brought from North Dakota in the 1950s.

My dad keeps a low level of light in the barn at night in case it's needed, so there should be enough to see without disturbing them too much."

DAKOTA WAS ALWAYS interested in looking at horses, but he thought Noelle wanted to avoid the group now headed their direction. Quite possibly it was her father and brothers, coming out to prepare for the hayride.

The air was somewhat warmer inside the barn, partly from being an enclosed space with large animals, away from the breeze, and partly because of the barn heater.

There were small lights along the base of the center aisle—enough illumination to navigate, while allowing the animals to rest in relative shadow. A colorful glow also rose in the far corner. One stallion looked over his stall gate and huffed a half-hearted challenge. At a soft word from Noelle, he withdrew and pulled a mouthful of hay from his feeder.

"I'm practically a stranger to them," she said. "But they're well-mannered unless they think you're an intruder who might be a problem."

"Do you get many intruders?"

"Not really. Once a stray dog got in during a late spring blizzard. She must have been kicked, because she ended up with two cracked ribs and a bruised patella. Still, it was better than freezing to death."

Dakota winced. "What happened to her?"

"The vet treated Moozie's injuries and Aunt Trish adopted her when we couldn't find the owners. We don't give up on animals."

"Even stray dogs that threaten your horses?" Right now, most of the animals were drowsing, but Dakota stroked a mare who looked out inquisitively. She was a chestnut beauty, with calm, sleepy eyes.

Noelle smiled faintly. "Moozie wasn't a threat. She was a beagle, probably lost from someone's car as they traveled through the county. The mares didn't know her and I doubt they would have been bothered except they had young foals at the time. We've had new cats move in and they don't pay any attention. One of our older geldings obviously decided Moozie was okay because we found them together in the morning."

They walked on and Dakota realized the glow of light in the corner was actually a Christmas tree. In a half circle around it were a couple of chairs and bales of hay. The festive tree seemed a surprise until he remembered how much the Bannermans loved the holidays. Perhaps this was a gathering spot for the family.

He lifted a faded quilt folded on one of the chairs. It seemed clean, so he wrapped the soft folds around Noelle.

"You should be wearing a heavier coat," he said.

"I'm not cold."

"You're shivering."

He'd seen Noelle's expression at the party, a haunted sadness that didn't leave her eyes, even when smiling. It was so unlike her, he was worried.

She pulled the quilt more closely around herself. "It's emotional, more than anything." She was quiet for a long moment, then sighed. "Have you ever kept something private, that didn't *have* to be private, and then realized by not telling, you may have made everything worse?"

Dakota suspected she was talking about family relationships, something he had little experience with handling. He had a tendency to keep things superficial with his brothers, at least when it came to his own life. Discussions like the one he'd shared with Jordan on Thanksgiving Day were few and far between.

Saul kept pushing, trying to talk, but Dakota wasn't interested, particularly when his grandfather asked about his leg and how well it was healing. He didn't trust the old guy. Jordan had originally suspected Saul was merely trying to get free labor from his grandsons and it remained a distinct possibility as far as Dakota was concerned.

"I don't know *exactly* what you mean," he said cautiously, "but it's okay if you tell me. You never know—I fixed a problem or two when I was in the Navy."

Noelle didn't say anything for a long moment, then sank onto one of the hay bales. "That's nice of you, but I'm afraid this *can't* be fixed. And I don't want you to feel as if I'm unloading all my private issues on you."

"I don't mind. Are you regretting your divorce?"

"No." The swift, firm denial reassured Dakota more than he liked to think about.

"Then what?"

"Um, well, have you ever heard of an ectopic pregnancy?" The unexpected question startled him.

"Not much I'm afraid."

Noelle nodded. "They're relatively rare. It's when the fetus attaches in the wrong place and inevitably can't survive, or be saved, and a woman may have trouble conceiving again in the future. And if she does conceive, there's a chance she could have another ectopic pregnancy. That…that's what happened to me earlier this year," she said in a rush. "It was the final blow to my already doomed marriage. Steffen blamed me and nobody could convince him I wasn't at fault. Or maybe blaming me was an excuse because he wanted a family and was afraid he might not be able to have one if we stayed together."

"Hasn't he ever heard of adoption?" Dakota asked, fighting to keep anger from his voice. He couldn't understand the man's unfairness, especially directed at Noelle, who must have needed love and support instead.

She was focused on the Christmas tree. "Adoption isn't a route some people want to take. I understand. The process often takes years and a huge amount of heartbreak can be involved."

Dakota was still appalled, though he admired Noelle for refusing to feel bitter toward her ex. In a world where divorce could be a battleground, she'd chosen acceptance.

He thought about the moments he'd held Daniel, fascinated by his tiny fingers and delicate features. Or when he'd spent time with Mishka, her sweet spirit filled with love for other people. Pain curled around his own heart for the child Noelle had lost.

"I'm guessing this is the part you haven't told anyone," he murmured. While he was no expert in family dynamics, he wondered how the Bannermans would feel if they learned she hadn't confided in them.

"No, I haven't told anybody else, so please don't say anything. Just keep it between us. I want them to be happy about Paige and Jordan having a baby without worrying about me. They feel bad enough about my divorce, which was unavoidable, no matter what. But even though I've tried not to think about the timing, the baby would have been due around my birthday. Maybe if Mom and Dad had known, they wouldn't have insisted on having the party."

Fresh realization dawned on Dakota. If everything had gone the way it should have, Noelle would either have given birth in the past few days, or still be expecting.

"It's silly," she murmured. "I didn't know

about the pregnancy until after I woke up from the surgery. I was fortunate—I could have bled to death if I hadn't gotten to a hospital in time. But even knowing that, I still think about all the might-have-beens."

Dakota sat next to her and traced the damp path of a tear on her cheek. "Maybe that's part of the problem—you didn't have a chance to process any of it, just grieve the loss."

She blinked. "I've counseled patients to let themselves grieve and tell them we each grieve in our own way, but applying that to myself is hard."

"Your way seems to be thinking about everyone else first. You went to the Himalayas right afterward, didn't you?"

"Not until I was cleared medically. I wanted to feel useful after it happened, but the biggest delay was waiting to sign the divorce papers. Everything was very civil. Steffen wanted out and so did I. We each kept what we owned when we got married and I told him to take the rest. Honestly, there wasn't anything worth wrangling over. And now—" She stopped abruptly.

"Now?" Dakota prompted after several seconds.

"NOTHING."

Noelle lifted the quilt around Dakota as well, enclosing them both in a cocoon of shared warmth.

She didn't want to express more of her doubts about returning to emergency relief work—maybe because she didn't want him thinking it had anything to do with her ex-husband. It didn't, though there was an irony to the situation. She was actually considering the shift in her career that Steffen had wanted her to make.

Dakota put his arm around her and she wondered how she could feel more for a man she'd known for less than three weeks, than the one she'd been married to for almost two years.

"I like the Christmas tree," Dakota murmured after a comfortable silence.

"Yeah. We used this one in the house during my childhood. When Mom wanted to get a bigger tree a few years ago, Dad said he'd set the old one up in the barn every December. He's even more sentimental than my mother and couldn't bear to let it go. I think he and my brothers sit out here discussing their plans for the ranch. Or maybe they tell each other ghost stories. You know, the kind where you shine a flashlight under your chin for effect and say in a portentous voice, 'this is a true story—it *really happened.*'"

Dakota grinned. "I remember Jordan doing that with me and Wyatt. He'd sneak into the room after Mom and Dad put us to bed. But his favorites weren't about ghosts and he didn't try to scare us. He liked the legends about gnomes and he made up stories about a magical wild horse that came down from the mountains."

"A magic horse is a nice image."

"I haven't thought about those nights in years. He said our horse was always there to protect us, even when the gnomes needed to go to sleep. It helped during those months when Mom was so sick. But he only managed to do it a few times after my grandfather got custody. Saul was a light sleeper and any sound would have him prowling the house."

It was touching that Dakota's older brother had been protective of his siblings, especially after their mother died and they ended up on the Soaring Hawk. Noelle enjoyed Saul, but the depth of his regret about his grandsons' childhoods suggested he'd made spectacular mistakes.

Jordan had turned out all right, enough for her sister to love him wholeheartedly and be loved the same in return. Nobody doubted that Jordan adored Paige and would do anything to make her happy. Noelle didn't know Wyatt, but Dakota had mentioned he was devoted to his daughter and deeply missed his wife.

And beneath Dakota's anger and frustration about his injured leg was a good, decent, courageous man with compassion for others. She hadn't intended to hear any of his discussion with Alex the other day, but she had. She'd left quietly, returning after a few minutes and calling out when she entered the barn. It seemed that he'd become a sounding board for the younger man—an understanding listener as someone who had been injured as well.

The ranch hands on the Soaring Hawk had quickly learned to respect Dakota. Not that he was a perfect boss. He'd reprimanded the employee who'd come to her for medical attention and his periodic moodiness bothered them—it was difficult to know where you stood with someone like that. Blair had even mentioned Dakota's mood set the tone each morning for the entire crew.

He also pushed himself far too hard. But the Christmas season was getting underway, and with Saul insisting his grandson become involved with the community activities, Noelle hoped there would be time for Dakota to relax and rest. He needed to heal. She'd seen the exhaustion in his face after a long day. While being tired wasn't unusual for a rancher, she knew part of it stemmed from physical pain.

"I almost forgot—I have something for you," Dakota said, shifting beneath the shared quilt to search in his coat pocket. He held out what looked like a shipping envelope. "It isn't wrapped, but happy birthday."

"You weren't supposed to bring a gift," she protested.

"I wanted you to have these."

Noelle's breath caught as she pulled out rolls of prayer flags printed with blessings.

"The flags are made by artisans," Dakota explained. "We can hang them when we drive into the mountains to cut fresh trees. You said the blessings are supposed to be for everyone, right? I thought maybe we could do it a week from Monday."

A measure of the sorrow inside Noelle eased. Of any gift she might have received, this was the most thoughtful. It gave her the oddest feeling that someone she'd known for such a short period of time could be so perceptive.

But then, Dakota was a whole lot more sensitive than he gave himself credit for being. A perfect example was his patience with the drama going on between Blair and Alex, even when they'd had a short spat in front of the other employees. In an aside to Noelle, he'd commented that they had more complications than many couples and he thought they needed a chance to work things out without him reprimanding them.

"You're amazing," she murmured.

"Amazingly hardheaded is as close as I come."

"Don't argue with me. Not when you haven't given me a birthday kiss," she said, looking up at him with a teasing smile. "Birthday kisses are allowed, along with mistletoe kisses."

"Good to know."

Without hesitation, he pulled her into a fierce embrace that took her breath away. Noelle could barely think, hazily realizing what she'd been missing all these years. Until now, nothing in her life came close.

When he finally pulled back a few inches,

she blinked and tried not to look as befuddled as she felt.

"Happy birthday," he whispered.

"Um, thanks."

Reluctantly she realized that she'd been absent from her own birthday celebration too long. It wouldn't be good to have the family asking questions.

"I hate saying this," she said, "but I should get back to the house."

"Do I get to ride with you on the hayride?"

"Yes, but no kisses," she warned. "There will be young kids along. The ride isn't intended to be a romantic couple's jaunt."

"How about this kind of kiss?" Dakota dropped a string of light kisses on her ear and hair. Her heart rate increased again.

"Better not. You'd make everyone start speculating we're involved. They're already going to wonder if we attend Christmas events together."

"Speaking of Christmas revelry, I know the Park Carolers are on Sunday. What else is going on this weekend?"

Noelle was still finding it difficult to concentrate with Dakota so close. Cuddling together under a quilt probably wasn't wise, however delicious it might be in the cold air of the barn.

"There are five craft bazaars tomorrow. Years ago they decided to have them all on one day, instead of spacing them out. The one at Fireman's Hall serves a lunch. The town's tree-lighting celebration is in the evening. First there's a lighted tractor parade around the town square. The mayor then makes an announcement and the Grand Marshal of the parade—which sounds grander than it is—flips the switch."

"So where should we start at the craft bazaars?"

Noelle tipped her head back and eyed Dakota's strong features. He resembled his grandfather, which meant he'd probably be just as attractive in fifty years as he was today. Saul—for all his long reputation as an ogre—remained a very good-looking man.

"Surely it would be all right if you skip the bazaars and only go to the evening events," she suggested. "Or maybe just one of them."

"Are you going to the craft bazaars?"

"Duh."

Dakota chuckled and his arm dropped from

around her waist. "In that case, shall I pick you up or meet you?"

He didn't seem bothered, so she shrugged. "I'm starting with the Mistletoe Market in the community center. It opens at nine. You can meet me there. With your own truck, leaving will be easier if it gets to be more merry than you can handle."

DAKOTA MISSED HOLDING NOELLE, but she was too tempting and he needed a little distance between them. "It isn't my kind of activity, but I can manage. After all, I've gone through survival training."

"I'm not sure you can compare this to survival training." She brushed a kiss on his jaw and it took a huge effort for him not to pull her close again. "You could be surprised at what you see. I haven't gone to the Mistletoe Market since college, but Mom says artists from all over Montana are participating."

Dakota thought there was a chance he might not be able to see anybody or anything except Noelle. She had a habit of grabbing his attention and not letting go. In fact, the hold she had over him was troubling. Less than a month into the arrangement with his grandfather and he was already getting sidetracked.

It wasn't like him.

His focus on an assignment had always been excellent. The perplexing part was wondering if Noelle was becoming more important to him than his agreement with Saul. And he was starting to think he knew the answer.

CHAPTER TWELVE

As NOELLE HAD PREDICTED, Dakota *was* surprised as he walked around the first Christmas craft market. Finely made wood toys, pottery, gold and silver jewelry—they had it all and more.

"Where is your family?" he asked Noelle as she looked at a pendant she was considering for Margaret Bannerman.

"My brothers aren't coming and the rest of us have an agreement to stay out of each other's way since gift shopping may be involved. Mom and Dad are going to the bazaar at Veteran's Hall first, while Paige, Jordan, Anna Beth and Saul are visiting the one at the school. It makes choosing gifts much easier. We just have to slide the opposite direction if we happen to cross paths and are carrying an item that isn't supposed to be seen until after it's wrapped for Christmas."

"I thought you shopped for your family in Bozeman."

"It would be fun to get something else for them. For years I've ordered all my Christmas gifts online and had them shipped directly to Montana in case I couldn't make it. This is more fun and personal and I get to wrap the packages, too."

"I'm going to use gift bags," Dakota confessed. "Wrapping isn't in my skill set."

"I happen to be an expert wrapper. We can set everything up in your office and put a sign on the door that says Santa's Workshop, No Entry Allowed."

"Sure," he agreed, pleased to see a sparkle of anticipation replace the lingering shadows in her eyes.

He focused on the goods being sold by various vendors, considering a wood train set for Daniel. His nephew was too young for toy trains, but it even came with a circular track. Dakota was fascinated by the toy, feeling like a kid again as he tested how smoothly it ran. After all, Jordan and Paige could put it away until the baby was old enough.

For his niece he had his eye on a large wood chest, decorated with carvings of cats and other animals. It reminded him of the work his father had once done, so in a way it would feel as if he was giving his niece something her paternal grandfather might have made for her if he was here.

"How about this for Wyatt's daughter?" Noelle asked after a while. She held up a patchwork quilt with a puppy theme on the border.

"You don't need to get a gift for Christie. Jordan and I are sending her and Wyatt a load of stuff."

"I want to." The quiet intensity in Noelle's voice stopped Dakota from making another protest. Naturally she wanted to get something for a child who had lost her mother.

He hadn't processed everything she'd told him the night before, but he knew how much she was grieving. Along with that was the pain she might not be able to have children in the future. He hurt about it, too, and wished he could have offered more comfort than just holding her.

It meant a great deal that she'd trusted him enough to share what she'd gone through. And he understood why she wanted to keep it private for a while.

"What about a quilt with kittens instead?" he suggested. "Christie has two cats. They're mostly black with bits of white."

Noelle diligently began looking through

the various patchwork quilts and found one with black-and-white tuxedo kittens pictured on the border. "Better?"

"The other was fine, too, but I don't think Christie has much contact with dogs. I'm considering a chest over there for Mishka. She could use it for toys or whatever else she wants."

"You already got a dragon figurine for her in Bozeman," Noelle teased as she paid for the quilt and the seller put it in a large plastic bag. "But let's go look."

The chest was made of hardwood and the animals carved into the surface were stained and polished to a satin finish, rather than painted. Though pricey, the workmanship was worth every penny. "This is great," Noelle said enthusiastically. "She'll like it when she gets older, as well as now." Yet an odd expression crossed her face as she looked at the back of the chest.

"Do you see something wrong with it?"

NOELLE SHOOK HER HEAD, but she thought the artisan's mark on the foot was almost identical to the Circle M ranch brand. Surely the resemblance was just a coincidence, yet she couldn't forget Saul's cagey expression when she'd first brought up the possibility of him finding his former son-in-law. He'd almost looked as if he knew where Evan Maxwell might be, saying he'd "heard" things.

And something else was ticking in the back of her mind, making her connect Evan Maxwell and the chest. She just didn't want to say anything and get Dakota's hopes up about finding his father when it seemed so improbable after all this time.

"Nothing's wrong—the work is beautiful."

"Yeah, it reminds me of the chess sets and Christmas ornaments my father used to carve during the winter."

Her pulse skipped. *That* was the connection. "Right. You mentioned he'd worked with wood."

"Dad liked keeping his hands busy. I guess that's what caught my attention. The ornaments and chess pieces were different types of animals, similar to the ones on the chest." Dakota turned his head to one side, frowning thoughtfully. "You know, I wonder if any of Mom's old Christmas decorations are still at the Circle M. Jordan has been working over there to get the place in better shape. No one lives in the house, but we want to look after it. I need to ask what was left there."

Noelle looked again at the small symbol on the wood, chills running up and down her back. Dakota paid for the chest and took it out to his truck along with her own purchases, saying he'd be right back. But as he walked away, she saw a larger version of the artist's mark on the bottom of the chest, as if burned into the wood with a branding iron.

While he was out of earshot, Noelle turned to the man tending the booth. "Did you make everything here?" she asked.

"Nah. We're a collective of artists. Doesn't make sense for all of us to come to one of these, so we take turns. I make the stained-glass kaleidoscopes. Most of us are artists part-time and have other jobs that pay the bills."

"I see. Do you have a business card for whoever carved the chest?"

"We have one for our group—Montana Full Moon Artists." He handed her a card. "Mike has always thought Shelton was too far, but he changed his mind at the last minute and contacted the organizers, asking if we could still set up a booth. Luckily they had a spot available and I was free. Mike does all of the woodworking in our group, including making the stands for my kaleidoscopes. I could only bring so much, but you can visit our website for more selection. Our shipping prices are reasonable."

Mike?

Disappointment replaced Noelle's anticipation that Evan Maxwell might have carved the chest. It was a good thing she hadn't mentioned the possibility to Dakota. The similarity to the Maxwell cattle brand must be coincidental or the artist could have seen it somewhere and adapted the design.

"Noelle?"

She jumped at Dakota's voice. "Um, yeah. Ready to keep shopping?"

"You bet. I want to get some of the crystal suncatchers for Mishka. Also that wood train set I saw on the other side of the hall for Daniel. I know he's too young to appreciate it right now, but he will when he's older. And maybe I'll get that patchwork quilt for him, too, the one with the puppies. Unless you want it instead."

"No, that's fine. There are plenty to choose from if I decide to get another. But just so you know, my grandmother makes quilts and has probably made one for the baby. She has for all her grandchildren and great-grandchildren."

"I can find something else." Dakota looked so excited about the shopping, Noelle forgot her disappointment and lingering questions about the chest.

Maybe he was finally catching the holiday spirit.

ALEX RODE INTO the hillier section of the Soaring Hawk on Saturday morning, pleased to be using one of the ranch's horses. Dakota had offered him the day off to attend the Christmas craft bazaars in town, but he'd asked if he could check fence lines instead.

Carmen Melendez was with him. Alex had GPS on his phone and didn't think he needed anyone along, but he hadn't objected. The boss's policy was to have ranch hands go out as a team, even though *he* almost always went alone. Nobody grumbled about having to pair up because it had been Jordan Maxwell's rule, too. The likelihood of a bear attack in Shelton County was low, and practically zero in winter when they were hibernating, but coyotes could be a problem, along with a few other predators.

Luckily Carmen wasn't too talkative. Alex wanted to think. He hated how things were between him and Blair, but he didn't know what to do about it.

A bunch of stuff in his life needed fixing. Like with his parents. After the last time he and Dakota had talked, he'd started wondering if he was wrong about why his mom kept bugging him to have more plastic surgery. Maybe she was just worried because he hardly saw anybody. She might be afraid he was becoming a hermit like old Mr. Hawkins had been for years and years.

Alex leaned forward and stroked Bingo's neck thinking that for someone who didn't actually want to be alone, he'd spent a lot of time making sure he *stayed* alone.

"Uh, Carmen, how well do you know Blair?" he asked, straightening.

"Well, enough to know she's seriously mad at you."

His heart sank. "You mean I've completely blown things with her."

"You'd be worse off if she wasn't upset."

He hadn't thought about it that way, but it might be a good thing—if Blair didn't still care about him, she wouldn't be angry. But did she still love him, or was she just upset at the way he'd acted?

With a sigh, he focused on the fences and

cows beyond. He'd believed he was pushing Blair away for her benefit, but he'd really done it because he was scared. He was still afraid they'd get married and someday she'd decide she didn't want to be with him any longer.

Of course, that wasn't different from any other couple. And how could it be worse than how he felt right now?

"What do you think I should do?"

"An apology would be a good place to start. Then go from there. I bet you never thought about doing anything romantic for her."

"You mean bring her flowers and poetry or whatever? Blair doesn't care about that kind of thing. She didn't even want me to give her an engagement ring."

Carmen rolled her eyes. "Sometimes people say what they think you want to hear. Anyhow, romance isn't just flowers. My mom says the best romance is about the little stuff you do to make each other happy."

Alex could think of several things his parents did for each other. Sometimes it was just sharing a special smile or kiss when they'd had a hard day. He used to think it was corny—now he wondered if he'd missed learning something important.

"Being romantic is hard when we're both working on the ranch and everyone is watching," he muttered. "Anyhow, it's too late. Blair likes Eduardo or Rod."

"You're just making excuses." Carmen slapped the reins, urging her horse to a faster pace.

Alex did the same, his head whirling with a blend of anticipation and dread. After the accident he might have wondered why Blair had fallen in love with him in the first place, but he'd never needed to do anything romantic—at some point they'd just begun talking about things they'd do when they were married. It made him think of something Mr. Hawkins had said about getting lazy when things were too easy, and that you should always make an effort, even when life seemed to be going well.

Looking back, Alex didn't remember which one of them had said "I love you" first. But no matter what, he was pretty sure he hadn't said it often enough.

"I'M BUYING," Saul declared at Fireman's Hall as they stood in line to get their meals.

Dakota's jaw jutted out. He hadn't been pleased when they all ended up in the lunch line together and he clearly didn't intend to let his grandfather pay for his food. "Absolutely not."

"It's my treat," Noelle said hastily. "For everyone."

"That isn't—"

"I've got it," her brother-in-law interrupted, pushing ahead to the cashier.

Noelle exchanged a look with her sister. Surely Jordan hadn't been as antagonistic as Dakota when it came to their grandfather, yet Paige seemed wryly amused and Noelle spotted Saul's wife nudging him, as if in warning. Maybe they were seeing reminders of Jordan's readjustment back to Montana.

Or not.

Dakota was different from his brother, even if a few of the circumstances were the same. His leg was part of the issue. Saul seemed to care about his grandson, but the way he asked Dakota about his injury kept putting his back up. She'd seen several of their interactions and there seemed to be little evidence of a thaw.

She just hoped something was happening underneath, because it would be best for everyone involved if they could live in peaceful coexistence. They didn't have to be buddies, just not at each other's throats.

Jordan returned with the meal tickets. The luncheon had changed over the years. Originally there was one choice—fried chicken, country fried potatoes, a square of gelatin salad and a couple of carrot sticks. Now the kitchen also offered turkey sandwiches and a green salad, along with a lighter soup and bread.

Saul gazed longingly at the fried chicken being served, but chose the soup. Then he gave Noelle a resigned look. "I'm trying," he said.

"I can see."

"What's that about?" Dakota murmured in her ear.

"Nothing to worry you."

Mishka asked for fried chicken and everyone else opted for the sandwiches. When they sat down, Dakota maneuvered to put Noelle and himself as far from his grandfather as possible.

Talk around the table turned to the handcrafted goods they'd seen so far. Her parents declared this was the best year yet, which might be true, but they always said that to be supportive of the organizers. Noelle was also aware of a few speculative looks in her and

Dakota's direction. Margaret and Scott Bannerman would love for their daughter to become seriously involved with someone local because they'd see her more often. But surely they knew it wasn't likely.

"This place hasn't changed," Dakota said after a while.

She looked around. Fireman's Hall was a meeting location for various groups and events, so they'd both spent a good amount of time here while growing up.

"A fresh coat of paint, that's about all," she agreed. "I'm glad they still have those wonderful old fireplaces. They remind me of the ones at the homestead house, especially the fireplace in the kitchen."

"What is it with you and fireplaces?"

Noelle ate a bite of salad. "I don't know. I guess they represent home and tradition," she said after a moment. "My aid organization is based in Atlanta, so I have a studio apartment there for when I'm between assignments. It's fine, but I'm not there often enough that it feels like a real home. What it *does* have is a small fireplace. I kept the lease, even after I got married…" Her voice trailed and she shrugged.

Maybe she'd kept her studio because she'd

subconsciously known her marriage was a mistake. Steffen hadn't seemed to care that she'd kept the lease after their first argument about where their careers were going. He'd been right in his own way, because how did you have a loving relationship if you were apart so much of the time and didn't try?

"I hope I'm not the reason you've eaten so quickly. Sorry for putting you on the spot earlier," Dakota said in a low aside.

Noelle blinked at her nearly empty plate. "It has nothing to do with you—the food is just really good."

"Yeah, it's tasty."

He ate his last bite and nudged her. "How about getting dessert at the next place? I've noticed a number of the vendors sell some type of sweets."

"Okay."

Noelle was itching to ask Saul if there was any chance that his son-in-law might be going by a different name and doing wood carving for a living, but it would be too awkward in front of everyone. Perhaps she'd have an opportunity at one of his daily exercise sessions.

She just didn't know if he'd give her a direct answer.

Blair spent the morning getting the Soaring Hawk website up and running, and in the afternoon she shifted to restocking the bales of hay and straw in the horse barn.

The weather had given them a break ever since the storm before Thanksgiving, with just a few flurries and not enough to add much accumulation. Feeding the cattle wasn't necessary—they were good foragers when the snow wasn't too deep—but horses were a different matter.

When she was done stacking the bales, she climbed to the top row and looked across the large space, feeling as if she was in a private hideaway of her own making. It was a fabulous old barn. Chances were it could still be standing for another hundred years or longer. In other circumstances she might have brought a book up here to read when she didn't have other tasks, but she hadn't since Alex was usually working with the horses and he clearly wanted to avoid her.

Blair waited for her anger to rise, but just felt a faint flicker. She sighed, knowing she needed to return the tractor and flatbed trailer to the equipment barn. Yet before she could move, Alex walked through the door.

"Blair?" he called.

"Up here. I just finished." She made her way down the high stack of bales. "What do you want?"

"Uh…" He shuffled his feet. "I want to apologize."

"For what?"

"Everything."

"Great. You've apologized. We're hunky-dory again."

"I mean it. Will you forgive me?" he asked.

He *seemed* sincere, but forgiving was complicated. Blair was willing to forgive Alex for mentioning her mother. It still hurt, but she knew he must have been upset being home. His mom had probably mentioned plastic surgery again. Donna Sorenson's intentions were good—she wanted to help her son and nothing else had worked. But Blair knew if Alex wanted more treatment for his scars, he'd do it without someone urging him.

Now he was asking to be forgiven for everything. Presumably that also meant pushing her away since the accident.

"Okay, fine. I forgive you," she said finally. "I'll see you later."

"Wait. I know you're still upset. Can't we figure things out?"

Now he wanted to talk?

Somehow that made her hurt more than ever. The best time for talking had been two and a half years ago. "Alex, this isn't a movie where you say *I'm sorry* and everything is okay. Forgiving is one thing, healing is another. I want a marriage that doesn't fall apart when something bad happens, because bad things happen all the time."

"I get that. What can I do?"

Blair made a helpless gesture. "I don't know. Maybe you're right—I *was* hanging on too hard. Because basically, you didn't trust me enough to know my own heart and stand by you for the right reasons, which makes me wonder if I can trust *you*."

Most of the color drained from Alex's face. "I promise you can."

She zipped her coat up, suddenly feeling colder. "You've promised a lot of things. So far, you've mostly broken my heart."

Blair could see it wounded him to hear that, but they weren't kids any longer. They had to be honest and find out if it was possible to put the pieces together again. She didn't want to pretend the accident hadn't happened; she just wanted to move forward and stop letting it define everything else in their lives.

"We can talk," she said finally. "But I'm working so it can't be now."

Aware of Alex watching her, Blair got onto the tractor and drove toward the equipment barn. She didn't know if she felt hopeful or tired, but at least they weren't still standing in the same spot.

DAKOTA WOKE EARLY on Sunday morning, realizing he'd been in the midst of a pleasant dream, rather than being caught in something darker.

A quiet sound came from Pepper, who must have recognized he was awake.

"Hey, girl."

He patted the narrow space next to him on the bed and she leaped up eagerly, head on his chest and tail swishing over his legs with happy wags. She was young and needed to be trained. Nevertheless, her instincts were astonishing; she was going to be a top herder.

A colorful glow suddenly poured around the curtains and he realized it came from the Christmas lights on the barn and other buildings, set to automatically come on for a few hours before dawn and then again in the late afternoon. As a surprise, Noelle had even put a small Christmas tree in the ranch office, along with other decorations—a tree featuring tractor lights and a shiny toy tractor beneath it with his name on a gift tag. The thoughtful gesture had given him a surge of emotion that still resonated.

She was stubborn. And the thing she was most stubborn about was Christmas.

No.

Dakota knew that wasn't quite accurate. Noelle was stubborn about life. She was obstinate about finding joy and sharing it with others, which was what Christmas was all about. And she was absolutely determined to see the worth in other people. He'd never known anyone like her.

But how long could someone with her loving spirit repeatedly work under such heart-wrenching circumstances without eventually being destroyed herself? A part of him wondered if that was why her ex-husband had wanted her to stop.

Pepper let out a whine, sensing the increased tension in Dakota's body. He stroked her head.

"It's okay, girl. I'm just finding out that caring about someone is even more complicated than I expected it to be."

Dakota rubbed his face, recalling a fragment of his dream. Except it was really a memory of Christmas before his mother had gotten sick. Funny, he'd barely remembered celebrating with his mom, yet now he was recalling how much she'd enjoyed the holidays and made them special.

A number of good memories were resurfacing, like the one about his brother sneaking in at night to tell him and Wyatt tales of friendly fantastic creatures.

It was as if Noelle had connected him to his early childhood again, allowing his memories to come out of hiding because they were finally safe. The fanciful thought made him shake his head, but it persisted. Remembering good times had been hard when there was nothing special in his life to hang on to.

Once most of the family left for church, he saddled Tucker and rode to the paddock on the other side of the equipment barn, Pepper running alongside. Except for trips into town, he rarely went anywhere without her these days.

The paddock was the best place to practice for the Shelton rodeo, being well away from his grandfather's critical gaze and out of sight of the main ranch. Winning an award meant little to him, but would likely impress Saul.

The old skill was coming back.

Dakota was working on reversing how he came off his horse so he could land on his left leg, which also meant reversing how he threw the rope. He was reasonably ambidextrous, so he thought it was possible. The real question was the speed required in timed events.

"Stay, Pepper," he said. She remained by the open gate, settling down and putting her head on her outstretched paws with an unhappy expression.

First he practiced roping the barrel, alternating with throwing the loop at an upended sawhorse, and dismounting as if going after a steer to tie.

When he felt more comfortable, his next big challenge would be to work on his bull riding skills. There was no training equipment on the Soaring Hawk and he couldn't contact the rodeo school run by Josh McKeon. Word might get back to Jordan and Paige since the McKeons were friends of theirs. But some of the most important skills in bull and bronco riding were balance and focus, so there were ways to work on that without additional equipment.

Anyway, once calving season started, there wouldn't be a minute to spare at a rodeo school or for practice. He already had a tough enough time finding a private hour between all the ranch work and Christmas activities. Today was a rare occurrence.

The loss of work time from doing "Christmas" should frustrate him, yet a smile tugged at his mouth as he thought about the previous evening. A string of colorfully lit tractors had circled the town park several times, onlookers cheering them on. Some had pulled floats with both children and adults in costume. The town's Victorian carolers had ridden sitting on hay bales, singing traditional holiday hymns. And candy was thrown out in great handfuls by a jolly Santa Claus on the fire engine, kids scrambling to get their share.

The tree-lighting ceremony had followed—the tree in the park had grown to an impressive height since he was a boy.

"Now they have to use construction cranes to put up the lights and decorations," Noelle had explained as they waited for the countdown to begin.

She'd huddled close to him as the wind chill factor increased through the evening. Everyone had been bundled in heavy coats and gloves and scarves, and snuggled to share a little extra warmth. He'd enjoyed having her so near to him.

The shopping flurry at the craft bazaars had also been fun until he'd been forced to sit down for lunch at the same table with his grandfather. But even that hadn't been as bad as expected. And not as awkward as the day Liam Flannigan had stopped by for his monthly "check" on Dakota's progress. Liam was a fine rancher and his honest reputation had made him the logical choice to be the third party who would decide if Dakota was meeting the terms of the agreement with Saul. He'd done right by Jordan, but Dakota knew it was early days for him.

Saul had listened to everything they were discussing, his dark eyes sharp and watchful. Finally Anna Beth had arrived and insisted her husband go inside the house.

Liam had smiled wryly when they were finally alone. "Don't be bothered by your grandfather. I can see everything is going smoothly here."

Dakota rode around and around the paddock, practicing his throws, and then jumping from Tucker's saddle. The motion had to be swift and seamless, or he'd lose time in getting to the steer and tying its legs.

Each leap from Tucker's saddle reminded him he was no longer a teenager, but he was determined to keep going. He still hadn't completely made up his mind to compete, but doing well at the rodeo was a way to show he could tackle whatever was needed to run the ranch, both to his grandfather and Liam Flannigan.

And maybe to himself.

CHAPTER THIRTEEN

NOELLE DIDN'T STAY for the Sunday potluck at church, instead going to the Soaring Hawk for her daily exercise session with Saul. He'd stayed home to relax, wanting to attend the evening festivities in town—he enjoyed being around people now, but acknowledged crowds were tiring.

She didn't know how necessary her encouragement still was, but she'd said she would help with his therapy while she was in Montana and intended to keep her word. Besides, with no one else around, talking about Evan Maxwell might be easier.

Since Saul no longer seemed as tired after a session, she'd begun repeating some of the exercises. He recognized what she was doing and complied with relative grace; he seemed to truly want a chance to see his great-grandchildren grow up, and if fitness was a part of that, then he was going to do his best.

But after they were done, she gave him a stern look.

"Okay, no more dancing around and saying you 'might' have heard something. Do you know where Evan Maxwell is living?"

Saul squirmed and finally nodded. "Well, er, *yes*. I sent him a message and we've talked. Can't say that was the easiest phone call I ever took," he muttered.

"I can imagine. How do you know where he is when Jordan and Dakota searched and couldn't find him?"

Saul frowned. "You're more direct than your sister, though I can't deny she gets her point across, too."

"You said I'm like Anna Beth. Which, by the way, I consider a compliment."

His exasperated expression softened. "The highest compliment. Evan is working as a ranch hand for someone I've done business with in eastern Montana. Not surprising, I've done business with most of the ranchers in the state. But Carlton didn't write until he learned Jordan was back in the area. He told me Evan was okay, he just didn't think he was ready to see family. I haven't known what to do. Then you urged me to get in contact and I went ahead."

Noelle sympathized; she knew how difficult secrets could be to hold, even with the best of intentions. "Is Evan working with wood again?"

"How do you know about that?"

"Because I may have seen some of his carvings at the Mistletoe Market yesterday. Is he going by Mike now, instead of Evan?"

"Michael is his middle name and he's employed under his mother's maiden name, rather than Maxwell." Saul heaved a sigh. "We talked for a while. He told me Victoria, Dakota's mom, had loved my old cane, the one my great-grandfather carved, so that's why he started carving himself. But since he'd sold quite a few chess sets and other pieces back then, he hasn't wanted his work displayed up here in case someone put two and two together, however unlikely. He's been in AA and sober for years, but he still thought it was kindest for the boys to leave things as they were."

"They aren't boys any longer—they're adults," Noelle reminded Saul. "And they should know about this. Evan must have changed his mind after you talked. Assuming it's the same person, he belongs to a cooperative called Full Moon Artists and is the one who arranged for them to be at the Mistletoe Market yesterday. It was their first time in this area. Dakota bought a chest for Mishka that has a maker's mark almost identical to the old Circle M brand. Someone is bound to notice sooner or later."

Saul frowned. "I asked Evan to Christmas as a surprise, but I don't know for sure he's coming. I'll speak with Jordan. Will you tell Dakota?"

"If you hope to have a relationship with him, you'd better tell him yourself. I'll find out where he's working this afternoon."

Noelle didn't know what to think when she left the house, worried how Dakota would react to the news. He wasn't in his office or the barn, but the stallion he used most often was gone. She saddled Stormy and rode out, wondering if he might be practicing his roping skills again in the old paddock.

Sure enough, thuds from a running horse rang out behind the equipment barn. As she rounded the large building, she saw Dakota on Tucker. Her eyes widened at the volume of dirt on his chaps. He also had large smears on his shoulders and arms.

"What are you *doing*?" she asked, afraid she already knew the answer.

Dakota reined Tucker to a stop and gave

her a level look. "The same as before, practicing my roping."

"You've got dirt and mud all over you. Does practicing require jumping from a horse as if you need to tie a steer's legs inside of a few seconds?"

Dakota's eyes narrowed. "What if it does?"

"Because it means you're practicing to compete in the rodeo, not polishing your ranching skills. You could reinjure your leg," she said incredulously.

Dakota had said the doctors agreed he'd eventually regain most of the strength in his leg, just not enough to serve as a SEAL. She recognized that adjusting to any limitation had to be hard for someone with his abilities, which was why she'd refrained from saying too much when he was climbing all over the barn roof putting up holiday lights. But she refused to be quiet about the rodeo.

"I do the same kind of work as a rancher."

"But it's not as fast or as dangerous."

Dakota meticulously coiled his rope. "Since everyone else seems to know about my agreement with Saul, I assume you do, too. I need to stand out. The All-Around Best Cowboy award could help. It isn't impossible—I won twice at the junior level."

Noelle glared and dismounted. Winning the All-Around Best Cowboy saddle required competing in everything from bull riding to steer roping. She cared about Dakota and the thought of him risking his leg for a rodeo was horrible. The risk wasn't just leaping from his horse—competitors could be gored by a bull, stepped on, kicked or any number of things. It was true those were risks also faced by ranchers, but the likelihood was much higher during competition.

"I don't see how competing proves anything," she said. "There are other ways to stand out. Ranching is demanding enough without deliberately inviting injury. Surgical techniques are improving all the time, but if you aren't careful, you could do damage that *can't* be repaired."

Pepper whined and looked back and forth between them. She was a smart dog, and animals had a remarkable ability to understand when something wasn't right.

Dakota set his jaw. "I don't expect you to understand. Success in the rodeo is one of the few times Saul showed approval when I was a kid."

"I understand that you and your grandfather are both bullheaded and totally impossible." She tried to keep her voice down but couldn't mask all her emotion. "Surely you've proven anything you need to prove, both to yourself and to Saul. You served with honor and courage. If Saul Hawkins is too blind to recognize that, he doesn't deserve to have you here in the first place. Where is the justice in having to start again from zero? You already did it once in the Navy."

"TIME DOESN'T STAND STILL. Most of us have to prove ourselves over and over," Dakota retorted, yet Noelle's staunch defense meant everything to him.

He rode to the fence and dismounted. The repeated leaps from Tucker's saddle had made his entire body ache. Once he'd nearly gone down on his right leg, but had managed to twist and land on his shoulder and hip instead. It was doubly frustrating when he thought about the rigors of his SEAL training and service. This was nothing in comparison, and yet he felt every bruise.

"Are you sure this is *just* about earning a share of the Soaring Hawk?" Noelle asked.

"What else? This is a valuable ranch and my mother loved it—heaven knows why after the way Saul disowned her for marrying someone he didn't like."

Noelle grasped the top rail of the paddock, seeming to have an internal debate with herself.

"For one, you seem to believe you could have helped your father with his drinking problem, even though you were just a small kid. Is that partly why you became a SEAL? If you couldn't help your dad, then you'd help other people. Maybe that's why you resent your injury so much, because it means you can't keep rescuing the world and trying to erase that illogical feeling of guilt. Or keep your..." Her voice trailed.

Dakota knew she'd started to say something about the men he'd lost on his mission. That he couldn't keep them safe.

Yes, he felt responsible—that was probably inevitable as their commanding officer. But he'd remembered enough of what happened after the explosion to know his team had behaved admirably. They'd not only saved *his* life, they'd completed their task and saved the other lives at stake. He might always feel a certain amount of guilt, but he could also take pride in their accomplishments.

"Not to throw fuel on the fire," he said mildly,

"but you have a compulsion to rescue people, too. I'm not one of your patients."

"You know I don't see you that way."

"And you should know I'm being careful."

"*Not if you're planning to compete.* What if you'd hurt yourself out here? You could have been lying there for hours before anyone found you."

Dakota nodded. Noelle was dealing with enough without him adding to her stress, and at the moment she seemed particularly upset. He went through the gate.

"Hey," he murmured, "I'm okay. The rodeo just seems like a good way to show I have the skills needed to run the Soaring Hawk. Actually, it's more than that. Competing would demonstrate I have the determination and drive to make the ranch a success, despite what happened to my leg. This place was a disaster when Jordan took over, but there are no big hurdles left for me to jump, so to speak."

"Since when is doing a good job not enough? Besides, you'd still have the Circle M, whatever happens to your deal with Saul."

"I only own part of the Circle M. Besides, it's a small ranch, barely enough to support one family. Jordan is married with two kids.

Wyatt has his daughter and expects to return to Montana someday. The more land and cattle we have to work, the better."

Noelle narrowed her eyes. "And maybe you also miss the exciting life you had as a Navy SEAL and this is meant to fill the gap. But ranching isn't easy. It's some of the most demanding work in the world—unrelenting, year round effort. There's no need to make it any harder."

Dakota had known that readjusting to civilian life could be difficult—it was for many soldiers—but he hadn't known the hardest part would be meeting a woman like Noelle and finding himself falling in love with her. He also suspected she was starting to feel the same way.

The timing couldn't be worse for either of them, though not because of what she'd told him about the ectopic pregnancy and what it might mean later on.

"We can't resolve this right now," he said quietly. "But I promise to reevaluate whether I should compete."

Then giving in to temptation, he pulled her close, uncertain if he was reassuring her, or himself.

NOELLE LET HERSELF lean in to Dakota for a brief moment. He was all right for now—no newly broken bones or apparent injuries and he'd said he might reconsider competing.

In a way she was surprised he hadn't told her it was none of her business. But maybe they'd gone beyond that.

"I'm sorry," she said finally.

"Why? For having a big heart?" His smiled warmed her. "More people should have hearts like yours."

"I'm supposed to be more clinical, whether or not I'm being a doctor. They did their best in medical school to teach me to be detached. One of my instructors said I'd be eaten alive if I wasn't careful. Her warning didn't do any good."

"Isn't compassion a form of medicine?"

"I think so." Noelle brushed some of the crusted dirt from his coat. "You're a mess and I completely forgot why I was looking for you, which is at Saul's request. He wants to talk."

Dakota stiffened. "About what?"

"Just go talk to him. It isn't about the ranch or that ridiculous agreement—I can tell you that much."

"Fine. Let's go back together."

They rode the short distance to the barn and she urged him to speak with his grandfather while she unsaddled the horses and took care of them, but he refused. The mare didn't necessarily need a complete grooming after such a short ride, but Noelle had been taught young to take care of her horse. Dakota said little as he worked on Tucker and she was distracted, thinking about what he'd said earlier.

It wasn't the first time he'd suggested that she shared his compulsion to rescue people. It was a fair argument. She'd planned to work in disaster relief since she first decided to become a doctor. Helping people was important to her, but that had nothing to do with her concern for him.

Dakota was compelling, with the same blend of strength and compassion she'd seen in other soldiers. Except she'd never felt drawn to them in the same way and couldn't bear to think about him being injured unnecessarily.

You won't be here to see it, an internal voice reminded.

Maybe.

Or maybe not.

She hadn't been willing to give up working in international relief for her ex-husband, but she was willing to do it for a life with Dakota. Not that he'd said anything about the future, but maybe it was time to come home, regardless.

Because of that, she was giving serious consideration to Dr. Wycoff's offer to join the Shelton Medical Clinic—even discussing the option with him and his daughter. Cheyenne was a fine physician and they were close to the same age, though because Noelle had gone to school so much younger, she had more experience, both in emergency medicine and general practice.

And, as it turned out, Cheyenne was scared to fly. She was thrilled at the prospect of having a partner who was comfortable with emergency medical flights—a not uncommon occurrence with Shelton being so far from a hospital. In fact, she and her father were offering generous inducements to convince Noelle to go into partnership with them. With Noelle's reputation, they felt it would be easier to get medical residents to come work in Shelton, too, easing the workload for all of them.

Cheyenne Wycoff's fear of flying was unfortunate, but it meant Noelle would have something unique to contribute. If there was one thing she'd done a lot of, it was flying in both large and small planes, in all sorts of conditions. Besides, a life saved was a life saved, whether it was here in Montana or somewhere far away.

Once Stormy and Tucker were in their stalls, Noelle headed for her SUV, only to have Dakota catch up and grab her hand.

"Uh uh. You're coming with me. Whatever is going on with my grandfather, you're obviously involved."

Her stomach roiled as they went inside. Looking into the open parlor, she saw Jordan and Paige talking. Jordan was shaking his head, a stunned expression on his face— Saul must have already shared the news about Evan Maxwell. It would be a shock to learn your father wasn't that far away after so many years of not knowing where he was.

They found Saul sitting in the front living room, staring at the Christmas tree by the window, a distracted expression on his face. He almost seemed unaware of their presence.

"You wanted to talk. What about?" Dakota prompted when his grandfather didn't say anything.

"Er, a few months ago I found out where

your father is living," Saul said, pulling his gaze away from the cheerfully lit tree. "I've asked if he'll come for Christmas, but he hasn't said one way or the other."

Dakota abruptly dropped into a chair. "I see."

"I don't know where he's been the entire time, but he's sober and working on a ranch. And not solely as a cowhand. Evan is doing his wood carving again."

Dakota looked at Noelle. "The chest I bought for Mishka. You seemed bothered by something you saw on the back."

She nodded. "The artist's mark resembles the Circle M's cattle brand, and there's a larger version on the bottom of the chest. I think your father deliberately sent some of his artwork to the Mistletoe Market on the off chance somebody would recognize it. Sort of a way to test the waters without actually having to face anyone. I didn't have a chance to ask Saul about it until this afternoon. I wanted to be sure before I said anything to you."

Saul leaned forward, a curious tranquility in his eyes. "Dakota, don't be upset with your father. If you want to blame anyone, blame me. Grief can eat you alive—no one knows that better than I do. But instead of helping

Evan when he needed it most, I took his sons away and did a miserable job of raising you."

Dakota released a heavy breath. "You were grieving for Mom, too, I guess."

"And for your grandmother, so I should have understood how lost Evan felt without Victoria. That's how I was when Celina died. While I didn't mess up with alcohol, I messed up in other ways. I'm sorry for all of it. I really thought you'd be better off with me, but it turned out I wasn't much of an improvement."

"Tell me where Dad is. I want to see him."

Noelle gently put her hand on his arm. "Dakota, no matter how long Evan has been sober, the prospect of seeing you could shake him badly. Don't force him before he's ready. He's reaching out in his own way and you should respect that, even if you're upset."

NOELLE SEEMED WORRIED, making Dakota want to hold her again.

What was he thinking? He wanted to hold her forever. But she might not be ready for forever and there were other considerations to work through. "I'm not upset with him," he said slowly. "I've always thought if Dad was still around, he might have trouble facing us. I just want to hear his voice and know that he's really okay. That's all."

"Maybe he'll come for the holiday."

"I got an idea." Saul fumbled for something in his pocket. "I saved a message from Evan. Paige and Anna Beth have been teaching me how to use this cell gadget. They want me to do some social media stuff for the ranch. Maybe we could talk about it and you could, uh, give me advice. It was real smart when you hired someone who could do that web thing for us."

Saul carefully pressed a series of buttons on his smartphone and held it out.

Dakota put the speaker to his ear and heard his dad's voice for the first time since he was a child.

Saul, Carlton tells me you want to talk and I guess it's a good idea. I'll try again later. Please don't let Jordan or Dakota know I called. Or Wyatt... I'm not sure if...well, I'd prefer you not saying anything, but I'll understand if you do. There was a pause. *Dakota is all right, isn't he? I heard he got hurt and was discharged. And I know Jordan and his wife and kids are living at the Soaring Hawk, but don't know anything about Wyatt. So any-*

way, um, bye. I hate these things. Never know when to stop.

The voice was older and more hoarse, but still Evan Maxwell.

Dakota forwarded the message to his own number before returning the phone to Saul. It gave him a minute to collect his emotions, and not just about his dad.

His grandfather was extending a huge olive branch. He'd contacted his despised son-in-law on behalf of his grandsons, had offered Dakota a compliment and asked for his input. In an awkward way, it seemed he was trying to make up for past mistakes.

Dakota even had to wonder if Saul's concern about his injured leg was genuine, rather than an attempt to question his ability to run the ranch. When he thought about it honestly, Saul didn't have a stake in him failing. Not at his age.

"Thanks for letting me listen to that," Dakota said. "I'll give Dad the time he needs. Maybe he *will* come for Christmas."

"I told him he's always welcome."

To Dakota's surprise, Saul thrust out a hand. Though Dakota was still wary, they shook. It felt like a new beginning—one he'd never expected.

Outside the house he looked at Noelle's solemn face. "Once again, I'm sorry I put you in the middle."

She wrinkled her nose. "That's okay. It suggests trust."

"I *do* trust you. Are we on for the Park Carolers tonight? I'd like to make it a real date. If the Hot Diggity Dog Café is open we could have an early dinner before going to the park."

Her eyes widened. "A real date? Wow. I'm impres—"

"Romantic?" a loud voice interrupted from the horse barn. It was Blair facing off with Alex, and even at a distance, her outrage was unmistakable. "Having Melody or Carmen leave your class ring in a fancy box on my pillow wasn't romantic, it was too much. I said we could talk—that didn't mean we were getting back together again. You've always believed you fell in love with me first. *Hah.* I'm the one who hung around until you finally figured it out. For once, *you're* going to have to do the work."

Dakota exchanged a look with Noelle. Obviously things weren't going well with the two ranch hands.

Alex held up his hands in a peacemaking

gesture. "I want you to have it, Blair, no matter what happens. I should have given you a proper engagement ring to begin with, so this is my way of saying I still care and want to try."

Blair lifted her arm and hurled something at him. Glints of gold sparkled in the weak winter sunlight.

"Jeepers, Blair, would you stop doing that?" he yelled, ducking. "That ring is heavy."

"You think I don't know it? I wore it around my neck for five years."

"Tell him, Blair," cried Eduardo. He was watching the altercation with Rod. Apparently they were her cheering section.

Alex glared. "Stay out of this, Eduardo."

"Nah. I'm taking bets on how long it's going to take you to crawl out of that hole you dug for yourself. I have to be around to keep track of who wins."

Dakota bent his head. "Am I in a hole, too?" he whispered in Noelle's ear.

"I don't think so. We haven't even gone on our first date." Her eyes were both amused and sympathetic as she watched the two cowhands. "But I'm having onion rings if we're going to the Hot Diggity Dog for dinner, so you're forewarned in case any kissing is anticipated."

"No problem, I'll order them, too."

His blood surged at the prospect of kissing Noelle again. He wasn't going to fool himself; they had plenty of challenges to overcome. Possibly more than Alex and Blair, though watching their argument had given him an idea—a just-in-case-I-want-to-be-prepared-with-an-engagement-ring.

"I'm tempted to say something here about the challenges of young love, but I'm not sure it's easier at any age. Besides, they're adults," she whispered. "And they've gone through more troubles than many older couples."

Alex and Blair had dropped their voices, but Dakota could tell the discussion had continued from the animated way they both continued to talk. He might have to speak to them once things calmed down. Making a scene in front of everyone wasn't the best idea. He'd overlooked it the first time, but repeatedly doing that in front of fellow employees could get to be a problem.

Melody came around the corner of the building and tapped both Eduardo and Rod on their shoulders, indicating the show was over. She was a good second-in-command;

it had been clear from the start why Jordan had relied on her so much. Dakota planned to officially make her his backup on the ranch, with a corresponding pay raise. It seemed the right thing to do and he didn't think his brother or grandfather would object.

He turned to Noelle. "I need to shower if I'm taking you to dinner. I assume the café is still a casual restaurant."

"As far as I know. Go ahead and clean up. I'll call to see if they're open today."

"Good idea."

Feeling remarkably pleased with life, Dakota headed for his quarters. Even the ache in his body from hitting the ground repeatedly didn't bother him, not with the prospect of an evening with Noelle.

THAT NIGHT A large number of people wandered between the brilliantly lit trees in the park square, admiring the community Christmas tree, along with the other decorations.

Noelle watched her breath fog in the air, which was suffused with the scent of evergreen, spice and chocolate. She didn't think there was a better fragrance in the world.

Dakota frowned at his cup of cocoa with a red-and-white candy cane sticking out of it.

He gave Noelle a skeptical look. "Doesn't the candy cane melt and get gooey?"

"That's the point. You use the cane to stir the cocoa and it gets all peppermintful. Then you refill the cup a few times and munch down the candy cane when you're done. If there's any left."

He grinned. "Peppermintful? I don't think there's any such word."

"My creative use of language is a time-honored tradition, starting when I got excited as a two-year-old and said something about Sainkerpat's day."

Dakota lifted an eyebrow at her. "Sainkerpat's day?"

"Saint Patrick's Day. I don't personally remember saying it—I was very young, but my family tells the story on a regular basis."

"You have a nice family. I've never seen Jordan happier than he is with Paige."

"We're fond of him, too. Come on, let's get a snipdoodle cookie. And no, I didn't make *that* one up. Snipdoodle is another name for snickerdoodle."

"I'm glad you're educating me on these issues."

"Don't look now, but we might be seeing Part Two, The Sequel," Dakota murmured after they'd each gotten a cookie and had their cocoa refilled.

"What? *Oh.*" Noelle saw what he meant— Alex and Blair were at the edge of the park and appeared to be in the middle of another dispute. "Come on, they don't need us watching them."

Noelle turned and headed for the bandstand where the others were gathering to hear the singers from the senior center. Nana Harriet was in the group and always sang with enthusiasm, if not a great deal of talent.

"You said you didn't see the point of Christmas," she asked Dakota as they waited. "Is that still true?"

"IT'S BEEN OKAY this year," Dakota answered cautiously. After all, how could he dislike a holiday that meant so much to her? "I should have told you that Saul got custody of us in December. So for me, the season is a reminder of how our lives got torn apart. Though that really happened when Mom died and Dad started buying whiskey to get him through the nights. Then it wasn't just the nights when he needed help, it was the days, too."

"I'm sorry." Noelle hugged his arm to her body, making him wish he hadn't worn such a heavy coat. There was too much fabric between them.

"It's okay," he said. "Doing this holiday stuff with you has reminded me about how much my mother loved Christmas. I guess it was easier not to celebrate, than to think about how things used to be. Maybe that's why Saul called Christmas a bother. But now those early memories feel extra special to me."

"I think your grandfather is realizing now how much he missed over the years. Regret is awful because we can't go back and change the past."

"His big concern was that my brothers and I would turn out like our father. Instead I turned into a grouch like him."

"I told you, you're not a grouch," Noelle protested. "But I'm glad you're getting in the spirit."

"Thanks. I think. Oh, I was going to move everything you want from the attic to the other house tomorrow, but do you mind if I take care of it on Tuesday?" He had an engagement ring to arrange if it was going to be ready for Christmas.

"No problem. I can make my fruitcake for the treat table at the homestead cabin. I already have the fruit soaking in orange juice, which I prefer over liqueur, though it doesn't hold as long."

"Fruitcake?" Dakota couldn't help making a face.

"You might be surprised. I'm using dates, dried apples, candied pineapple and cherries instead of citron. It's an old family recipe and very popular. Not the least bit dry. But I'm also serving molasses cookies, applesauce cake, gingerbread and Victorian sponge cake with raspberry filling. I'll fudge a little on my historic theme and add fresh fruit and veggies for the healthier-minded."

"I can go along with the rest of the menu. Do you have your dress yet?"

"It should arrive soon. Paige had a good idea about contacting the high school drama department, but the costumes were tossed after the roof leaked six years ago. I found something on the internet instead."

Just then the choir began singing, drawing both their attention.

Because he knew it would please Noelle, Dakota decided to order an Edwardian-style suit for himself, or to look for one in Bozeman when he was there tomorrow. Making her happy had become his priority.

CHAPTER FOURTEEN

"You okay, bro?" Jordan asked as Dakota cleaned manure from a horse stall, late that evening. Quite unnecessarily, since two of the hands had already mucked them earlier.

"I'm fine."

Jordan picked up a pitchfork and joined in. "Big news today about Dad. I suppose you're angrier than ever at Saul."

"I'm still making up my mind."

"Dad was a wreck back then, you know. Driving drunk, getting arrested for bar fights and other trouble. It was also his choice to stay away all these years and not get in contact."

"Saul could have helped him, instead he was left alone."

"Which Saul understands and is sorry about," Jordan said seriously. "But I'm not sure Dad wanted help. He was self-destructing in front of us. Maybe he had to hit absolute bottom before he could get up."

Dakota frowned. He'd idolized Evan, but *could* the presence and encouragement of his sons have made a difference? Jordan was saying the situation had been much worse than his younger brothers had known. He must have shielded them from the worst of the gossip between their classmates, or else they hadn't paid attention, too lost in their own troubles.

"I remember nights when Dad wasn't there."

Jordan nodded. "And other nights when the sheriff brought him home so drunk he could barely walk. Sheriff Cranston did his best. I know he was worried. He'd bring us gallons of milk and bags of burgers from the Hot Diggity Dog Café, concerned we weren't getting enough to eat. So the truth is, sooner or later the authorities would have taken us away. Probably sooner. We might not have resented Saul as much if he hadn't been the one to initiate the custody issue, but we still would have ended up on the Soaring Hawk or in foster homes." Jordan lifted the handles of the wheelbarrow filled with manure. "I'll run this out to a compost heap and get fresh straw. Back in a minute."

Dakota appreciated having a couple of minutes alone. The thought of foster homes was disturbing—they could have been separated or sent to different communities. Life at the Soaring Hawk may have been grim, but at least they'd been together.

He'd taken for granted how much the three of them had relied on each other. Even as adults, when serving in different parts of the world, they'd video chatted, emailed or sent a quick text when they weren't on a mission. For that matter, while new sailors weren't generously paid, when Jordan enlisted he'd arranged for his younger brothers to have spending money and a cell phone that only they knew about. Talking hadn't always been possible in case Saul caught them and took it away, but they'd texted often.

It was another nice recollection he hadn't pulled out in a long time. Noelle was having quite an impact on him.

He *did* have good memories, even from when they were living with Saul. Their grandfather had loosened up after Jordan enlisted, letting Wyatt and him spend more time with friends and take part in the rodeo and the Shelton Youth Ranching Association.

As the Maxwell brother who'd looked like Saul's estranged son-in-law, Jordan had gotten the worst end of everything. He'd enlisted at seventeen, right out of high school, believing his brothers' lives would improve if he was gone. He deserved the life he had now with Paige and the children.

Dakota wiped his forehead. Was there any chance he deserved a life like that with Noelle? If they couldn't have kids the regular way, he was fine with adoption. Plenty of children needed homes.

"You have an interesting expression on your face," Jordan said as he returned with the straw. "Does it have anything to do with my lovely sister-in-law, with whom you've been spending so much time lately?"

"I'd say it's none of your business, but you're my brother, so I'm going with, how did you guess?"

Jordan chuckled. "You have the same bemused expression I used to see in the mirror when Paige and I were getting to know each other. The Bannerman women are a force to be reckoned with."

Dakota agreed. "Except it's a little complicated for me. Noelle is an international relief doctor and I'm a ranch foreman. A *new* ranch foreman."

"You don't have to stay in Montana."

"I do for the next year. I signed a contract with Saul."

"Contracts can be renegotiated. Saul might be willing to count the time you spent working here after high school, waiting for Wyatt to graduate."

Dakota began pitching the fresh straw into the stalls to replace the small amount of soiled bedding they'd removed. "Except I wouldn't feel as if I'd done my part in earning the ranch. Noelle calls the agreement ridiculous, but the Soaring Hawk is valuable. Maybe I *should* prove I have what it takes to be a cattleman. All that aside, she's only been divorced a short time. I don't know that she's ready for another commitment."

"Paige believes her sister's marriage was doomed from the start."

"Yeah, because her ex asked her to stop being who she is," Dakota retorted. "I'd never want Noelle to change or stop doing something she believes is right."

"And I'm sure she wouldn't ask you to stop being a cattleman. It's who you are at heart. She grew up on a ranch and must understand."

Dakota recalled the gut sensation he'd felt about needing to check the herds on Thanksgiving Day and the cow he'd found tangled in polypropylene twine. Life on the ranch was becoming second nature again, the sense of being connected to the land. It was a good sensation, one that had been missing in his life.

"I should have asked before, did someone call Wyatt about Dad?" he asked.

Jordan's face turned solemn. "I called before we left for the park. I couldn't say too much, only that we know where dad is living. He just learned he's being transferred again after the New Year, so that's his immediate concern. I told him I'd fly out after Christmas to lend him a hand with packing and looking after Christie, but he refused. Says he can't let me be away with Daniel still being so young."

"Why can't they leave him in Hawaii longer?"

"Because the Navy puts someone where they want them to be, not the other way around. You know that."

Dakota hunched his shoulder. He did know that. His brother wasn't going to tell him anything he didn't already know. Or probably be as forthright about it as Noelle had been. A *furious* Noelle, he thought, thinking about the flush in her cheeks and how her golden-brown eyes had flashed fire as she called him out for taking unnecessary risks.

She hadn't been a doctor talking—she'd been a woman, worried about a man.

All right.

It was possible that becoming a Navy SEAL had helped assuage the feeling he'd failed his father, or at least the conviction that being together might have made a difference to his dad's drinking. But he'd been six when his mother died. Dakota understood why Evan hadn't been able to comfort his sons, but Noelle was right that it hadn't been his children's job to save Evan.

A weight seemed to ease, along with a measure of the other guilt he carried. He would never duck responsibility for his own actions, but he also didn't have to carry a weight that didn't belong to him.

"—extra weekend between Thanksgiving and Christmas."

Dakota realized his mind had drifted while his brother was talking. "What's that?"

"I was saying we were lucky to have an extra weekend between Thanksgiving and Christmas this year. It made getting ready for the ranch homes tour easier for Noelle."

"She's taking it in her stride. I thought the

crew would be unhappy about the additional work of decorating, but they seem to love doing it for her. By the way, I'm giving Melody a pay raise and officially making her my backup as of January first. Seems only right to recognize she's been given extra responsibilities."

"Excellent. She's gotten bonuses, but I'm sure she'll appreciate having the situation formalized." Jordan yawned. "Sorry. Daniel is sleeping better, but not always through the night."

"As if you mind."

Jordan grinned. "Not a bit. Paige and I have discussed whether to have another baby, but at the moment, we're enjoying the two children we already have. Not to mention being run off our feet with them. See you tomorrow, bro."

"Night."

Dakota put the shovel and pitchfork away, along with the wheelbarrow, and adjusted the barn's lights. After taking out his phone, he checked to see if he'd gotten a response to his email to the jewelry designer. He had. She was excited to work on his project and willing to deliver before Christmas, except she didn't know if the gemstones he wanted were available. Good emeralds were rare. She'd already sent inquiries to suppliers and had created several designs for him to evaluate.

Excellent.

He'd go into town tomorrow and speak with her in person, choosing which design he wanted. This particular jeweler at the Mistletoe Market had impressed him. He'd bought a pair of earrings and a pendant of gold holly leaves accented with rubies for Noelle, which had given him the idea for something else.

He just hoped Noelle would have faith that no matter what, they belonged together.

THE FOLLOWING SUNDAY evening Blair was still resisting Alex's determined romantic assault. It wasn't that she didn't love and forgive him, but she needed to be sure they wouldn't have a future built out of cards, collapsing the next time a challenge was thrown their way.

He'd brought her roses, a crystal Christmas ornament and a dozen other gifts. They were nice, but they were just things.

Because the decorating on the ranch would require a burst of activity this coming week, Dakota had given them extra time off over the weekend. Yesterday the Christmas Bake-Off had seen a huge turnout, with Alex's mother winning a grand prize for her sweet potato cheesecake in one category and a blue ribbon for her raspberry orange scones in another. She'd beamed and hugged all of them, whispering "Thanks" in Blair's ear.

Blair couldn't take complete credit for Alex being at the Bake-Off. Besides, he'd still been wearing his coat and a turtleneck sweater pulled high up his neck, though it was warm inside the community center and there was no need to stay so heavily wrapped. There might be a few curious looks in the beginning if he stopped covering up so much of his neck and jaw, but it would probably be because people had forgotten what he looked like after so long.

Tonight Blair had driven into town alone to watch the Park Carolers. She just wished Alex would be more patient. He'd put her through over two years of heartache; he shouldn't blame her for wanting to be sure that whatever happened, they could weather it together.

The town's amateur barbershop quartet was singing, but Blair hovered at the edge of the park, looking up and wishing stars were visible to wish on. Instead it was dark overhead and tiny bits of snow were swirl-

ing as if she was in the middle of a giant
snow globe.

"Hey, Blair. I brought you a candy cane."

She sighed and accepted the candy from
Alex. As usual his neck and jaw were wrapped
with a thick scarf. It was cold, but not *that*
cold. Though…maybe he was more suscep-
tible because of the scarring, something she
might know if he hadn't avoided her since the
accident. At least they were finally talking.

Alex cleared his throat. "Are you mad at
me again?"

"I'm not sure I've ever stopped being mad,
to be honest."

"That's fair. But I'd still like you to give us
another chance."

Blair glanced around the park, hoping her
aunt and uncle weren't around. Or her cousins, who had a habit of being overprotective—
though admittedly, even if she didn't need
their support, knowing she had it was nice.

"I just don't understand why you pushed
me away in the first place," she said finally.
"We should have been able to get through this
together. I wanted to be there for you because
I loved you. Nothing else."

For the first time Alex seemed less defensive, more thoughtful. "Okay. Confession time.

When I woke up and finally understood what had happened, I got really angry and sorry for myself. Then I started thinking how beautiful and caring you are. It used to seem like you were the popular one and people just included me for your sake. I didn't mind before the accident, but I was afraid you'd feel sorry for me now that I was going to have all these scars. And I felt guilty, so deep down, I didn't think I deserved you, either."

Her eyes widened. "Guilty about the accident?"

"Yeah. When they were putting me into the ambulance I heard the deputy tell someone that I didn't cause the crash, but a more experienced driver might have prevented what happened."

Blair sighed. "You could say that about almost anything. We can always find a reason to feel responsible. I felt guilty because if I hadn't gotten stomach flu, we might have gone riding together, instead of you driving that load of hay. And your father felt guilty about the tire blowing. He agonized, thinking he might have missed seeing a problem or left a maintenance issue undone."

"It wasn't his fault—I hit a piece of metal on the road."

"You didn't tell anyone that."

Alex looked chagrinned. "I've made a lot of mistakes. I didn't want to talk about it and figured everyone knew because of what the deputy had said."

"Sometimes life stinks," Blair said, "and if you don't trust the people who love you, then it's going to stink even more. If we're going to have a future, you have to promise we're a team. You can't make decisions for both of us—we have to share in the good and the bad."

"I get that. Do you still love me?"

His face was so yearning and hopeful, that she wanted to hug him. "Yes, but we need to get to know each other again. We've barely been together since you were in the hospital. And I don't know how you could think people were only friends with you because of me. I figured other kids were putting up with me because we were buddies."

"No way."

"Yes, way. I wasn't born in Montana and I didn't fit in for a long time. But you were always there and had my back."

"You did fine at college by yourself. I looked at your social media postings for a while, but it hurt too much. You were constantly doing something with somebody—a lot of somebodys I'd never met."

"I hoped you were looking. It was the only way I could tell you what was happening. And maybe I also hoped you'd get upset and call me," Blair admitted.

"I wanted to a thousand times. But the longer I didn't get in touch, the more it seemed you didn't need me."

Blair shook her head. "Oh, Alex, those were just photos of friends and things I was doing. I missed you so much, but I had to keep going, hoping you'd remember how much I loved you."

Alex seemed to steel himself, then he pulled the heavy winter scarf off, exposing his jaw and neck. "You love me, even with this? There are more scars, even worse. This is what you'd be living with if we work things out." He took off his coat and unbuttoned his shirt, pulling the fabric aside to reveal the extensive scarring on his chest and shoulder. The white lights strung on a nearby tree illuminated them in stark clarity.

Her eyes burned, but not because she was repulsed. Showing her was an act of trust and most of the hurt in her own heart eased with the understanding.

After stepping forward, she kissed his jaw and put her hand over the worst scar on his shoulder.

"The only reason these matter is because of the pain they caused," she whispered. "I see you, Alex, not scars. You want to know why I fell in love with you? It's because you were kind and decent. Because you made me laugh in the middle of being mad at the world and my mother for dumping me. I loved the guy who could name all of the constellations in the night sky and wanted to be my friend, even when I barely knew one end of a cow from the other. I fell in love for a million different reasons and none of them had to do with how you look."

"Me, too. I mean, you're beautiful, but I'd love you no matter what, because you're amazing." He shivered. "Uh, maybe I should put my coat back on."

"Yeah, you're going to freeze."

Alex hurriedly rebuttoned his heavy flannel shirt and donned his coat again. He left the scarf lying on the ground.

Though he didn't realize it, revealing his scars was the act of trust Blair had needed… the one thing that could convince her they still had a chance.

She grabbed his arm. "Let's get some hot chocolate to warm you up. My treat."

He laughed. "It's free."

"So is love."

A happy, easygoing smile filled his face and she saw the Alex she'd fallen in love with again, just a little older, and hopefully a little wiser.

She had a feeling they were going to succeed this time.

"DEFINITELY THAT ONE," Noelle said, looking at the pine tree Dakota had suggested he cut.

They already had four trees stacked on the bed of the pickup, and needed two more. At the crest of the hill above them rows of prayer flags blew in the breeze between tall pines, colorful symbols of the good wishes she was sending for the world. Luckily a small snowstorm had blown itself out by midnight the evening before, and the morning had dawned clear and bright. She wanted to honor the beliefs of the people in the Himalayas and had hoped to hang the flags under the right circumstances.

As it turned out, the timing was even better than she'd thought. The reason Dakota had suggested they come today was because he'd done his own research—the tenth day of the lunar cycle was considered an auspicious day to hang the flags. Instead of thinking she was being foolishly sentimental, he was supporting her and the wonderful people she'd met and their traditions.

She watched him cutting the pine and fell in love with him even more than before. He did everything so simply, without fuss or posturing.

Dakota lifted the large tree onto the pickup. The tallest ones extended well over the tailgate, perfect for either side of the horse barn doors.

She was having a decorating party tomorrow evening. Finally she'd have everyone—family, friends and ranch hands—together, drinking eggnog and wassail and eating treats with Christmas music wafting through the air.

Dakota had laughed and agreed *not* to do everything himself with his crew like they'd done when her evergreen swag and garland was delivered. They'd done a nice job of putting it up, but she wanted at least one communal evening where they were all working and decorating together. She'd gotten them all *thank-you* gifts and would give them out then.

Saul was excited by the prospect of having a party and had ordered several four-foot long sandwiches from the town deli, though Anna Beth had insisted on making green chili stew to go with them.

Noelle stretched and yawned, feeling her old energy bubbling again. Maybe it was Christmas. And maybe it was Dakota.

Or both.

"You look happy," he said.

"I am. This is my favorite time of year." Noelle gave him a serious look. "But even though I love the holiday trappings, it's the underlying spirit that matters most. You get that, right? I mean, all this decorating is fun and beautiful, but the real treasure is from something we don't see."

He hugged her close. "I understand. At least, I do now."

Noelle had never seen his eyes so warm and tender. Hope blossomed in her heart, more intense than it ever had before. She was still concerned about him committing to a relationship that might not include children, but she couldn't think about that now.

Besides, it was something he would have to decide.

The last week had been more enjoyable than she had imagined. The homestead cabin was lovely, with just enough furniture to give it a homey feel. A wedding ring quilt adorned one of the beds, and the other was spread with one in the old Dresden plate patchwork pattern. Nana Harriet had insisted on making two sets of eyelet dust ruffles and pillow shams, saying someone in the family would want them.

Noelle had expected to grieve terribly while making up the baby cradle, yet the pain had been eased by Dakota's presence. He'd helped her spread the antique bedding, followed by a kiss that made her heart soar.

He'd also guessed her secret wish to have the kitchen china hutch and old dishes brought over. She'd found the hutch had been given a place of honor, the blue-and-white china sparkling clean, standing up on the plate racks. Ever since, she'd felt the spirit of Ehawee Hawkins in the house, smiling because her beloved home was no longer empty and forgotten.

And on the front doorway was a cluster of

mistletoe, put up by Dakota. He'd swept her into a passionate embrace beneath it, saying they were obligated to honor the tradition involved or it was bad luck. He'd used that excuse several times since then—not that she was objecting.

"Shall we pick the last tree?" Noelle asked lightly.

"Sure. How about that one?"

He pointed to a likely fir, but when she got close, Noelle wrinkled her nose. "I don't think so."

"What's wrong?" he protested. "It's the best one we've seen. Great shape, nice, full branches. Just the right height."

"Yeah, but a skunk has sprayed here recently. Smell it?"

Dakota stepped and closer made a face. "That's pretty bad. Even worse than a pair of old, reeking boots."

"It would make an interesting addition to the Christmas home tour, but not one people would enjoy. I can see guests dashing away, wondering if a certain black-and-white animal is going to appear. And I don't mean Buddy."

He chuckled. "Buddy would probably be hiding under my bed if there was a skunk. He encountered one last summer evidently and it took forever for him to stop smelling awful, even though Jordan and the veterinarian did their best to clean him up. Must have been tough with a cat. They aren't known for co-operating. Maybe that's why Buddy is extra friendly now—he remembers being persona non grata with humans and beasts alike."

"Poor Buddy. I'll have to give him some extra attention."

DAKOTA MIGHT HAVE been jealous of the cat, but one of the great things about falling for Noelle was knowing she had plenty of love to share.

He tied ropes across their cargo and drove back toward the Soaring Hawk until he saw a promising stand of pines.

Noelle hopped out of the truck and began evaluating the various trees. "Let's take this one," she said. "Not as good as the other one, but the branches are nicely spaced for deco-rating."

Dakota cut the tree and put it on top of the others. He sniffed around the load, trying to detect any hint of skunk, but it just smelled like Christmas.

Christmas?

Yeah, Noelle had done her magic.

He was completely hooked by the holiday spirit…and by the amazing woman who'd come into his life like an unending shower of shooting stars.

CHAPTER FIFTEEN

ON THE NIGHT of the first tour, Noelle did the finishing touches on the serving table, pleased with how everything looked. She would re-stock the platters as the evening wore on, assuming they had that many visitors. The treats were spread out in the room to the right of the front door, which might have served as a less formal gathering area for the family when they expanded the house.

The tours would be today and tomorrow evenings from five to eight, and repeat the following weekend, concluding on the twenty-third. She was keeping her fingers crossed that the weather would cooperate.

Dakota had lit the fireplaces early in the day, keeping them going while she worked on other tasks for the evening ahead. The temperature was comfortable, if not toasty warm—old fireplaces were lovely, but they weren't the most efficient way to heat a home by modern standards.

She was surprised when the front door opened since it was a half hour before guests were supposed to begin arriving. The air whooshed from her lungs at the sight of Dakota dressed as an Edwardian gentleman from head to toe. He even wore a black top hat and carried one of the fine walking canes she'd seen in photographs from the era.

"Good evening, Miss Bannerman." He bowed slightly.

"Good evening, Mr. Maxwell. You're elegant tonight."

"And you are as always lovely."

Noelle adjusted the white tie above his white waistcoat. "Very fashionable," she murmured. "But I didn't think you'd want to dress the part."

"Is that why you didn't ask? I wondered. Yet how could I resist when I knew you would enjoy it so much?"

"Sweet-talker. You like my gown, then?"

"Wild about it."

She lifted her eyebrows. "Did you even look?"

"It's red."

He was partly right. She wore a long, flowing red dress with a black lace and bead overlay falling from her shoulders and again from her waist. Her only jewelry was a pair of re-production chandelier earrings with green-and-clear crystals. The dress and strands of black crystals in her upswept hair sparkled so much, she didn't need anything else.

The rest of the ranch glistened with modern Christmas lights, but inside the original house she'd used electric bulbs that simulated old-style gas flames. The Christmas trees on the porch and inside the house were illuminated by strings of lights formed to look like candles, while red velvet ribbons and strings of "pearls" were entwined with garland throughout. She hadn't ignored the second floor—though it was blocked off, each window had a trio of faux candles glowing in welcome. Retro-styled solar lamps lighted the walkway to the porch.

The ranch crew had volunteered to take turns directing traffic. There was coffee and other treats in the ranch office for when they needed to get warm or just wanted to kick back and relax.

The decorating party on Tuesday had turned out the way Noelle had hoped, ending with a light snowfall that frosted the trees and made the place look even more like the snow globe she'd gotten for her sister. The snow had continued until the next morning—not a blizzard, but enough to slow travel. Luckily the weather had cleared before noon as predicted—she'd seen Dakota's tension through the morning as he debated whether he'd made the right choice not to put out feed for the herd. But the snow still wasn't so deep the cattle couldn't easily get to the dry grass beneath.

"We might not have as many visitors over here," Noelle said, wanting to be prepared. "The main house will be the most popular, and having two places to visit on one ranch is unusual, though the tour committee seemed excited by the idea and immediately advertised."

"That's okay. More for me." Dakota took a slice of fruitcake from the platter and popped half into his mouth.

Noelle grinned. Ever since he'd cautiously tasted her fruitcake the first time, he couldn't get enough. She'd made several additional batches, along with other treats, to keep him fed with all the Christmas goodies he hadn't been able to enjoy since he was a little boy.

The flashing of headlights through the window caught her attention and she looked out. A stream of cars was pulling into the main ranch and the ranch hands came out, pointing and directing them to parking areas.

"Hey, look," she said. "Your crew is wearing Santa hats and light strings around their necks."

"They wanted to add something to the tour. You were so thorough with the decorating, they had trouble finding something you hadn't already thought of doing."

"That's sweet."

She was delighted to see several large groups headed in their direction first, laughing and talking.

Dakota kissed her cheek. "Looks like the show is starting."

Noelle nodded and squeezed his hand. Things were going well between them, so well she was almost worried. But with everything they'd both gone through the past year, surely they were due for their share of Christmas joy.

And falling in love had to be the best Christmas gift of all.

DAKOTA WOKE EARLIER than usual on Christmas morning and promptly got up to work in the horse barn. The steady, familiar task of cleaning after the horses was peaceful. It was even festive with the decorations Noelle had put up.

Noelle.

He paused a moment to make sure the jeweler's box was in his pocket, delivered just few days earlier by the designer. The ring wasn't a traditional engagement ring, but he hoped it would suit a woman so devoted to Christmas.

A truck drove into the main ranch as he started pitching straw in the cleaned stalls. Probably one of the ranch hands, coming back for something they'd left behind. But twenty minutes later footsteps sounded. He looked up and froze.

"Hello, son. Merry Christmas."

Dakota dropped the pitchfork and grabbed his father into a fierce hug, the years falling away.

Noelle had already shown him Christmas magic, and this was simply another demonstration.

"Merry Christmas, Dad."

"I'm so sorry," Evan whispered. "Can you ever forgive me?"

"Sure. Just don't ever go away again."

They stepped back a few inches and grasped

forearms, son and father, looking into each other's face, unwilling to let go.

"Saul has offered me a job here on the Soaring Hawk," Evan said finally. "You're the foreman, so if it's all right with you, I'll accept."

"Of course it's all right."

"My needs are simple these days. A place to work and sleep, and if it isn't too much trouble, a spot to work on my larger carvings when I'm not otherwise occupied. Saul thought I might set up a work bench in a corner of the equipment barn, subject to your approval."

"You've got it."

"The important thing is the chance to know my sons again," Evan said gravely. "And to get acquainted with Jordan's wife and children, and maybe Wyatt's daughter, someday."

Dakota nodded. He hoped by the end of the day, Evan would have a future daughter-in-law.

They stopped at the foreman's quarters for Dakota to wash and change, then went up to the house where Evan had already briefly greeted the family. Mishka promptly hugged her new grandpa and wouldn't let go of him.

Noelle smiled at them. She'd arrived early,

ahead of her parents and brothers, and Dakota pulled her against his chest, hoping his arms would never feel empty again.

NOELLE LOVED THAT Dakota wasn't shy about holding her in front of his family. Aside from wrapping gifts together in his office, they'd found little time alone since the first evening of the tour. Work on a ranch never ended and Dakota refused to ask more of his employees than he was willing to do himself.

The tours had been a big success, visitors loving the period feel of the homestead house and refreshments. More local residents than usual had bought tickets—for many it had been their first opportunity to see either home at the Soaring Hawk. The committee was already talking about next year.

She and Dakota had also gone into town for the Park Carolers and every other holiday event. The crowded celebrations had offered no chances for private snuggles or intimate conversation, but the look in Dakota's eyes had given her delicious shivers.

Quite obviously, Alex and Blair hadn't worried about privacy in a public setting. They'd been too busy kissing to pay much attention to onlookers, seeming determined to catch up on lost time. But when Noelle had spotted a shiny engagement ring on Blair's finger, she'd managed to get a confirmation from the couple.

Yes, they were engaged again, to be married in June.

Noelle was afraid that meant Dakota was losing his two newest cowhands. But there *had* to be other men and women wanting to work for him. He'd swiftly earned a reputation for fairness, and now Evan would be employed at the Soaring Hawk. She expected Dakota's periodic moodiness would ease now that his health and outlook were improving, but time would tell.

"You've been claimed by your granddaughter," Noelle said to Evan as he held Mishka, who was enthralled with the carved Christmas cat ornament her newfound grandpa had given her.

Evan smiled. "I can't think of anything better. She's lovely."

"We think so. Daniel is as cute as can be, too. You'll see when he's awake."

He shook his head, looking bemused. "Hard to believe I'm a grandfather three-times-over. The thought never crossed my mind when I was nineteen and raising a ruckus all over the county."

Noelle liked Evan. The years and his own demons had been hard on him, but there was peace in his eyes. Like Saul, he'd weathered the storms of loss and grief and finally found his feet again. But while Evan looked like an older version of Jordan, his personality, muted by years of drinking and hard living, reminded her the most of Dakota.

"I've heard about your practical jokes," she said lightly. "Like when you put a half-grown bull in the bride's room at the church before a wedding."

Evan looked rueful. "I feel bad about that."

"Maybe it made the day even more memorable. Your old pranks aren't too different than the ones Dakota pulled in Shelton, so he was just keeping up the tradition."

"What?" Dakota whispered in her ear.

She cocked her head. "Did you think nobody else knew you were responsible for those pranks? *Everybody* knew except Saul. Sheriff Cranston cleaned the water tower himself. He didn't want a fuss made."

Dakota looked stunned. "I don't know what to say."

"It's okay. Everyone understood, and nobody wanted you to get in trouble at home."

BECAUSE OF NOELLE, Dakota had begun appreciating his hometown again. The idea that everyone, including the sheriff, had understood his rebellion and protected him from Saul was another revelation.

Shelton wasn't perfect, but it was a great place with people who cared.

Saul didn't seem bothered by having his formerly estranged son-in-law in the house. The two men even put their heads together and talked cattle for a while. But when Saul suggested they play a game of checkers, Anna Beth put her foot down.

"My husband is a wizard with checkers and I'm not having him trounce anyone on Christmas."

"Victoria used to say it was her father's favorite game." Evan got up and took one of the gifts from under the tree. "Saul, I made this for you after we talked that first time."

Saul opened the package. Inside was an inlaid wood checkerboard and playing pieces. "Almost too nice to use," he said. "But I'm not gonna let that stop me."

Dakota caught his grandfather's gaze and was amazed to see tears swimming in his eyes. In that moment, he understood the depth of regret Saul felt about the past and his recognition of how much he had missed. But with Noelle next to him, Dakota didn't feel triumph, just a sense of life falling into place.

Saul wasn't a bad person, he'd simply made mistakes, the same way Evan had made mistakes. Dakota could only hope he didn't make mistakes just as big.

The rest of the Bannerman family arrived and they decided to open gifts with everyone taking turns playing Santa and handing out presents one at a time. When Dakota received a beautifully wrapped package, perfect in every detail, he didn't need to look at the card to know it was from Noelle.

Her note said, *I know it isn't the same, but you can start a new tradition.* Inside he found an antique fourteen-karat-gold pocket watch. He gave her a swift kiss, whispering "Thank you" against her lips.

"Dad, look at this." Dakota showed his father.

"That's just like the one I used to have." Evan gave Noelle a smile. "Dakota loved that watch."

The watch was passed around and admired, along with the other gifts, which included items for Evan. When Noelle and Paige discovered he might be there for Christmas, they'd wanted to be sure he felt included.

Noelle gasped when she opened the gold holly leaf pendant and earrings Dakota had gotten her. After the family admired them, she put them on and got up to see how they looked in the foyer mirror.

Dakota followed her and collected their coats from the coat tree. "Let's get a breath of air," he murmured. "I need to talk to you."

"OKAY," NOELLE AGREED with a last look at the beautiful gold holly leaves adorned with ruby "berries." She didn't wear much jewelry, but couldn't imagine anything more perfect.

Outside, Dakota led her to a wicker love seat behind one of the outdoor Christmas trees, a private nook where they couldn't be seen from any of the windows.

"You're missing Christmas with your dad," she said.

Dakota traced her lips with the tip of his finger. "There's plenty of time. I'm thrilled my father is here, but this is more important."

"It is?"

"Yes. I never thought I'd say this to a woman, but I'm in love with you, Noelle. Absolutely, head over heels, love-you-forever in love. The kind of love I didn't believe I was capable of feeling. Will you marry me?"

Noelle's heart skipped. She'd hoped for a proposal, yet now she hesitated, wanting to be sure. "I've talked to Dr. Wycoff and his daughter about practicing medicine in Shelton. They've offered me a partnership."

Dakota shook his head. "I'd never ask you to stay in Montana. It's your choice. Whatever we need to do, we can make it work. I'll get a job somewhere else, maybe as a consultant. Ex-SEALs can write their own ticket with security companies."

"You already know I was considering my options. I *want* to come back," Noelle insisted. She hadn't cared about having a long-distance marriage with her ex-husband; it was a different matter entirely with Dakota. "The Soaring Hawk is part of your heritage. I just need to be sure you understand I might not be able to have children." Her voice broke as she said it.

Dakota looked into her eyes. "Noelle, if we can't have kids the usual way, I'm completely okay with adoption. Please take a chance on me." He reached inside his coat and took out a jewelry box. "This might be an unconventional engagement ring, but I had it designed especially for you."

Noelle held her breath. Designed for her? Then he'd been thinking about marriage for a while.

She opened the box and saw a ring with dazzling marquis emeralds and round rubies, set to resemble a cluster of holly leaves and berries. And inside the band she saw the words, *To Noelle, My Christmas Joy.*

Dakota slid the ring over her finger.

"I talked to Saul about us living in the old homestead house," Dakota said. "Not because I expected it, but as a 'just in case' scenario. We can do any updates needed. So, will you take a chance on a beat-up ex-Navy SEAL who loves you with all his heart? I can't guarantee perfection, but to borrow a little from Charles Dickens, I'll honor the spirit of Christmas throughout the year and do everything possible to make you happy."

Noelle put her arms around Dakota's neck.

"Then yes. I love you, too," she whispered. "With all my heart and soul. But we'll make each other happy. It isn't your responsibility alone."

"All right. I hope you aren't interested in

a big wedding, because I don't think I can wait too long."

"You'd be surprised at how fast my mother can work. How about New Year's Day? Can you wait until then?"

"Barely," he whispered after another long kiss.

* * * * *

If you missed Jordan's story,
The Cowboy SEAL's Challenge *from
acclaimed author Julianna Morris,
visit www.Harlequin.com today!*

Get 4 FREE REWARDS!

We'll send you 2 FREE Books plus 2 FREE Mystery Gifts.

FREE Value Over **$20**

Both the **Love Inspired®** and **Love Inspired® Suspense** series feature compelling novels filled with inspirational romance, faith, forgiveness, and hope.

YES! Please send me 2 FREE novels from the Love Inspired or Love Inspired Suspense series and my 2 FREE gifts (gifts are worth about $10 retail). After receiving them, if I don't wish to receive any more books, I can return the shipping statement marked "cancel." If I don't cancel, I will receive 6 brand-new Love Inspired Larger-Print books or Love Inspired Suspense Larger-Print books every month and be billed just $6.24 each in the U.S. or $6.49 each in Canada. That is a savings of at least 17% off the cover price. It's quite a bargain! Shipping and handling is just 50¢ per book in the U.S. and $1.25 per book in Canada.* I understand that accepting the 2 free books and gifts places me under no obligation to buy anything. I can always return a shipment and cancel at any time by calling the number below. The free books and gifts are mine to keep no matter what I decide.

Choose one: ☐ **Love Inspired**
Larger-Print
(122/322 IDN GRDF)

☐ **Love Inspired Suspense**
Larger-Print
(107/307 IDN GRDF)

Name (please print)

Address   Apt. #

City   State/Province   Zip/Postal Code

Email: Please check this box ☐ if you would like to receive newsletters and promotional emails from Harlequin Enterprises ULC and its affiliates. You can unsubscribe anytime.

Mail to the **Harlequin Reader Service:**
IN U.S.A.: P.O. Box 1341, Buffalo, NY 14240-8531
IN CANADA: P.O. Box 603, Fort Erie, Ontario L2A 5X3

Want to try 2 free books from another series? Call 1-800-873-8635 or visit www.ReaderService.com.

*Terms and prices subject to change without notice. Prices do not include sales taxes, which will be charged (if applicable) based on your state or country of residence. Canadian residents will be charged applicable taxes. Offer not valid in Quebec. This offer is limited to one order per household. Books received may not be as shown. Not valid for current subscribers to the Love Inspired or Love Inspired Suspense series. All orders subject to approval. Credit or debit balances in a customer's account(s) may be offset by any other outstanding balance owed by or to the customer. Please allow 4 to 6 weeks for delivery. Offer available while quantities last.

Your Privacy—Your information is being collected by Harlequin Enterprises ULC, operating as Harlequin Reader Service. For a complete summary of the information we collect, how we use this information and to whom it is disclosed, please visit our privacy notice located at corporate.harlequin.com/privacy-notice. From time to time we may also exchange your personal information with reputable third parties. If you wish to opt out of this sharing of your personal information, please visit readerservice.com/consumerchoice or call 1-800-873-8635. **Notice to California Residents**—Under California law, you have specific rights to control and access your data. For more information on these rights and how to exercise them, visit corporate.harlequin.com/california-privacy.

LIRLIS22R2

COUNTRY LEGACY COLLECTION

19 FREE BOOKS IN ALL!

EMMETT
Diana Palmer

COURTED BY THE COWBOY

THE RANCHER AND THE BABY
Marie Ferrarella

Cowboys, adventure and romance await you in this
new collection! Enjoy superb reading all year long
with books by bestselling authors like
Diana Palmer, Sasha Summers and Marie Ferrarella!

Get 4 FREE REWARDS!

We'll send you 2 FREE Books plus 2 FREE Mystery Gifts.

FREE Value Over **$20**

Both the **Romance** and **Suspense** collections feature compelling novels written by many of today's bestselling authors.

YES! Please send me 2 FREE novels from the Essential Romance or Essential Suspense Collection and my 2 FREE gifts (gifts are worth about $10 retail). After receiving them, if I don't wish to receive any more books, I can return the shipping statement marked "cancel." If I don't cancel, I will receive 4 brand-new novels every month and be billed just $7.24 each in the U.S. or $7.49 each in Canada. That's a savings of up to 38% off the cover price. It's quite a bargain! Shipping and handling is just 50¢ per book in the U.S. and $1.25 per book in Canada.* I understand that accepting the 2 free books and gifts places me under no obligation to buy anything. I can always return a shipment and cancel at any time by calling the number below. The free books and gifts are mine to keep no matter what I decide.

Choose one: ☐ **Essential Romance**   ☐ **Essential Suspense**
                   (194/394 MDN GQ6M)   (191/391 MDN GQ6M)

Name (please print)

Address   Apt. #

City   State/Province   Zip/Postal Code

Email: Please check this box ☐ if you would like to receive newsletters and promotional emails from Harlequin Enterprises ULC and its affiliates. You can unsubscribe anytime.

Mail to the Harlequin Reader Service:
IN U.S.A.: P.O. Box 1341, Buffalo, NY 14240-8531
IN CANADA: P.O. Box 603, Fort Erie, Ontario L2A 5X3

Want to try 2 free books from another series? Call 1-800-873-8635 or visit www.ReaderService.com.

*Terms and prices subject to change without notice. Prices do not include sales taxes, which will be charged (if applicable) based on your state or country of residence. Canadian residents will be charged applicable taxes. Offer not valid in Quebec. This offer is limited to one order per household. Books received may not be as shown. Not valid for current subscribers to the Essential Romance or Essential Suspense Collection. All orders subject to approval. Credit or debit balances in a customer's account(s) may be offset by any other outstanding balance owed by or to the customer. Please allow 4 to 6 weeks for delivery. Offer available while quantities last.

Your Privacy—Your information is being collected by Harlequin Enterprises ULC, operating as Harlequin Reader Service. For a complete summary of the information we collect, how we use this information and to whom it is disclosed, please visit our privacy notice located at corporate.harlequin.com/privacy-notice. From time to time we may also exchange your personal information with reputable third parties. If you wish to opt out of this sharing of your personal information, please visit readerservice.com/consumerschoice or call 1-800-873-8635. **Notice to California Residents**—Under California law, you have specific rights to control and access your data. For more information on these rights and how to exercise them, visit corporate.harlequin.com/california-privacy.

STRS22R2

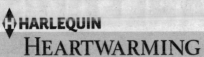

HARLEQUIN
PLUS

Announcing a **BRAND-NEW** multimedia subscription service for romance fans like you!

Read, Watch and Play.

Experience the easiest way to get the romance content you crave.

Start your **FREE 7 DAY TRIAL** at <u>www.harlequinplus.com/freetrial</u>.